Praise for

Diamond Rings Are Deadly Things, Book #1

"Mystery, suspense, murder and romance all intriguingly tied together in one very fun walk-down-the-aisle cozy mystery!" – *Shauna Wheelwright*, reviewer

"As a longtime fan of Rachelle Christensen, I always love her stories and characters, and this novel is another thrilling mystery to add to my collection. Adri faces bridezillas, wedding dress disasters, and murder. Find out what mashed potatoes and crafts have to do with suspense in *Diamond Rings are Deadly Things*—and don't be surprised if you have to stay up all night to finish the book!"--*Rachel Ann Nunes*, Author of *Before I Say Goodbye*

"This is a terrific story with quirky characters, fun crafty ideas, and a mystery that will keep you wondering through all the twists and turns." --*Heather Justesen, author of Brownies and Betrayal*

"Author Rachelle Christensen does an excellent job of keeping the reader guessing and throwing out unexpected twists into the story. Great suspense and plenty of romance make this book an excellent escape!" – *Heather B. Moore, USA Today Bestselling author*

Veils and Vengeance

Other Works by Rachelle

Diamond Rings Are Deadly Things (Wedding Planner Mysteries #1)

Proposals and Poison (#3)

The Soldier's Bride (A Music Box Romance #1)

Carve Me a Melody (A Music Box Romance #2)

Hawaiian Masquerade (Destination Billionaire Romance)

How to Fetch a Fiancé (Must Love Dogs Series)

Wrong Number
Caller ID

Novellas:
Silver Cascade Secrets

Double Take
Hope for Christmas: An Echo Ridge Romance

The Kiss Thief: An Echo Ridge Romance

The Princess Bride of Riodan: An Echo Ridge Romance

Coming Home to Love: An Echo Ridge Romance

Nonfiction:
What Every 6th Grader Needs to Know: 10
Secrets to Connect Moms & Daughters

Lost Children: Coping with Miscarriage

Ultimate Life: Create a Life Worth Living in 9 Simple Steps

Veils and Vengeance

A Wedding Planner Mystery #2

RACHELLE J. CHRISTENSEN

Thrills for the *Heart*

FOR A LIMITED TIME

Sign up for Rachelle's VIP Mailing List

to get your *FREE* book.

Get started here:

www.rachellechristensen.com

For Kyle

Your darling baby smiles and cuddly hugs make it all
worth it.

Acknowledgments

Every book is a journey and this one took years, but I enjoyed every step. I especially enjoyed visiting the beautiful island of Kauai, and I have my brother, Patrick Jolley, to thank for that adventure.

Thanks to my first readers who cheer me on and give great feedback to make the story better: Patrick and Necia Jolley, Nichole Giles, Rachel Ann Nunes, and Heidi Taylor.

To my friend, Dominique Etcheverry, and her wonderful family for answering questions about the Basque language and heritage. Thank you for helping me get my facts straight.

I'm grateful to the community of support I have within LDStorymakers, Authors Incognito, and so many incredible writers in my area. I love getting together to talk words with people who understand the work of writing.

This book took a journey with fantastic editorial support from Heidi Brockbank and Sabine Berlin. Thanks to Eschler Editing for helping me polish my story. Kelli Ann Morgan is a superstar at designing covers, and Kimberly Anderson's illustration is delightful! Thank you to Bob Houston eBook Formatting for a job well-done.

To my parents, Tim and Andrea Jolley, thank you for reading my manuscript, brainstorming ideas, and for your unwavering support.

My children inspire me and I'm so grateful I get to take part in their creative energy every day. My husband, Steve, deserves huge thanks for making writing retreats possible and recognizing how important writing is to me. He is the hero in my book.

I'm grateful to my Heavenly Father for each day of life He grants me, and for the opportunity to see that each day is full of miracles and possibilities.

Chapter 1

SAND AND SEASHELL BOTTLE

Create a unique conversation piece by filling a tall skinny bottle with beach sand and sea shells. Alternate layers so that you can easily view the shells amidst the sand. Vases or hurricane glass can be used but it's recommended to find a bottle with a stopper or lid to protect against spills.

Courtesy of www.mashedpotatoesandcrafts.com

I kicked off my flip-flops and burrowed my toes into the sand at Tunnels Beach. The anticipation of standing on a beach in Hawaii had been building for the past seven months, and it was definitely more beautiful than I imagined.

My dad claimed I could get a nice tan in our Idaho desert sand while lying next to his horse, Fellar, but I disagreed—

especially since it was February. A destination wedding on the island of Kauai was at the top of every wedding planner's make-believe resume, and I would've gone through a lot more than the grueling seven-hour flight for this opportunity.

"What do you think, Adrielle?"

I turned and saw Jonathan Connelly studying me with a grin. "It's gorgeous. Call me Adri." I smiled at the bride's future brother-in-law, thinking that the beach wasn't the only gorgeous thing around. Malia Wright's fiancé, Kyle, was good-looking, but she hadn't prepared me for his older brother Jonathan. He was close to six feet tall, with a muscular surfer-type build, and a contagious grin. Jonathan spent more time on Kauai than the rest of his family, living in his parents' vacation home while they split their time between Hawaii and the mainland. I figured that explained his sun-bleached blond hair and bronzed skin.

"I will if you'll call me Jon."

With a lift of one eyebrow, I held out my hand. "Deal."

He chuckled and shook my hand with a firm grip, leaving my palm gritty with sand. I tried to brush it off on my towel, but several tiny granules still clung to my fingers.

"Ah, your first discovery—the sticky sand of Kauai." Jon motioned to my fingers. "Be prepared. You'll be home a week and still shaking the beach out of your hair."

"When it dries, it'll come off," I replied.

Someone laughed behind me and I turned just as Jon's dad, Neil Connelly, dropped the bags full of snorkeling gear at my feet. He smiled, and I could see a tinge of gray in his neatly trimmed mustache that I hadn't noticed in his light brown hair. "The innocence of youth." Neil leaned down and scooped up a handful of sand and held it out. "Take a look, Adri. You'll see that the beach here isn't just sand, but tiny bits of broken shells and volcanic rock." He let the sand fall into my outstretched palm.

The granules of sand were actually reddish brown, and as I studied them, I saw what Neil meant. There were larger pieces of smooth white bits that must be sea shells and black flecks that could only be lava rock.

"Neil, she only just got here and you're already making her study the sand?" Heather Connelly rolled her eyes at her husband as she crouched to unzip the gear bag. She wore a dark blue bathing suit that complemented her chestnut hair. Heather looked a bit younger than her husband, probably closer to fifty while Neil appeared closer to sixty.

"Uh-oh, don't get sucked in." Kyle Connelly stepped forward and patted my shoulder. "Feign disinterest, and he might give up and go away."

I laughed. "But I am interested. I've never seen beach sand like this before."

"No, Adri. Don't get him started." Malia shook her finger at Neil with a grin. "She's here to finish planning my wedding, so don't load her brain with a bunch of useless facts."

Neil held up his hands. "I surrender. Let's go snorkeling instead."

Malia had informed me that Neil and Heather Connelly enjoyed scuba diving, but they'd opted for snorkeling so

3

everyone could be included in the pre-wedding activities. Mostly that meant Malia and me, since neither of us were divers.

"That will be difficult to do without the wetsuit jackets," Heather said with a hard edge to her voice. "Adri and Malia will freeze."

"Oh, did I forget those?" Neil bent over the bags and emptied them, pulling out fins, masks, and a couple beach towels. "Sorry, hon."

"I have my rash guard. That will help," Malia said and glanced at me. My strappy turquoise swimsuit left most of my back exposed to the sun.

Heather narrowed her eyes toward Neil. "I reminded you twice."

The tension was picking up, so I stepped forward. "I'll be fine. The water's warmer than the Snake River, and I never used a wetsuit there."

"You can borrow mine." Jon moved to pull off his swim shirt.

"No, that's okay." But he'd already taken it off and placed it in my hand. I glanced at his toned chest—okay maybe more than a glance—and felt my face heating up. I looked away and mumbled, "Thanks."

"That's a good idea," Kyle said. He stood next to his brother, and I noticed that Jon was almost a head taller than Kyle. "Trust me, Adri, I've been diving here dozens of times. You'll be shivering, but you won't want to come in to shore because it's so incredible."

4

"He's right. The water is warmer here, but it's still only about seventy-two to seventy-eight degrees year-round," Neil said.

"Thanks, Mr. Factual, but what we really needed was for you to use your brain and remember the jackets," Heather muttered as she zipped one of the bags shut. "Tunnels Beach isn't meant for a quick snorkel." She turned to Malia with a frown. "We usually like to stay out for an hour because there's so much to see."

I pulled on Jon's rash guard and crouched near the sand, letting my hair hide my face, which was flaming by now. I shouldn't be embarrassed, but Heather's anger toward Neil made me feel even more awkward.

"Give us a few minutes, Mom," Kyle said. "I want to take some pictures of Malia by the ocean, and she said I had to do it before her hair got wet." He sensed the tension too, and was creating a diversion for everyone.

Heather nodded, and I watched Malia kiss Kyle as they walked down the beach with fingers intertwined. Malia was part Hawaiian, so her skin glowed in the tropical sun, unlike my own fair complexion. She ran a hand through the thick, loose curls at the base of her neck. I wondered if she had decided to wear her hair up or down for the ceremony.

Their wedding would be lovely. Malia had sought me out at her friend Natalie's wedding last June. I couldn't turn her down when she told me she wanted to have a destination wedding in Hawaii. Even though her cousin was Luke

Stetson—the divorce attorney who thought he wanted to date a wedding planner.

I shook my head. I wasn't going to think about Luke and his emotional baggage or the fact that he'd be arriving in Kauai in three days. Or the dimple in his chin. Or how he looked when he was out for a run with his shirt off. Gritting my teeth, I turned my thoughts back to the bride's family.

"Beautiful, isn't it?" Jon murmured.

"Mm-hmm." I was lost in my thoughts, unaware of the scene before me.

Jon pointed to a lush green mountain ridge. "The Na Pali coastline has some wicked hiking trails. If you get up about 5,000 feet, the vantage points are unbelievable."

"It'd be fun to do a tropical hike." I cleared my mind and refocused on the verdant seascape before me. "I love that the mountains are right here by the shore—such beauty together with the ocean."

"I never get tired of watching the waves," Jon said. "Malia and Kyle don't like hiking much, but maybe I could take you. There's one at the top of Waimea Canyon. You usually get rained on, but it's worth it."

A breeze ruffled his sun-bleached curls, and I tried to keep myself from staring at the contrast of his golden skin next to my white arms. He was waiting for my answer. My heart sped up. I was here to coordinate Malia's wedding, but she had assured me there would be time to play. Jon was harmless—I could look. Twelve days until I would return to Sun Valley, Idaho and a mountain of work prepping for six June weddings.

"I'd like that. You're talking about the Wai'ale'ale Crater, aren't you?"

"You've done your homework."

"I bought *The Ultimate Kauai Guidebook* so Malia and I could figure out the details for her wedding."

"Yep, I've seen tourists with that blue guidebook—it's a good one." Jon nodded. "I'm happy for Kyle. It's funny that he met a Hawaiian girl in Idaho who's never been to Kauai. Malia seems like a nice girl, though— she'll fit right in."

"She is. They're a great couple."

"I'm ready to snorkel," Neil hollered.

"My parents are like fish." Jon chuckled. "You ready?"

"Absolutely."

Ten minutes later, we swam out along the coral reef that made Tunnels one of the best sites for snorkeling on the island. The feeling of floating on the salt water while looking down at the fish was infinitely more amazing than I'd imagined. So much life thrived just under the surface. My fingers buzzed with excitement. I had to keep reminding myself to slow my breathing down to a normal pace. We followed a sandy path through the coral with Neil and Heather leading the way, Jon and I in the middle, and Kyle and Malia bringing up the rear.

I'd practiced snorkeling in a pool with Malia back home, but this was completely different. Just when I was feeling comfortable watching fish skirt over the sandy bottom an arm's length away, we swam around a large rock and the ocean floor dropped away.

Neil had prepared us by telling us about the tunnels that carved through the ocean floor. Only fifteen feet behind us, the water had been maybe ten feet deep, but the tunnel before me must have been forty feet down. Someone grabbed my hand and I turned to see Jon. He looked at me and gave a thumbs up. I returned the okay signal, but didn't want to let go of his hand. I squeezed his fingers as he was about to release mine, and he looked back at me and gripped my hand tighter. There was something unsettling about swimming where the ocean floor wasn't clearly visible—so deep that in places the bottom looked murky and dark.

Jon turned and kicked his fins to the right and pulled me along a huge line of rocks. He pointed and I watched Neil dive down with a waterproof camera. He snapped a picture near a rock—I saw several fish swimming in and out of holes—then he surfaced. Seconds later, there was a tug on my hand, and I lifted my head out of the water next to Jon's.

He pulled out his mouthpiece. "How are you doing?"

"This is like another world." My voice sounded hollow, reminding me that I still had my mouthpiece in. I removed it. "Thanks for helping me. I wasn't prepared for how deep that was, even though Neil told me."

"Yeah, it blew my mind the first time. I just kept telling myself, ten feet, forty feet—it's all the same."

"I guess." I chuckled. "I had to remind myself that I'm a great swimmer, and this is salt water."

"Hey, Jon," Neil interrupted. "Dive with me. There's some bright pink coral your mother wants to see." He pointed to where Heather was floating on the surface of the water.

Jon looked at me. "You probably noticed that most of the coral is that tan or yellowish color. It's fun to see something different. Would you like to come?"

"Sure."

"You'll have to kick hard. It's almost impossible to stay under the water without weights, and you'll need to use your arms, too," Jon said. "We have a lot of practice, so we can stay down almost a minute."

"Okay, I'll try, but if I can't get down, don't worry about me. I'll just float here."

"You're a good sport, Adri," Neil said. He swiped beads of water from his mustache and pointed to his left. "Kyle and Malia are right over there if you get separated from us."

"Ready to go?" Jon squeezed my hand.

I nodded and readjusted my mouthpiece, blowing air through the pipe before dipping my face back in the ocean. Jon and Neil dove, and I followed Heather as she swam through the water with strong arms. The force of the salt water was unbelievable—I got down to where I could feel a little pressure on my eardrums before I was forced back up. Blowing the water out of my tube, I tried again, this time kicking harder. As I approached Jon, he waved and pointed at the pink coral. He gripped a rock with his other hand. So that's how he could stay under for a minute.

They were still a few feet below me, but I had caught a glimpse of the coral, so I let myself be jettisoned to the surface once more. Proud of myself for spewing the water out of my breathing tube, I continued along the reef in the direction Jon had indicated Malia and Kyle were swimming. I couldn't see them ahead, but I wasn't ready to resurface yet. A mint green fish with a bulbous horn protruding above its eye flipped past me. I followed it and turned to see a long silver fish snaking its way along the top of the water. I sucked in a breath, startled at the proximity of the slender fish.

I lifted my head, and waited for the droplets of water to slide down my mask. There were several snorkelers out today and it took me a full minute before I identified what I thought was Malia's dark ponytail bobbing along the water with Kyle next to her. I had been heading in the wrong direction. They were a lot farther than I thought they would be. It looked like they were much closer to the beach.

I ducked my head back under the water and began swimming in their general direction. The buddy rule nudged me as I surveyed the area. With a slow breath, I looked right and left at the shelves of coral and rock surrounding me—no sandy paths in sight. *You're doing fine. Just swim along the rocks until you see a path to the beach*. I reminded myself to slow my rapid breaths to a quieter rate.

I kicked past the shelf of lava rocks cascading to the bottom some thirty feet below. Something caught my eye and I held perfectly still. A rainbow fish. I'd seen the blue fish with neon green and orange stripes in a picture. It nosed around the coral and my smile widened until I remembered to bite down on my mouthpiece. The fish was maybe ten feet below me. It would only take a minute to dive closer, and then I would resurface and find the shore like a good girl.

The fish swam through a coral tunnel, and I wished that my assistant, Lorea, was with me to examine its beautiful markings. Or that I had spent a little more money to buy the waterproof camera I'd had on my wish list. I made a mental note to buy a disposable one before we went on our next snorkeling trip. The salt water forced me nearer the surface, but I kicked down once more, blowing out the reserve of air in my lungs. With practice, maybe I could get as deep as Jon and his parents.

The rainbow fish darted in front of me, and I stopped kicking. It looked at me, and I gazed at its glassy eyes for about two seconds before I began to rise back to the surface. I searched for the rainbow colors and saw a flash as it swam around a large boulder. From behind the rock, I noticed an object protruding from the side, floating near the rocky shelf. I blew out the water in my tube and blinked to clear my eyes.

Sucking in a noisy breath, I kicked forward against the current. A blue flipper floated near the boulder, but what had my heart rate accelerating was the arm moving in a slow wave on the other side of the rock. Lifting my head out of the water, I scanned the area around me. The beach was probably two hundred yards away, and I thought some of my snorkeling buddies were near the exposed reef west from me. They were too far away, and I couldn't leave until I checked if my goggles were clear. My brain didn't want to accept that what I had seen looked like a human arm.

Gulping a huge breath and kicking down hard, I dove back under the surface. The pressure on my ears increased as I dove deeper. The saltwater continually pushed me toward the surface, but with one more forceful kick, I grabbed onto the boulder. With my feet above my head, I pulled myself around and caught sight of the flipper—and the arm. It was attached to the body of a woman.

A black scuba mask covered her face, and behind the glass lens, her eyes were open. They stared forward into the darkness of the water where the tunnels delved deeper through the coral. Chains encircled her body with a weight resting next to her in the sand. Her arm moved again in the current, and a glimmer of metal caught my eye. I tried to focus on the object—it looked like a bracelet or maybe a watch. My lungs tightened, begging for oxygen.

I released my hold on the rock and allowed myself to float back up to the surface. The chains wrapped around her body were etched into my mind as I broke through the water. Ripping off my mask, I gulped in air and let loose the scream I'd been holding since I focused on those sightless eyes behind the mask.

"Help! Call 9-1-1! Help!" I waved my arms frantically and then paused. I needed to mark my position—though this area was calm, the current was still strong enough to move me several feet in less than a minute. The beach was dotted with several people lounging and walking. There was a chair on the sand with a red and white umbrella behind it, shading a man who was reading a magazine. He was directly in front of me, and I noticed the cluster of trees behind him, the way the sand formed a steep bank, littered with bits of driftwood. Hopefully he wouldn't move before help arrived.

Someone swam toward me with fast, clean strokes— Malia. She was followed by the rest of the snorkeling party. When she bobbed next to me, I yelled, "There's a body down there. It looks like a woman."

She pulled her mouthpiece out. "What? Is she hurt?"

"No, she's dead. Wrapped in chains and some kind of weight."

Malia gripped my arm. "Are you okay?"

I hadn't noticed, but now everything came into focus. My teeth chattered and my shoulders tensed with shivers. "I don't know." Tears pricked my eyes. "I saw a flipper, and then her arm. Her eyes—she was . . ."

"Is she hurt?" Heather asked as Neil, Jon, and Kyle surrounded me.

I thrust my hand into the water, pointing downward. "She's dead."

"Who?" Jon came closer and gripped my hand.

"I don't know. There's a body down there by a big rock. I saw the chains."

Heather pulled off her mask and glanced at Malia. "Is she okay?"

"No!" I yelled. "She's dead. Didn't you hear me? Her arm—it was floating."

Jon grabbed my other hand and shook my arm. "Adri, they're talking about you. You look really pale. We need to get you to shore."

"But we need to call 9-1-1."

"We will, as soon as we get you out of the water."

Jon ducked his head under the water and then resurfaced. "It's too shallow and the shelf is too narrow here. She'll have to swim back around the reef." His voice echoed through his breathing tube.

"I don't know if that's the best idea right now," Neil said. "She looks like she might be in shock."

"No, I'm okay." Another shiver rippled across my shoulders.

"If you swim toward the mountain, there's a wide path leading straight to the beach. You'll be able to skirt the coral." Heather pointed to the beach. "Head for that family building sand castles."

"We can take her." Malia looked at Kyle and he nodded.

"First, can you show us where you found the—the body?" Jon asked.

Panic. That's what I was feeling. I didn't want to put my face in the water again and see those eyes staring up at me. Salty tears mixed in with the briny water coating my lips. The beach chair—I blinked my eyes and looked for my landmark. "There, the red and white umbrella. I was directly in front of it when I surfaced."

"Okay, Malia, you stay with Adri. We'll see if we can find whatever she saw." Jon pressed his mask against his face.

"I think you should head for shore now," Heather said. "You've been in the water too long. You must be freezing."

Numb was more like it.

"We'll be quick." Neil dove under the water with Kyle.

Jon prepared to follow, but I reached for him. "Look for a blue flipper, and her arm—"

He squeezed my hand. "It's okay. Make sure you're taking slow, easy breaths." He followed his father.

"Be right back." Heather's flippers made a splash as she swam downward. Less than a minute later, she reappeared and pulled out her mouthpiece. "They've found something. My mask started leaking." She tightened the straps. "Malia, take Adri to shore now and call for help." She dove back down before we could answer.

My teeth chattered and I clamped my jaw shut. I noticed goose bumps on my arms. "I'm afraid to go underwater again."

Malia clasped my hand. "You'll be fine. We'll kick fast, and I bet we'll be back to the beach in less than five minutes. If you get too scared, you can keep your head up."

There was a splash and Kyle resurfaced. "Let's go!" He shouted. His eyes were wide. He'd seen the body as well.

"Lead the way," Malia said.

She waited while I readjusted my mask over my face. The pounding of my heart increased as the water lapped against my arms. With my pinky finger, I wiped the inside of my mask to clear it, then I sucked in through my nose for a tight fit.

"Ready?" Malia's voice sounded hollow.

I gave her a thumbs up and leaned over the water, biting hard on my mouthpiece. As soon as my face hit the water, I closed my eyes, afraid of seeing the body. Malia jerked on my hand, and I opened my eyes. She pointed at a school of white and blue fish. For a moment, I forgot to be scared as they flitted in between the rocks and bunches of coral.

Malia tugged on my hand again, and I began kicking my feet, remembering not to bend my knees. Kyle swam ahead of us and we followed—the fins moving us through the water rapidly. We reached the sand tunnel, and I noticed how loud my breathing was in the tube next to my left ear. I focused on one thought: *don't panic, just breathe.*

When my knees hit the sand, I lifted my head out of the water and ripped my mask off. Crawling forward out of the surf, I struggled to hold in the tears.

"I'll run to the lifeguard station," Kyle called over his shoulder as he sprinted across the sand.

"Adri, why don't you lie down for a minute? I'll call for help." Malia removed her snorkel gear and pointed down the beach. We had left our cell phones stowed safely in the gear bags about three-hundred yards away.

I nodded. "Okay." Malia jogged across the beach. All I could do was watch her and remind myself to suck in another mouthful of air. Outside of a funeral viewing, the only other dead body I'd seen was that of my best friend, Briette. I'd been planning her wedding when she was murdered. With a shake of my head, I pushed out the memory like I'd done so many times over the past two years. I tried to think of something else. I turned my head and watched how the sun shimmered on the ocean waves.

The image of that arm kept coming to the forefront of my mind. And then I would see the mask, and even though I would try to stop myself, I would see those eyes—I think they were green. With a shudder, I moved my focus back out to the water.

Jon and his parents were out there somewhere. Were they trying to bring the body to the surface? My gaze flitted across the groups of snorkelers. There were probably about fifteen people out today. Neil had mentioned that even though Tunnels Beach was the best place to snorkel and scuba dive on the whole island of Kauai, not many tourists knew about it because there was limited public access. We had parked on the other side of a private drive and walked about ten minutes to the beach. All I wanted was to go back to the hotel and lie down, but I wondered how I would find the strength to walk across the sand to our vehicle.

I'd prepared for this wedding for months, working to avoid problems and stress so that I could enjoy the trip—I didn't plan on finding a body. The image of the woman came to mind again, and I remembered the chains wrapped around her torso. It wasn't just a dead body that I had discovered. It was murder.

Chapter 2

WEDDING CARD RECIPE

1. Fold 4 ¼" x 11" piece of brown cardstock in half to make 4 ¼" x 5 ½" card base.

2. Stamp heart images randomly across card base.

3. Now stamp desired image (flower, bird, etc.) on white or other colored cardstock scrap. Punch with medium oval punch or cut using decorative edged scissors. Adhere to center of card front with glue.

4. Utilize a favorite quote, printed on cardstock for the inside message of the card.

Example: Of all forms of caution, caution in love is perhaps the most fatal to true happiness.

-- Betrand Russell

Courtesy of www.mashedpotatoesandcrafts.com

Malia returned before Kyle, holding a cell phone tight to her ear. I had spotted the Connellys out in the gentle swells of the ocean. Jon waved at us—he must've seen Malia approaching.

"They're right there," I said. Malia stopped next to me and looked toward the water. Their gestures indicated they had found the body and were staying put until help came.

"Hold on a minute." Malia moved the phone and crouched next to me. "Kyle should be back soon." She turned around and squinted down the beach. "I see him. He's with someone—must be the lifeguard." She motioned to her phone. "They're contacting the Coast Guard."

Ha'ena Beach park adjoined Tunnels so that was quick thinking on Kyle's part, although a lifeguard wouldn't be much help to someone already dead.

"I can see Jon out there." I pointed to his rhythmic waving. "They must have found her."

Malia straightened and waved back at Jon. Kyle and the lifeguard drove up on an ATV.

"How are you holding up?" Kyle asked me as he pulled his mask and flippers back on.

"I'm okay. Warming up." I didn't want to say more because my lip trembled with the effort of holding in a sob.

"I'm heading out with the lifeguard, but more help is on the way." Kyle stared at me for a second. "It's okay. Everything will be fine."

I wrapped my arms around my legs and rested my chin on my knees. I wanted to believe him, but I didn't know if I was strong enough. Not even a year ago, I'd been through more trauma than I could have imagined. My life was threatened multiple times, and I had a scar on my chest to prove it. Broken pieces of Adri were held together by a thin coating of glue that threatened to disintegrate. I was supposed to be improving by going to therapy and sorting out my issues. And now this. I tried not to think about the police, the questions, the taste of fear in the back of my throat.

I refocused on my surroundings. Tunnels Beach was extraordinary because the reef was so large that the surf didn't break for at least a quarter of a mile out from the beach. The roaring of the waves was subdued by the distance which was probably why I heard the sirens approaching a few minutes later.

Men in scuba gear swam out to the Connellys. I watched Heather, Neil, and Jon approach a few minutes later, accompanied by one of the Coast Guard officers in a wetsuit. The officers wrapped towels around them—the Connelly family had been in the water too long. Another officer asked them questions and took notes.

"Miss, are you the one who found the body?"

The deep voice startled me, and I looked up to see a Polynesian man, his gold badge glinting in the sunlight. His black hair receded above his high forehead.

"Yes." My voice cracked, and I coughed to clear my throat, but I couldn't hold the tears back. "She's dead."

He crouched beside me on the sand. "It's fortunate you found the body before something else did. We don't know who she is yet, but I'm sure her family will be grateful to know what happened to her."

My shoulders shook with sobs, but I concentrated on his words. It was true. Although the woman had most likely been murdered, at least her body hadn't been washed out to sea or eaten by crabs. "But someone killed her," I whispered. The impact of the crime stole my breath. Refilling my lungs with air, I looked at the officer. "I saw the chains."

"That's what I heard, but we won't know for certain until we investigate further." He held out his hand. "I'm Officer Kinau. Can I ask you a few questions?"

I nodded and swallowed hard. My hand was limp in his firm grasp. There wasn't much I could tell him. Some part of me realized that I was experiencing shock, and I kept trying to tell myself to calm down.

"Why don't you take a few deep breaths?" The officer tapped my hand. "Look at the patterns of sand on your fingers. Focus on that for a minute, and see if you can feel your breaths slowing."

"Okay." I stared at the sand and recognized the fragments of sea shells and black flecks Neil had shown me earlier. The granules blurred before me, and I took a deep breath. It hadn't been long ago that I had faced a situation much more dangerous than this one. My fingers traced the raised line on my chest where the knife blade had entered. I was stronger than these bits of sand on my fingers.

My breath slowed and I closed my eyes. Immediately, the image of the dead woman came to mind. I forced it out, searching for something good to pull to the front of my consciousness. Luke Stetson's face. That dimple in his chin. His broad shoulders and that concerned look on his face when he'd sat next to me in the hospital. He had saved me and then he asked me on a date. In between breaths, I thought about the past several months. I'd been too busy with my wedding planning business and with healing emotionally and physically to worry about dating. Luke knew that and he hadn't asked again after I turned him down the first time, but I wondered when he might get the nerve to ask me again.

Wait. I didn't want to think about Luke either. I opened my eyes.

"That's better." Officer Kinau crouched next to me. "Now tell me what happened."

I told him how I followed the rainbow fish and noticed the flipper—and the body. "And her arm. It was loose, moving through the water." I stopped. There was something else—something about her arm. What was it? Or was it her mask?

"Anything else that you noticed?"

I squeezed my eyes tight, allowing the image of the woman to fill my thoughts. Focusing on the memory of her arm moving through the water, I struggled to recall whatever was tickling the back of my brain, but there was nothing. With a frown, I opened my eyes. "I don't know. I kind of freaked out. It was my first time snorkeling here."

"I'm sorry about that." He handed me a notebook. "I need a signed statement from you—this is standard procedure.

Would you mind taking a few minutes to write things down now, while they're fresh?"

"Sure." I took the pen he handed me along with the notebook.

"I'll be back in a few minutes. Thanks for doing this." Officer Kinau stood and brushed sand from his pants. He headed over to join the other officer questioning the Connelly family.

I tried to keep the lines of the paper from blurring as I began to write. Rehashing the same conversation I'd just had with Officer Kinau made it a little easier to know what to write. The page was nearly filled by the time a shadow blocked out the glare of the sun. I glanced at Officer Kinau and finished my last sentence.

"I hope this helps." I handed the notebook and pen back to him.

"It will. Thank you." He pulled out a card. "Take this. If you think of anything else significant, let me know. I'd also like to take down your contact info in case we have more questions."

"Okay." I gave him my number and told him I was staying at the Grand Hyatt Resort in Poipu. Shivering in the sunlight, I took another ragged breath.

"Thanks again for your help. Try to enjoy the rest of your vacation."

"I will." I tried to appear like that was a possibility and gave him a weak smile.

After he left, I squeezed the card and noticed the red and brown sand falling from my fingertips. A few minutes later, the officers finished up their questions with the Connellys and Jon hurried to my side. "How are you holding up?"

"I don't know. I'm trying to relax." The calm I sought had eluded me. It was work just to swallow the shudders from my frightened sobs earlier.

"Why don't we get you someplace where you can rest?" Jon held out his hand and helped me up.

Kyle and Malia had gathered all of our stuff along with the snorkeling gear. Malia gave me a hug. "I'm sorry, Adri. You did great, though."

Everyone looked out to the reef where several men were diving. A small crowd had gathered on the other end of the beach to gawk and the officers held them back.

"Come on, we don't need to stay to see this." Heather took Neil's hand. He appeared to be torn for a moment, but then he glanced at me and nodded.

"She's right, guys. That officer said we're free to go." He turned to Heather. "It's a good thing, since he didn't seem too happy that we had touched the body."

"I was checking for a pulse," Heather replied.

"I still don't understand why you guys bothered checking," Jon said. "It was obvious she was dead."

"She could have had a tank and been stuck down there," Neil said. "We needed to make sure."

"I wonder who she was. The poor girl," Heather murmured.

With one glance back at the ocean, I turned and followed Jon to the road. I had been so excited to see the waves and colorful fish, but now all I could think about was the woman with green eyes and how there was something I should remember, but I couldn't.

Chapter 3

WATERMELON SALAD

6 cups mixed field greens
1/2 cup thinly-sliced red onion
1/2 cup carrot curls (or shreds)
1/4 cup diced, toasted macadamia nuts
1/2 cup crumbled Gorgonzola cheese
1/2 cup per serving seedless watermelon, cubed

Raspberry Vinaigrette
1/4 cup seedless raspberry jam
1/4 cup strawberry purée (fresh or frozen)
1/4 cup apple cider vinegar
1/4 cup balsamic vinegar
1-1/4 cups salad oil (olive oil or vegetable)
salt and pepper to taste

In a small bowl, whisk all ingredients. Set aside. Yield: 2 -1/4 cups.

Toss greens in large bowl with just enough raspberry vinaigrette to coat the greens.
Divide greens into liberal portions on 4 plates. Garnish greens with remaining ingredients. Serve chilled.

Courtesy of www.mashedpotatoesandcrafts.com

It was almost four o'clock by the time we reached the resort in Poipu. The entryway of the Grand Hyatt exuded elegance with a rectangular chandelier that must have been the size of two large dining tables put together. The spacious area invited natural light for extra illumination, and as I walked through the courtyard, the heat warmed my skin.

Malia had chosen the resort for her wedding activities and reception because it was close to the Connelly's beach house in Koloa. The actual marriage would take place on the beach outside the hotel in a secluded area.

The heady scent of plumeria welcomed me as I entered my room. Jon had given Malia and me each a lei at the airport, and the maid had draped mine over the lamp near my bed. I leaned closer and breathed in the scent. Then I remembered my camera. I took the lei and positioned it on the desk so that I could take several photos of the beautiful flowers to post on my blog.

I busied myself with that task, struggling to keep my thoughts from dipping back into the ocean where I'd found the woman. After taking several pictures, I decided that the only relief I would find from the haunting images was to work on final wedding details. Grabbing a notebook and my planner, I left my room and headed for the front of the hotel.

I approached the line of concierge desks. "Hi, I'm Adrielle Pyper—the wedding planner for the Connelly/Wright wedding. I'd like to go over a few things."

"Oh, what an exciting time. We love weddings." A young woman straightened her chair and looked up at me. "Who have you been working with?"

"Chelsea has been my main contact. Is she in today?" I glanced at the four other concierges, wondering which one might be Chelsea. One of the reasons Malia had selected the hotel was because they had plenty of expert staff who made it possible to do most of the planning from the mainland.

"As a matter of fact, she is right there." The young woman pointed at the end of the concierge desk to another young woman with dark hair plaited in neat corn rows that went halfway down her back.

"Thank you." I walked a few paces over, admiring her hair and wondering how much upkeep it took.

"Chelsea? I'm Adrielle Pyper, the wedding planner from Sun Valley, Idaho."

Chelsea popped out of her chair and held out her hand. "Adri, it's wonderful to meet you in person." She shook my hand vigorously.

"I've been looking forward to meeting you too."

"I bet you're busy—it's crunch time now." Chelsea tapped her watch and grinned.

"Malia and Kyle are counting down the days. All the major planning has been done, but there are a few housekeeping items I needed to follow up on."

"I jotted down a few things from the last time we talked. Let me get to my notes." Chelsea sat down and motioned for me to follow. I slid into the cushioned chair and placed my planning binder on her desk.

"Okay, here it is. Malia Wright and Kyle Connelly." She tapped the end of her pen on her cheek.

"As arranged," I started, "the wedding party will all be attending the luau on Saturday night. I want to make sure there are enough leis for the guests. We had planned for thirty-five, but I think we need forty-two." I let my hand hover over that item in my planner, waiting to check it off.

Chelsea flipped through her book and then studied her computer screen. "Hmm, just a minute." The clicking sound increased as she opened new documents and shuffled through papers. I noticed her dark skin looked flushed, and she swallowed several times. Finally she turned to me. "I'm sorry, but there's been a mistake. If you'll excuse me for a moment." Without waiting for an answer, she turned and practically ran toward the front desk.

Reminding myself to take deep breaths, I attempted to rein in my worries. Whatever it was, it couldn't be that bad. After a few minutes of running crazy scenarios through my mind, I flipped to a new page in my planner and double-checked the list of things I needed to do tomorrow.

Ten minutes later, Chelsea approached. I stood and clutched my planner tightly to my side.

"Ms. Pyper, it seems that we've run into a little trouble."

I dragged my palms along my shorts, and reminded myself that it couldn't be anything serious. Lorea had assisted me in going over final arrangements with Malia just before we left Idaho. But then I noticed the way Chelsea's hand trembled as she flipped absently through her notebook again.

"One of the other concierges who worked here for only two weeks scheduled an event the same day as your private luau."

"What? But that's impossible. We've had this scheduled for over six months."

She cleared her throat. "It looks like their luau was scheduled three weeks ago."

I lifted my eyebrows. "And I don't see the problem."

"We need your help." Chelsea leaned forward and lowered her voice. "We'll work with you, but we can't cancel the other booking."

"But I've had this planned for six months. Thirty people are flying over from the mainland to attend the wedding."

"Which is why we're going to do everything to make sure you're happy." She removed an invisible piece of lint from her waistline. "Please, will you sit down with me for a moment and see if we can get this worked out?"

My blood pressure was rising, and heat flushed my neck. "Everything *has* been worked out. As I said, we reserved rooms and times over six months ago."

"Believe me, if there was any way we could cancel the other booking, we would, but it just isn't possible." Chelsea hesitated and looked me in the eye. "We're prepared to upgrade your rooms and provide you with added amenities and upgraded service for your events."

"Why is this other client more important than my bride and groom? We've already paid very good money for the deposits." I was having trouble keeping the frustration out of my voice. I liked Chelsea. On one level, I knew this wasn't her fault, but she was the one who could help me fix it.

She looked down at her feet and spoke softly. "They aren't more important. We will look at each and every reservation and see where either party can budge."

"So you're not going to tell me who they are?" I slumped down into the chair.

Chelsea sat across from me and toggled her mouse. "I can't. I'm sorry."

"Yeah, you've been saying that a lot," I snapped. I rubbed my forehead and tried to readjust my thinking. It sounded like there was no way out of the problem, so I needed to figure a way around it.

"We've come up with a few ideas and some extras we'd like to add to help smooth this over," Chelsea offered.

"I don't need extras. I need to know why my booking is suffering because of someone else's error."

"Here's a list of alternate times for your wedding luau. Could you at least consider if any of them might work?" Chelsea handed me a paper with times circled in red.

Every part of me wanted to rip the paper to shreds and throw it back in her face, but my training reminded me that this scenario wasn't her fault. I took a few steadying breaths and tried to switch my viewpoint.

Malia had wanted a sunset wedding with a luau afterwards, but now it looked as if that was no longer an option on Saturday night. There were offered times earlier in the day on Saturday and also Friday and Sunday night, but none of those would work. Some guests wouldn't arrive until Friday and others were leaving Sunday night. Malia and Kyle were planning to fly to Maui Sunday morning for the rest of their honeymoon.

The words blurred before me. I was too exhausted to figure it out, but still I kept trying to think of an alternative. I would have to break the news to Malia—the thought made me want to cry. I wondered if we could switch venues, but at this late date, it was doubtful anything could be secured. Then I thought of something.

"We have a contract—you have to honor our arrangements."

Chelsea nodded. "Of course, it's our every intention—"

"No." I held up my hand. "Let me finish. We will be having a luau on Saturday night as planned. There are no other alternatives for my wedding party. You will have to hold two luaus on that night or find a way to combine the two parties, yet keep some elements separate."

Her face looked splotchy with heat patches popping up on her cheeks, nose, and chin.

"The grounds here are large enough that you could extend the other luau farther down, closer to the beach front. I'm confident in your abilities. I'll stop by first thing in the morning to see the new sketches for the layout you've drawn up and work out seating arrangements."

"But, Ms. Pyper. Please." Chelsea addressed me formally, but I noticed the tremor in her voice.

I stood. "And thank you for making certain that I'm happy with my choice of wedding venues." I walked away as she continued to sputter.

They would figure it out. That long line of concierge tables might be running madly, but they could do it. I was reminded again that it wasn't the resort's fault, but I knew they would make it right. I wasn't going to worry about it any longer.

Thankful that the Connellys hadn't planned anything else for the evening, I retired to my room. The restaurants didn't appeal to me, but ordering room service in my pajamas did. My cell phone buzzed just as I pulled the elastic from my hair. It was Malia.

"This is Adri."

"How are you feeling?"

I swallowed and thought about the double-booking fiasco, then realized she was asking me how I fared after finding the body. With a shudder I answered, "Ready to forget this whole day."

"That's what I thought. It's really not fair—this is our first official day here." Malia said. "I'm not ending it like this. Will you meet us for dinner?"

"No, you and Kyle go on ahead. You don't want me there. I was about to call room service and change into my pajamas."

"Uh-uh, you're coming to dinner with us—all of us. Everyone is upset about what happened, so Neil and Heather wanted us to go out. Jon is especially worried about you."

My stomach flipped when she mentioned Jon, and I chided myself. "I appreciate it Malia, but you go on ahead."

"Adri, I'm not taking no for an answer. Jon is on his way to pick you up. Neil pulled some major strings, and we're meeting at the Beach House Restaurant. It's famous because as you dine, you can look out and see the sun setting over the ocean. Get ready, 'cause you don't want to miss this!"

She hung up before I could protest again. I groaned and fell back on my bed. I was tired, but I accepted that I didn't have much choice in the matter since I was the employee in the situation. If I called Malia back and begged, she might relent, but it was best to humor her happy demeanor.

Already half-undressed, I looked longingly at my cotton pajamas, then turned to my closet and pulled on the hot-pink maxi dress I'd purchased just for this trip. It was fitted around the bust-line and then fell to just above the floor in a silky, soft polyester that would look nice for the restaurant and keep me cool at the same time.

My hair was unruly and the humidity had doubled the amount of blonde curls I usually dealt with. Back home in the dry desert air, I sported an ugly wave, but I had to admit the curls induced by humidity made me feel pretty. I grabbed a silver headband and slipped it into place. My hand had just closed around my tube of mascara when a staccato knocking sounded on the door. Malia hadn't been joking when she said Jon was on his way.

What to do? I wanted to touch up my makeup, but I needed to find my sandals too. I thought about hollering "just a minute," but I didn't want to leave him standing awkwardly in the hall. Leaning close to the mirror, I swiped on my mascara and then hurried to the door.

When I pulled it open, Jon stepped back. "Wow, you look amazing."

Tingling warmth swept up the back of my neck, and I forgot what I was going to say.

Jon held out his hand. "Are you ready?"

I stared at him. His sun-bleached hair still held the tousled look, and he sported cargo shorts and a white and blue-striped button-up shirt. The top two buttons were undone, and he wore a simple white seashell necklace that was indicative of all things Hawaiian—it looked nice against his golden skin. I stood there staring until my brain registered that he'd asked me if I was ready. "Um—yeah."

"You sure?" He glanced down at my feet and winked.

My face went up a few degrees in heat. "Give me one minute." I turned to re-enter my room. The door clicked shut—he would have to stand in the hall while I got a handle on myself.

Fanning my face, I grabbed my sandals and slipped them on, checked my reflection in the mirror, and commanded myself to act natural. It wasn't the time to go gaga over Jon Connelly or *anyone* for that matter. I squared my shoulders and opened the door.

Jon was all smiles. "Ready now?"

I allowed myself to relax. "Yes, thanks for waiting. Malia didn't give me too much of a heads up."

"She didn't want to give you an opportunity to bomb out." He chuckled. "She told me to make sure I didn't leave the hotel without you."

After working with someone as closely as we had for the past six months, it was safe to say Malia knew me well. I thought of my assistant, Lorea, and how she was always encouraging me to step outside my comfort zone. I missed her, and wished again that she could have come along. Malia had offered to fly her out too, but Lorea's sister was getting married the same day as Malia and Kyle. There was no way around it, so Lorea had stayed in Idaho, citing that the Zubiondo family gatherings were better than any beachside luau.

I glanced at Jon as we exited the hotel. "Thanks for coming to get me. I'll be honest—I didn't want to come."

"But it'll be good for you." He touched my elbow, guiding me toward a silver convertible. "Here's our ride."

He opened my door with a flourish and I slid onto the leather seats. "Is this a rental?"

"It's mine." Jon beamed. "For now. I leased it—cheaper than renting all the time. The restaurant is only about five miles away. Hope your hair doesn't mind driving with the top down."

"No, my *hair* doesn't mind," I replied. "And neither do I."

"Did I mention that you are smokin' hot?"

My cheeks flushed even as I told myself not to take him seriously. Jon was just flattering me. "Thanks, I think."

"Really, you were turning every head on our way out of the hotel."

"Maybe they were looking at you—surfer boy."

He grinned. "I'm not that great at surfing—more swimming, scuba, snorkeling."

"It'd be fun to try surfing, but I like swimming." I almost said snorkeling, but then remembered why we were going to this impromptu dinner and swallowed instead.

Jon seemed to notice the shift in the conversation too, because he started pointing out different trees: a flowering bush in full bloom with dark pink flowers trailing over glossy green leaves, another tree with a vine of purple flowers twisted around the trunk. "Nothing like driving off into the sunset to set the mood for the evening, eh?"

I rolled my eyes. "You should have been a comedian."

"Not trying to be funny. It really is a nice evening, and here we are." He pulled up to the Beach House Restaurant and helped me from the car. "I'll show you why people like to come here."

I followed him around the side of the restaurant where the waves lapped at a shoreline littered with boulders. A few patches of sand were occupied by sunbathers, but by the amount of swimmers in the water, I figured it must be a great place for snorkeling. Jon pointed toward the ocean. "Watch carefully and I bet we'll see some turtles."

"Really?" I took a few steps closer to the edge of a steep drop off and looked out at the water that was about ten feet below us.

"There's one," Jon said, pointing to a splash in the surface.

I squinted and leaned closer when a turtle's head bobbed above the surface. The dark outline of his body moved lazily through the current. "There he is." My voice pitched higher in excitement, and I bit my lip, not wanting to sound like a kid at the zoo.

"I could watch them for hours," Jon said.

Immediately, I felt at ease. He wasn't judging me, and I didn't need to feel insecure around him.

"It's nice to see you smile again." Jon nudged my arm. "Look, there's three turtles right there."

I studied the water and relaxed a couple more notches. We watched for a few more minutes until Jon said we should probably join the others inside.

The rest of the Connellys were just being seated when Jon and I walked in. The Beach House was flanked by a large open veranda, where guests could dine right by the shore. The sounds of the waves breaking blended with light music and people talking in the gorgeous setting. The warm atmosphere welcomed me to relax as I surveyed the dimly lit dining area. I would have termed it romantic, but that sounded so unoriginal coming from a wedding planner.

"Adri, thanks for coming," Malia said. Her full smile was outlined in a deep burgundy shade of lipstick that brought out the rosy hue of her skin.

I bit back my retort about being commanded to show up and instead said, "Thank you. I've heard of this restaurant before, and I can see why."

"Wait until you taste the food," Heather said. "It's scrumptious."

We settled in with our menus and there was some small talk, but I sensed that everyone was trying not to think of the discovery earlier. I caught myself glancing out at the vast ocean and wondering what else might lie beneath the waves.

Neil cleared his throat. "I know we're all skirting the issue of the body we found today at Tunnels, so I just wanted to say that I've been in contact with the police again. They haven't discovered her identity, but hopefully will soon."

I gripped the cloth napkin tightly while trying to push the images from my mind. A light touch on my fingers snapped my focus back on what Neil was saying. I looked down and saw that Jon had covered my hand with his. He squeezed my hand and the tension in my neck and shoulders relaxed a bit.

"We're not going to let this ruin our celebrations," Neil continued. "But we won't pretend it didn't happen either. I'll keep you updated on whatever I can find out. Now, let's order and then we'll go out and enjoy the sunset."

Heather leaned over and kissed Neil, and he whispered something to her. They both looked my way, and Neil tipped his chin toward me. I smiled to reassure them. They were worried about me, so I needed to put on a good face, otherwise I'd be roped into family dinner every night during my stay on Kauai.

When Jon released my hand to pick up his menu, I noticed the absence of his fingers curled around mine more than I wanted to admit. After ordering a watermelon salad and an entree with chicken and a rice pilaf, I spent the next few minutes lecturing myself on staying focused and not getting ideas about certain tanned gentlemen. The restaurant grew louder as several people headed outside past our table.

"It's almost sunset," Neil said. "Shall we?" He helped Heather from her chair and they strolled outside together followed by Malia and Kyle. Jon and I brought up the rear. I marveled at the beauty before me.

The sunlight was fading. Shimmering strands of golden pinks and purples cascaded across the ocean waters. The light illuminated a stand of palm trees in the distance, and I had my camera up snapping pictures before it sank any lower.

"Let me take one of you," Jon said. "Come over here and we'll wait our turn."

Several people had the same idea. They stood on the edge of the lawn overhanging the ocean with the brilliant sunset glowing behind them. Several couples kissed as a picture was snapped, and I was pleased to take one of Malia and Kyle that would make a cute impromptu shot to add to their wedding video. Jon took a picture of me, and we stood and gazed out as the coral globe of light sank beneath the ocean.

"Here let me take a picture of you two." Heather held out her hand for my camera. I handed it to her, feeling awkward about having my picture taken with Jon. "You two look cute together."

"Mom, no match-making." Jon grumbled.

Heather laughed. "It's just a picture." She handed me my camera and patted my hand. "How are you holding up, dear?"

I lifted one shoulder. "I think the adrenaline has finally worn off. I'm kind of tired."

"Please let me know if there's anything we can do to make your stay here more comfortable." She studied my face with that motherly concern I'd seen before. "I feel so bad that things started off this way. I'm afraid to go to sleep tonight after all that."

I nodded. "I keep seeing her face and her arm—there was something colorful." I closed my eyes, studying the image in my mind before shuddering. "I guess it's probably best if I try not to think about it anymore, but the officer kept asking me questions about what I'd seen."

"He asked all of us a lot of questions," Jon said. "I didn't understand why when the body was right there for them to examine."

"I think it might have had something to do with them wanting to record the evidence before they moved the body out of the water," Heather offered. She frowned. "It's disturbing. That poor woman. She looked so young."

I blinked back the moisture in my eyes and saw that Heather was doing the same. She patted my arm. "We don't have to worry about it anymore. Let's go back inside. Thankfully the police here are very good at their jobs."

When we walked back inside, the waiter was just placing our salads on the table for us. The presentation of the food was magazine-worthy, so I snapped a few pictures. Red slices of watermelon mixed with spinach and dotted with Gorgonzola cheese and grated carrots made a mouth-watering photo.

"Here, let me take a better picture for you," Kyle said. He held out his hand for my camera. "Now smile. You too, Jon."

Jon leaned in beside me. Kyle took the picture and handed me my camera. Now I had two pictures with Jon and me. If I sent them to Lorea, she'd be bugging me for details non-stop. I decided to send one to her for kicks.

"Thanks, Kyle. I wanted to take a few pictures of the food to post on my blog."

"A blogger, huh?" Jon draped his arm over the back of my chair. "Do you blog about your wedding stuff?"

"That and much more," I said. "My site is called Mashed Potatoes and Crafts. My mom and I blog about all kinds of crafts, sewing, card making, and cooking."

"That sounds like something Malia would like."

Jon was humoring me, but I couldn't resist sharing a little bit more information about my favorite little guilty pleasure—

blogging. "You'll have to visit the site and check out our special Idaho mashed potatoes recipe."

"That sounds yummy." Jon rubbed his stomach. "And you sound like a very talented lady."

His praise was genuine, and I appreciated the small thrill it gave me. "Thank you."

The food was as delicious as it looked, and soon everyone seemed more relaxed after our adventurous day. I saw Heather and Neil watching me with concern, but by the time we had dessert, I think they were assured that I was no longer in shock.

Malia and Kyle left before everyone else for some island star-gazing. We all laughed, and Heather shushed us but Jon nudged my elbow. "You'll see on the way back. The stars are incredible here—not many lights to interfere."

And he was right. I leaned my head back and admired the glittering masses in the blackness above. The Tiki torches were burning as Jon pulled up to the resort. He jumped out and opened my door, taking my hand to help me out. "Come over here," he said. With a tug on my hand, he led me across the drive to a small pond and pointed toward the heavens. "Venus is right there."

My throat constricted. It was like trying to swallow several jagged rocks at once as a memory washed over me— another night of star-gazing with someone who seemed genuine and kind—but he wasn't. I pulled my hand out of Jon's grasp and took a few stumbling steps back toward the hotel.

"Adri! Are you okay?"

He rushed to my side, and I recognized the panicked feelings I'd experienced so many times over the past six months. I stopped, closed my eyes, and took a deep breath, remembering what the victim's advocate had told me—the relaxation practices I'd mastered could help rescue me from an oncoming anxiety attack. Jon stayed near me, but thankfully he didn't say anything until I opened my eyes.

He cocked his head to one side. "I get it—it's been a rough day for you. Let me help you inside. I'm sure you're exhausted with the time difference and everything."

Biting back tears, I let him take my hand and guide me into the resort. It was such a simple thing. He wasn't trying to push me, just make me feel normal when I didn't, and I appreciated it. Jon thought it was all because of earlier, and most of it probably was, but gratitude that I didn't have to try to explain the past to him welled up inside me.

"You promise you're going right to bed?"

I nodded. "Thanks, Jon."

"No prob. Maybe I'll see you in the morning."

As I sank into the bed, I covered my eyes with my arm. This wasn't like me. I was a take-charge woman, full of confidence. I didn't break down at the slightest memory. Tomorrow would be better. After a good night's sleep, I'd be back in control.

As I approached the unconscious realm of sleep, it almost felt as if I were still floating on the water, the waves pushing me gently back and forth.

Chapter 4

LOREA'S CROCHETED INFINITY SCARF

Materials: 1.5 skeins yarn blend, use crochet hook N for bulkier yarns.

For more info on how to decipher a crochet pattern (and its abbreviations), see the website.

Instructions: Ch 18. In the 3rd chain from the hook, work dc, ch 1, dc in the same ch. *Skip two chains and then in the next ch, work dc, ch 1, dc in the same ch. Repeat 3 more times from * to end, then in the last ch, work 1 dc, ch 1, 1 dc in the same ch.

Row 1: Turn, ch 3 and work hdc, ch 1, hdc in each of the chain 1 spaces from the previous row (center of each "V"). At the end of the row, finish with a hdc in the last space (ch 3 turning space).

Repeat row 1 until 60 inches long or desired length.

Courtesy of www.mashedpotatoesandcrafts.com

The clinking of dishes woke me at just after seven the next morning, and I jumped out of bed—rubbing away the nightmares on the fringes of my consciousness. I had planned to get up at six-thirty for a little exercise and be back in time for a fruit plate, courtesy of room service. The light knock on the door indicated that my breakfast was served. Exercise would have to wait.

I scooted the food tray into my room. Then I rinsed off my face and gargled with cool water, allowing myself a few minutes to fully wake. Feeling more alert, I plopped down on my bed for breakfast. As I savored the fresh pineapple and mangoes, I thought about what I needed to accomplish for the day.

First thing, conquer the booking dilemma and find out who in the heck thought they were more important than *Adrielle Pyper's Dream Weddings, Where happily ever after is your destination*. I rolled my shoulders back, enjoying the imagined confidence I needed at the moment, pretending as if everything were on track for a successful wedding.

The deep waters from yesterday beckoned to me with their murderous secrets, but I took a cleansing breath and forced them out of my mind. Neil said he would keep us updated on what the police found—I had to control my morbid curiosity and trust that the police would uncover the details of the woman's demise.

Even as I struggled to rein in my thoughts, I recalled the nightmare from last night. I had been in the ocean again, but this time the woman wasn't dead. She grabbed my arm and pulled me toward her, motioning to the chains on her torso. Her eyes were frightened, and she spoke, but bubbles came out of her mouth, and I couldn't understand what she was trying to say. I had awoken with a feeling of danger and an urgency to discover what the woman wanted. The questions spinning through my brain demanded answers, but I didn't know where to start. I could only go to sleep after I turned the lights on and checked my room for bogeymen.

A shiver ran down my spine, and I shook off the vivid memories of dreams mixed with reality. I needed to concentrate on something else. My room had a small balcony, and I stepped outside and breathed the floral scented air. Everything in Hawaii smelled so fresh.

A rooster crowed. The sound transported me back to mornings on the Idaho farm. I smiled when I thought of my parents. They'd never been anywhere as exotic as Hawaii. They relished their farm life, but all the same, I hoped I could convince them to take a well-earned tropical vacation sometime soon. I allowed myself a few more minutes of relaxation to clear my mind, and then hurried to get ready. Malia had said she would be by the hotel after nine, so I had just enough time to go to battle with the concierge.

I glanced at my craft bag with bits of charcoal gray yarn sticking out near the handles. On the flight I'd worked on crocheting an infinity scarf, and I was almost finished. I wanted to give the scarf to Lorea as a thank you for the extra work she was doing while I was enjoying the Hawaiian sun. I'd envisioned having a bit more time to myself in the evenings to relax and finish my project, but things had turned out to be much more exciting than I planned. I tucked the craft bag back in my suitcase—there would always be time on the flight home.

Repeating a mantra of confidence, I prepared for battle. My off-white capris and a turquoise top gave me a professional yet comfortable appearance. I pulled a brush through my curls and tied my hair back in a messy bun. The shimmery eye shadow I used accented the deep brown of my eyes, and I took care to make sure I got some mascara on my nearly invisible blonde eyelashes before scooting out the door.

I walked with purpose toward the front desk, but just as my sandals echoed across the tile I collided with another woman.

"You!" Her voice was caught between a shriek and a growl. She raised her hand and smoothed her perfectly coiffed, bleached-blonde hair and glared at me.

I stepped back. "I'm sorry. Are you okay?"

"You." She pointed at me. I raised my eyebrows and looked behind me, hoping she meant to point at someone else.

The woman wore a dark pink power suit that accentuated her large bust and tiny waist. I pegged her for forty, trying to pull off thirty, but it was hard to tell under the copious amounts of makeup lining her beady eyes. She jabbed her

finger towards me. "You're the one messing up all my plans."
She spoke with an English accent and a slightly nasal tone.

"Excuse me?"

"Don't be fresh with me, young lady. I know that the
resort double-booked our events, but you could have
rescheduled."

For a moment, my mouth hung open, then I remembered
how unladylike that looked so I clamped my jaw shut. So this
was the woman behind whatever company or celebrity had
booked over the top of Malia's wedding plans. My blood
pumped faster, like the tick-tocking of the clock on a bomb
about to go off. With a breath, I stopped the heated
acceleration of my heart. She had been the cause of my
indigestion last night, and I wasn't about to let her ruin my
good morning mood. I squared my shoulders. "Ever heard the
phrase, 'Lack of planning on your part does not constitute an
emergency on mine? '"

She lowered her pointing finger and her eyes narrowed.
"Of course, but we all know that isn't the case for little people
like yourself. You are supposed to cater to me."

I sucked in a breath. "Is this some sort of joke?" The
woman couldn't be for real, could she?

"That's your problem. You aren't taking me seriously."
She pursed her lips and tapped the toe of her pink heels.

Okay, obviously no joking going on.

She pointed her finger in my face and I took a step back.
"You'll change your reservation for the luau on Saturday

night, or you'll have me to deal with me. My company is far more important than your little wedding."

Enough was enough. I stepped forward again, swiping her pointing finger out of my way. "I have no idea who you are, and I definitely don't know who you think you are, but as far as I can tell, you're a human being just like me."

She opened her mouth, then closed it and narrowed her eyes.

"I've had this wedding celebration planned for over six months. If you have a problem, take it up with the staff, but if you threaten me again, I'll call security."

"I'm not threatening you, Ms. Pyper. My conversations are never idle, and I always hold to my word." She pressed her lips together, and a bit of the blood-red lipstick adhered to her tooth when she spoke. "You will change your luau to Friday, and my company will foot the bill. I don't have time to discuss this further. I'll check with the concierge later to see to the revised plans."

She turned to go, but not before I replied. "I won't be changing anything, but I will be contacting security right now."

The woman laughed. "You do that." She lifted a brow. "I tried to warn you. You should know that people who mess with me often end up hurt." Her heels clicked sharply against the tile as she made her way across the mezzanine.

Of all the borderline crazy people I'd worked with, this woman took the cake. She was psychotic. The gleam in her eye was unnerving, but she didn't know who she was dealing with. I hadn't spent the early years of my career working at Bellissima Wedding Dreams in San Francisco without learning how to deal with celebrity types and people with 'royal pain' personalities. I smoothed the front of my shirt and took a deep breath. It'd been almost three years since I left Bellissima and being my own boss was wonderful. But standing in front of this woman made it hard to ignore the churning in my stomach.

A second later, I realized why she was so angry. The Hyatt must have worked out a way for Malia and Kyle to hold their luau as originally scheduled. I nearly skipped to the security desk, but then remembered I was on my way to report her—I adjusted my facial features accordingly.

A moment of weakness overcame me just as I reached the front desk. What if crazy lady wasn't really crazy? The woman had already posed a formidable opponent if I examined what she'd made the resort staff do. I still didn't know who she was or why it was so important for her to have the luau time on Saturday night, but my competitive nature and hard-nosed upbringing had me rising to the occasion. I didn't care if the woman was Queen of Persia or some other great thing, I wasn't backing down.

First thing first. I had to find out who she was. I marched up to the front desk. "I need to speak with security. I've just been threatened."

The woman gasped. "Are you okay?"

"I'm fine," I assured her. "But I would like to report the incident because the woman seemed dangerous."

"I'll get someone right away." She reached for her phone, but a concierge—my new friend Chelsea, stopped her.

"That won't be necessary. I'll handle this." She turned to me with what I recognized immediately as a fake expression of apology. She inclined her head and relaxed the creases in her forehead, but her Adam's apple thumped with nerves. "Adri, I apologize for Mrs. Harper's behavior. She's really harmless, but she does go to great lengths to get her way. Could you step over to my desk with me?"

I tried to think of something smart to say, but I was too shocked to comment. She must have witnessed the entire exchange—pointing fingers and all. I couldn't believe that she hadn't interfered. Maybe she knew the woman was all bark, no bite. It was a hopeful thought that was extinguished as soon as I met Chelsea's serious gaze.

"I guess that Mrs. Harper has made you aware of her apparent need to have her company luau on Saturday night?"

"And I'm grateful that you are honoring your commitment to my clients. Thank you." I was totally bluffing, but when she sighed I knew that the schedule really was holding.

She pulled out a few pieces of paper. "Here's what we worked up, but Mrs. Harper is furious about this. She threw an absolute tantrum." Her nose crinkled as if she smelled something unsavory. "But my manager told her she'd have to deal with it."

"Uh-yeah, apparently her way of dealing is a little different than most. She basically threatened me with my life if I didn't let her have the luau time on Saturday night."

"Don't let her get to you." Chelsea straightened the page outlining the beach and the seating areas for the luau. "She'll still have her party, but it will be a bit more crowded than she wanted."

I studied the diagrams and nodded. "Thank you. I hope you understand that this is also an inconvenience for my wedding party. We specifically booked a private luau and I'll expect extra concessions on your part to make up for this."

"Of course. We've added a few of the specialty items to the buffet that you said were too expensive, we'll provide leis for all the guests." She ticked off imaginary items on her fingers. "We're bringing in some extra fire dancers and we'll have freshly chopped coconuts to drink available later in the evening." She paused, waiting for my reaction.

"I think those are some nice touches. I appreciate that."

"Good. I've been worried ever since Mrs. Harper's tantrum. There is one other slight adjustment we're working on." She rubbed the palms of her hands on her dress pants.

Noticing that the tension had suddenly increased, I glanced around us—no psycho woman in sight, so that meant— "Are you kidding? You're not really asking me to change something else, are you?"

Her forehead tightened. "It's a small thing, really. The library—"

"No. No way. Kyle has some of his friends coming over to play the gig."

"Please consider it. The overlap is only an hour. If you could possibly push it back one hour later. I'm so sorry for the inconvenience."

I tapped my foot. "This is beyond inconvenient." Then I could see it. She'd already made the change in her mind and bowed to Mrs. Harper. For a second, I wanted to lash out. My temples throbbed with the heightened emotions, and I mentally stepped back from the situation. This was one place where we could budge.

The original coordinator had asked that we start the evening's events at seven and Malia thought it would be pushing it to be there on time. I knew this, but I wasn't about to volunteer the info. If I didn't put up a fight, Mrs. Harper would steamroll me, and Chelsea would buckle under the pressure.

Flipping lightly through the pages of my planner, I double-checked the notes I'd made and saw the window of opportunity. I also saw the dream wish Malia had that all of the guests would enjoy the spa at the Hyatt during their stay—not just the ones who could afford it. Leaning back in my chair, I leveled a flinty gaze at Chelsea.

"I want free spa services for the guests—give them a wedding package, and I might consider making an adjustment to our already adjusted contract."

She opened her mouth to speak, but closed it just as quickly. "We'll do it." She thrust a piece of paper into my hand. "Thank you. There shouldn't be any other problems."

I glanced down at the paper as she walked away. It was a revised schedule for our wedding party and I was right—the time for the library reception had already been changed. I hoped I hadn't given in too easily.

The hair on the back of my neck tingled, and I turned around. I felt like someone had been watching me. A dozen people walked across the foyer—it could have been any of them. A Polynesian man glanced my way and passed between the pillars. I made eye contact again as he walked across the lobby. Something like a tremor moved through my body. Had he been watching me?

I was about to go after him when I spotted Malia coming in the glass doors. Sending up a prayer of thanks for the bride with a sunny personality and remarkable forgiveness skills, I embraced her.

"You look better this morning," she said. "Maybe a bit flushed—something exciting going on?"

"You could say that." I motioned to a chair. "Can we sit for a minute?"

Malia looked concerned, but eased into the chair, running a hand through her dark brown hair absently.

"There are a few small changes to our wedding plans that have caused me a bit of stress, but it's been handled, and I think you'll be happy." I pulled out my planner and began crossing out and scribbling notes as I filled her in on the crazy antics of Mrs. Harper.

"She really threatened you?" Malia narrowed her eyes. "We need to file a formal complaint."

"What we need to do is find out who she is, because she has some kind of power over the people here. When I went to notify security, the concierge was there waiting to intercept me and advised me on another change of plans."

Malia listened patiently as I outlined the delay in the library reception and squealed when I told her about the finagling I did so her wish could come true. She clapped her hands and hugged me. "Adri, you are the absolute best. I'm sorry you've been stressed, but I hope you can enjoy the rest of your day."

Her eyes sparkled when she said that and warning bells went off momentarily, until I glanced at my checklist and remembered what I needed to do next. "I still haven't received the file on the new logo design and templates from Neil's company that I'm supposed to use on the napkins and stuff at the reception. Do you know anything about that?"

"Jon and Neil went to the office to check on a few things. I guess Neil's personal assistant, Charly, is missing and she has all the files on the new logo," Malia said. "It might be a no-go if they don't find her soon."

"What? I was planning on contacting her today to get the final prints." Before my blood pressure could fully come down from the first incident, this new information had it rising again. I hated the feeling of being out of control and at everyone else's unorganized mercy.

Malia shrugged. "Obviously I'm not going to cry real tears if the Tri-C company logo doesn't show up for its V.I.P. seating at my wedding." She rolled her eyes.

"But your father-in-law is footing the bill for the luau so he might cry—or something." That had been foremost on Neil's requests for the wedding breakfast, and the bill was ginormous, so I couldn't shrug it off as Malia had.

"You already have the company lined up waiting to print the image, right?"

"Yes, but—" I protested.

"No, buts, you need to take a break." Malia shook her head and smiled. "I don't want you to worry about this. Jon said he would let us know as soon as they figure out what to do."

I gripped my planner and tried to keep my voice calm. "But if I don't get it ordered they won't be here in time."

"Call the company and tell them you're going to need a rush order. Find out when the last possible minute is that you can send them the file."

"Good idea."

Her phone started playing a calypso tune and she answered it with a cheery, "Aloha!" She held up her finger and walked a few steps from me while she continued her conversation.

I redirected my attention to the revised wedding schedule and amenities. A few minutes later, Malia returned and patted my hand. "Sorry about that." She sat back down. "Now I want to say something. You're in Hawaii. You're an amazing wedding planner who is so organized that even these setbacks won't throw you off track. I know everything will be okay." Malia gave me a thumbs up.

I sensed that she was working hard to keep up her usual cheerful nature. "Malia, you can be angry—I am."

She took a deep breath. "Nothing is going to interfere with the happiness that Kyle and I are celebrating. I decided that if something didn't work out, it wasn't meant to be."

I started to say something, but she held up her hand. "No, it's my wedding. Now I know these things are stressing you out, and you can't do anything about it right now, so I made some other plans for you."

"What? When?" Shaking my head, I eyed her phone. "That's okay. I have plenty to keep me busy." The ticker tape in my mind ran through all the items I needed to double-check before the wedding. Malia was right—this wedding had been planned down to the tiniest detail long before we ever boarded the flight—but I didn't want to let go of those carefully laid plans for some company with a larger payroll than mine.

"Adri, you aren't listening to me," Malia interrupted my thoughts. She took my hands and looked me in the eye. "You have two hours, maybe three tops, and then I want you to take a break for the rest of the day. We both know if you don't, you'll end up stewing all day over problems you can't solve."

"Why can't every bride be like you?" I asked, and sincerely meant it.

Malia gave me a hug. "I know my wedding will be beautiful. Thank you for everything you've done." She stood and pointed at me. "No ditching."

"How can I ditch if I don't know what I'm ditching?"

She laughed, but didn't offer any more information. "Kyle and I are going on a sunset catamaran ride, so I probably won't see you until tomorrow. Text me if you need anything."

"Have fun." I waved. "Take a picture of a dolphin for me."

I walked back to my room, wondering what Malia had been scheming—maybe something with the hotel staff. Informing her about Mrs. Harper had gone well. I had a feeling it would, but I still had a bad taste in my mouth every time I thought of the well-pressed, ornery woman. There must be some way to find out who Mrs. Harper was planning her luau for, but so far no one had let that information slip. I had a few tricks up my sleeve when it came to sleuthing. Maybe I'd have to use them.

Chapter 5

VEGETARIAN ISLAND SANDWICHES

Sliced red, yellow, and green peppers; bell, Anaheim, or banana peppers are a favorite
Gouda cheese
Mustard and mayonnaise if desired
Garnish with alfalfa sprouts, baby spinach leaves, and sliced avocado, seasoned with sea salt, pepper, and olive oil infused with coconut
Serve on Hawaiian sweet rolls, hoagie buns, or your favorite sandwich bread

Courtesy of www.mashedpotatoesandcrafts.com

The next couple hours I spent holed up in my room, working at the desk with an ocean view. I made phone calls and double-checked that everything would be ready for the wedding on Saturday. The company printing the new logo on the napkins, place cards, and other paraphernalia could do so as late as Friday. I sat on the balcony feeling oddly relaxed despite the problems with the upcoming nuptials. I decided it was because I was only worrying about one wedding at the moment instead of six or seven as had been the norm lately.

I was just about to text Lorea to check on the Zeeman/Benson wedding—our next big gig happening in June, when someone rapped on the door.

I checked my watch, and grabbed the doorknob. It had been two and a half hours since Malia had warned me about relaxing. Maybe this was someone from the spa with a surprise appointment, or room service with fresh pineapple. I opened the door and my smile froze.

Jon Connelly stood there dressed in blue swim trunks and a black rash guard that accentuated his toned chest muscles. "Aloha." He flashed me the Hawaiian hang loose sign and grinned. "That look means Malia didn't tell you I was coming, right?"

I shook my head slowly from side to side wondering what he wanted, then I remembered. "Oh, did you find the file with the new logo?"

He frowned. "Sorry, but my dad has some people working on it. Don't stress—Dad's doing enough of that for everyone."

"Okay, then I won't stress. So what did you need?"

He stuck his hands in his pockets and smiled. "I know things have been pretty crazy for you. Malia said I might help prevent a nervous breakdown, so will you go on a date with me?"

No way. I couldn't believe that Jon was what Malia had been referring to when she gave me the "no ditching" command. Was she that worried about me? I would have to tell her that I liked being alone, having time to relax. I didn't need to be entertained. "I don't do well with pity dates."

"This is not a pity date. I didn't word that right. Adri, I think you're a talented woman and you have gorgeous brown eyes. I'd like to get to know you better. I want to take you on the bike trail down to Donkey Beach. It's a relaxing ride, and the scenery is gorgeous." He tilted his head to the side. "Please?"

I couldn't help but laugh. "Why did Malia put you up to this? I'm totally fine."

He looked confused. "Malia didn't put me up to anything. I've been bugging her since you got here. She called me a couple hours ago and said that you had some free time this afternoon. She wouldn't give me your phone number, said I had to come take you on a date to get that info."

My shoulders tensed with that news, but I softened when I thought about how easy Malia had been to work with. She wanted me to have fun and part of her meddling came from her knowledge of my history—which was still pretty fresh.

Jon stepped forward. "Please. I know I should have asked you outright, but I figured you'd say you were too busy with the wedding plans."

He was right. I wouldn't have accepted, based purely on how it looked. I came to Hawaii to work, not play with the groom's brother. "Well, Malia is technically my boss, and she did give me an order before she left today."

"What was that?"

"I think her exact words were, 'no ditching.'"

He laughed. "She's awesome. Kyle's a lucky guy."

"I agree. Malia is solid gold."

"So, can I claim your afternoon?" Jon held out both hands. "The bike path is easy—right along the shoreline."

"That does sound like fun, and I need some more pictures for my blog."

"Then it's a date. Can I come back here to pick you up in fifteen minutes?"

"Sure." I was just about to say that I needed to grab my suit—it was nice of him to allow me time to get ready. "I can probably be ready in ten—I hate to keep you waiting."

"No problem. I have one quick errand to run, so take your time." He lifted two fingers in a wave and hurried down the hall.

A jitter of excitement flowed through me as I changed into my red tankini and pulled on a cover-up and another pair of flip-flops from my selection—black with red elastic bands. The plans were most likely a pity date, despite what Jon said, but all the same, I would get to see more of the island. And Jon wasn't hard to look at.

I sent a text to Lorea: **Going on a date!**

She would be proud of me, and then she couldn't hassle me so much when I wanted to set her up with someone back home. Her fear of commitment ran deeper than mine, although mine wasn't necessarily a fear of commitment—I think most people would be a little gun-shy if their last boyfriend had tried to kill them.

I pulled my hair back into a ponytail and applied raspberry lip gloss. Jon arrived right on time. "You look great," he said as we walked toward the elevator.

"Thanks." I experienced a moment's hesitation about going out with Jon—just the two of us. I hoped he was truly looking forward to time spent together. The elevator doors slid shut with a soft ping, and I told myself to act natural.

My morning had been far from natural, though. I thought of the strange incidents from earlier and the conflicts with Malia's luau. I hadn't thought about Mrs. Harper, the crazy lady, since I returned to my room. I'd been so busy—first working and then getting ready for my impromptu date—that the encounter had been out of focus. But now her sneer came back to center stage and my eyes tightened as I relived her harassment.

The identity of her company was top secret for some reason, but I had ways of figuring things out. They couldn't hide forever. Someone at the hotel was bound to slip up. I didn't like the sensation of fear and anxiety my encounter with that woman had brought on. A line from my therapist came to mind. "The best way to overcome fear is to recognize it, identify it, and define it. Pull back the scary layers and face the source of the fear." That's what I had to do—discover the company trying to trump Malia's wedding, layer by layer if necessary.

I wondered how much Jon knew about my crazy day. "Did Malia tell you about Mrs. Harper and her mysterious company trying to trample the wedding plans?"

"Yeah, I was really surprised. Malia said you handled things well—that you came out on top."

"If you don't count the threats."

"Really?"

I nodded. "I told her not to threaten me, and she said she wasn't." The elevator doors opened and I saw a flash of hot pink and stiffened. Jon noticed immediately.

"You okay?" His voice was a low murmur. He gave my hand a gentle squeeze.

"Uh, you know how we were just talking about psycho-lady?"

His eyes widened and he looked around. "Is she here?"

"I thought I just saw her, but I'm not sure."

"C'mon." He tugged on my hand. "There's another way out."

He led me around a large tree and exaggerated checking to see if the coast was clear. I covered my mouth, but a laugh still escaped.He grinned as he led me through the shopping areas and out a side door. "I feel like a spy or something," he whispered.

"I wish you were. It's really bugging me that I don't know what company that horrible woman works for."

"Tell you what—forget her, enjoy the day with me, and when we get back, I'll see what I can find out. No one should get away with that kind of behavior."

I studied his face. He wasn't teasing—there was a tightness around his eyes that indicated he was serious and maybe even concerned for me. "That sounds great."

We drove to a little bike shop where we rented two cruisers with oversized, cushioned seats. Jon shouldered a backpack that he said contained secret spy food and rolled his bike into the street. I laughed when I straddled the pink bike, and Jon began ringing the little bell attached to the handlebars of his baby blue bicycle.

Less than five minutes later, the ocean roared nearby and a cool breeze brushed my skin as I pedaled leisurely alongside Jon.

"Having fun?" he asked.

"This is awesome." It had been too long since I had taken a real vacation, and even though this was classified as work, it felt like a break to me.

We passed other bikers, runners, and several people out for an early afternoon stroll. A large green bush with dark pink blossoms trailing toward the ground caught my eye. It was the same type I had seen in several places on the island. "What is that flowering bush called?"

"That's bougainvillea." Jon pronounced it bogan-viya.

I grinned. "I've read about those flowers in so many books, but I never knew how to pronounce the word. I've always wanted to see one in real life."

"They're everywhere. Some people keep them trimmed for hedges. There are some red ones by the resort."

I breathed in, rolling back my shoulders as I pedaled. "The air smells like flowers here."

Jon smirked at me. "I think someone's a romantic."

I pushed the lever on my bell and raced past him. "Not me, but don't tell my clients."

He laughed and caught up with me. "So tell me more about the Adri outside of wedding planning."

"I like the outdoors, running, hiking. I love my family. I'm a farm girl."

"Hey, I know some things about farming."

I rolled my eyes. "Ha, how many sprinkler pipes have you moved?"

Jon placed a hand over his heart. "Ouch, did you just call me a wimp?"

"'Fess up, city boy. How dirty do your hands get with your so-called farming?"

"I feel threatened," Jon said. "Malia told me, 'Adri is a sweet, beautiful girl.'" He pointed at me. "This chick has attitude."

I laughed so hard I snorted and that set Jon off. He braked and leaned over his handlebars. He had a great laugh, and when he slapped his thigh I was reminded of my dad. We continued riding, and I asked him about the company his father owned. I had learned that Tri-C was a GMO—one of several companies specializing in genetically modified organisms, or GMOs as they were referred to on the isle of

Kauai. But Malia had insisted the Connellys had a unique approach—I was interested to find out why they thought their approach was different than the other companies on the isle.

"I still don't understand why your parents don't live here."

"Part of the year they do." Jon stopped pedaling so I could catch up. "My dad likes to keep up with the competition. He does a lot of work monitoring crops in several different areas of the country."

"How did your dad start the company?"

"Tri-C is a huge company—my dad is only part owner—there are actually four other guys who are part-owners. They all went to school together at Stanford. My dad studied agronomy and genetic engineering. Two of the guys are agronomists from Utah State University. When they transferred over to Stanford with big ideas, the company was formed."

I coasted past Jon and pulled the lever on my bell. "I watched a documentary a few years back and no offense, but I came away with the opinion that GMOs are bad guys."

Jon chuckled. "Yeah, my dad loves those films—don't bring it up, by the way, but our company is different. At least my dad's vision is different. He's not trying to drive small farmers out of business and take them to court for "stealing" genetically modified seed. The mission of our company is to create smart seeds that produce more nutrient dense plants.

"But I thought the soil was in charge of the nutrients."

"It is, but our smart seeds work with the soil to take the most important trace nutrients into the plant. For us, it's not all about creating a weed-proof, bug-proof plant, but one that produces a true organic food."

"That sounds a lot more noble than I suspected."

He grinned. "Well, if you talk to any of the islanders, you might get a different story. GMO is a bad word here because pretty much all the farmland is tied up in crop testing. Kauai is almost completely dependent on imports for its sustenance."

We passed by a young couple snapping pictures of the shoreline. I rang my bell as I caught up with Jon again. "Hmm, now who is the tour guide of little known facts?"

"Sorry, I didn't mean to bore you." He tilted his head and gave me a crooked grin.

"Actually, you're not. I think it's very interesting, considering my family homesteaded in Rupert. My grandparents had to clear out the sagebrush and plant around lava flows to get a good crop."

"See, now that's interesting to me. Kyle has been trying to explain the desert terrain in that region of Idaho—it sounds fascinating."

We continued to talk about farming and my Idaho roots until we reached the end of the bike path. The path continued on in to a narrow red-dirt path, but our cruisers weren't equipped to do much off-roading.

"I thought you said we were going to the beach." I motioned to the red dirt trail beyond us and then to my bike. "This is not a mountain bike."

"We are. We passed the trail head about a quarter mile back. I just wanted you to be able to say you rode the entire Kauai bike trail." He turned his bike around and began pedaling back the way we had just come. "We can bring a mountain bike on our next date if you'd like."

With a shake of my head, I followed him. Jon was easygoing, and I liked his fun personality, but I wasn't sure about his ideas of future dates. I was here to put all of my plans for Malia's wedding into action, not chase after her brother-in-law. If only his toned surfer's body didn't look so good. I bit my lip when I noticed how the bronze color of his skin contrasted with the unruly curls at the nape of his neck— my internal debate was heading in the wrong direction.

"We'll leave our bikes right here." Jon rode off the paved trail into the grasses on the side of the hill. He hopped off his bike and laid it in the grass. I followed suit. We were at the top of an incline overlooking the ocean.

"Beautiful." My feet itched to feel the cool water and warm sand. The day had heated up nicely. It was time to reapply sunscreen.

Jon stood next to me. "That's Donkey Beach. The waves can be rough, so it's not great for swimming, but it's a nice place for a picnic."

"Sounds good to me."

We walked down the hill and through a border of trees that lined the edge of the sand.

"Oh, I forgot to lock up the bikes—my gorgeous date distracted me." He squeezed my hand. "Go on down near the water. I'll catch up with you."

"I can come back with you, it's not that far."

"No problem. Here take my pack. Pick out where you'd like to set up for lunch." He shrugged off the backpack and handed it to me.

I was surprised at how heavy it was. "Wow, there must be some picnic in here."

"Don't get your hopes up, my mother—the vegetarian—volunteered lunch." He pointed toward the beach. "There's a big piece of driftwood right there. I'll be right back if you want to head for a good picnic spot."

He jogged up the hill, and I kicked off my flip-flops, grabbed them from the sand and began walking barefoot across the warm sand. The noise of the surf and waves pulling back and forth across the shoreline gave me a thrill. I loved the ocean. It was so powerful. I wanted to dip my feet in the water, but first I deposited the backpack near the driftwood and stretched out my legs. I re-applied sunscreen and decided to set up lunch.

The backpack held two reed mats, sandwiches, sliced pineapple, and what looked like two homemade smoothies in insulated mugs. I set everything out and then watched the waves for a few minutes, and still Jon hadn't returned. Every few seconds, I turned my head to look back toward the trees at the base of the hill. I was just getting up to go and see if everything was okay when he jogged through the trees.

"Sorry about the wait," he said when he reached the picnic spread. "I dropped one of the keys in the grass. It took me a few minutes to find it. There may have been some swearing involved."

I grinned. "I won't tell if you don't."

"Thanks. Now let's eat."

I was starving by the time we unwrapped the sandwiches. "I've never had a Hawaiian picnic."

"Well, I wouldn't call this Hawaiian," Jon mumbled around a bite. "But these are my mom's specialty island sandwiches."

I took a bite and nodded. Mine had red and yellow sliced peppers, gouda cheese, spinach, and avocado. It was delicious on the sweet roll that was now warm from the sun.

"At least my pack will be lighter on the way back." Jon motioned to the water bottle I'd just guzzled.

"Oh, I'm sorry, should I have saved some?"

"No, there's two more in the pack. I'm just teasing."

After we finished eating, I removed my cover up and Jon raised his eyebrows. "Now who's on the pity date?"

I threw a handful of sand at him and leaned back on my mat. Jon tried not to be obvious in his staring as he pulled off his shirt and reclined on his mat. A smile pulled at the corners of my mouth, but I didn't say anything. Instead, I closed my eyes, dozing under the tropical heat. I was almost asleep when the image of an arm moving slowly with the current of the water invaded my senses. I opened my eyes and sat up. "Do you think the police found out who that woman was?"

Jon shaded his eyes with his hands. "I haven't heard anything yet. It's been bothering me too." He sat up and leaned toward me. "I know it was disturbing, but I don't want it to ruin your visit."

I swallowed. I wouldn't admit that the nightmare last night was too vivid. When I awoke with sweat dripping down my back, I felt compelled to find out the identity of the dead woman. Flicking some sand off my knee, I turned to Jon. "I'm still upset by it. I think she was young."

"Did you get that good of a look at her?" Jon sat up straight. "I didn't realize you were able to get down that close."

"I grabbed onto the rock and pulled myself close enough to see the chains wrapped around her. I think she had green eyes." With a shudder, I closed my eyes and my throat went dry.

"Don't do that to yourself."

I opened my eyes and blinked rapidly.

"Hey, it's going to be okay." His voice was soft and he tilted his head to look at me.

I met his gaze. "But someone killed her. Someone took her life." The pitch of my voice rose, so I paused, whispering, "Why?"

Jon shook his head. "I don't know. It's a crazy world, but you finding her was a good thing. Now the police can investigate, and whoever is missing her will get some closure."

"I guess." I dug my toes into the sand and watched it reshape around my feet.

"C'mon, let's get your mind off that." Jon took my hand and pulled me up next to him. I wobbled and leaned into his chest as I got my footing. It was only for a second, but the warmth of his chest sent tingles through my arms as we walked down to where the waves were crashing into the shoreline.

The water caressed my feet and for a moment we stood there letting the bubbly surf wash over our ankles. "Wanna jump a few waves?" Jon asked.

"Sure." I rubbed the back of my neck where the sun warmed my skin. "I haven't done that for at least five years, but that was in California."

"Warmer here, and we won't go out too far."

"Oh, I meant to take my ring off and leave it in the backpack." I motioned to the amazonite ring I had purchased from a vendor at the hotel. "It doesn't fit quite right, and I don't want it to fall off in the water."

"Give it to me. I have a zippered pocket in my shorts." He motioned to his dark blue board shorts.

"Thanks." I handed Jon my ring and watched him slide it into his pocket and zip it closed. Then he reached for my hand and when our fingers intertwined, I made eye contact with him again. The light blue color of his eyes looked almost crystalline in the bright sun, and I studied the flecks of green that created an almost turquoise hue. My face flushed. I looked back to the ocean.

"You sure you're okay?" He squeezed my hand gently.

I nodded. "Thanks for this. I needed a break today."

"Well, let's go then." Jon broke into a run, pulling me with him. I gasped when the water hit my thighs. The first wave was cold, but after a few minutes I didn't notice as swell after swell rose and broke on the sand. We jumped a few waves, but Jon didn't think it was a good idea to go too far out.

We returned to our beach mats which were pretty much covered with sand. My breath came in short puffs. Jon was quiet as he caught his breath. We watched a group of guys trying to catch a good wave, but mostly getting pounded a little ways out.

"The ocean's angry today," Jon said. His voice was soft, and I had to lean closer to hear him above the crashing waves.

"I think it's beautiful. I wish I could capture it in a picture, but it's something you just have to see in person."

"Mm-hmm, I could say the same thing about you." He put his arm around me.

It felt good being close to him. I rested my head on his chest and allowed myself a few deep breaths. The inner struggle returned, with the good, no-nonsense Adri reminding me that I didn't have time to date Jon, and the bad Adri thinking about how it might feel if he were to kiss me right then.

He rubbed his hand up and down my arm, sand flaking off with the movement. "If I helped you, could you make time for a hike in the next couple of days?"

I lifted my head. "Help me?"

"Yeah, with your work. Maybe I could run errands for you? Or better yet, see if one of my dad's secretaries could."

With a smirk, I pounded his shoulder. "I should make you come and pick out flowers just for that. But you know what would help me is if I could track down your dad's personal assistant."

Jon stiffened. "She quit."

"What?"

"It was sudden, and my dad's not happy about it."

"She was my main contact person for the files and the new company logo. Your dad wanted me to make sure they were on the napkins and some new bracelets for the wedding party. Do you know who I should contact now?"

"Uh, I do remember hearing something about the logo, but I'm not sure what's happening with locating it. Let me talk to Dad—I can definitely do that for you." He looked at me and the tenseness in his face relaxed. "Will that earn me another date?"

He was staring at my lips. It took all my willpower not to look at his mouth. Instead, I dropped my gaze. "I'll see what I can do."

"Adri," he whispered and I lifted my eyes to his. He leaned toward me, and I felt the electric pull of a kiss about to happen. My eyelids fluttered, but I didn't close them. I swallowed and Jon hesitated, his lips inches from mine. He lifted his hand to my cheek. "Why are you afraid?"

It all came crashing back then. The reasons my heart was *definitely* not ready to go where Jon was trying to lead it— even if it was just a kiss. The last person I'd kissed was my boyfriend—someone who had proclaimed his love for me. I didn't even want to think his name, let alone speak it aloud. After stalking me for months, he'd tried to kill me. He was in prison now, and I was safe. My chest tightened. I sucked in a breath, leaning back. My movements were jerky as I started to pull myself to my feet—what was I going to do, run away? I sank back into the sand and with a noisy exhale, rested my head on my knees.

The images were colliding into each other—the crazy boyfriend, the knife, the dead woman at the bottom of the ocean. The tension in my head increased, and I forced the scenes from my mind, searching for something to replace them that would comfort me. Luke filtered into my thoughts, and even though I didn't want to, I recognized a yearning for his presence. We weren't dating, and our friendship felt safe. At least that was something I could focus on that wouldn't hurt me.

"Adri?" Jon was still there, of course, and he sounded worried. "Are you okay?" The warmth of his hand on my back brought me out of my panic. I blinked, trying to clear the tears clinging to my lashes. He would think I was an emotional basket case.

Malia knew something happened to me last summer, but maybe not all the details. Jon didn't know anything about me, but my scar would have been impossible to miss in my red swimming top. When he hadn't said anything about it, I figured it was because Malia had filled him in. But maybe Jon was just as polite and kind as he seemed. I considered the chance that Malia didn't know as much of my history as I'd assumed—if she stayed out of the news loop, it was possible.

"I'm sorry," Jon said.

"You didn't do anything wrong," I mumbled.

"Adri, please, what's the matter?"

I heaved a great sigh and lifted my head slightly. "I have issues."

"Don't we all?"

I groaned and swiped my eyes with my hand.

"Do you want to tell me about it?"

"Did Malia tell you anything about me?"

He studied me for a moment, his brow furrowed. "Besides, 'Jon, you have to meet my wedding planner. She's incredibly gorgeous and the nicest girl.'" He leaned forward. "She was right, you know. You are gorgeous, but you're authentic too. That's rare and I feel so lucky to be able to spend some time with you today. Sorry I ruined things."

I thrust my hands into the sand. "You didn't ruin anything. It's been a wonderful day—just what I needed." I paused, trying to think how to explain my behavior. My fingers traced my scar, did I want to tell him? He was watching me again, waiting for me to say something.

Finally, he cleared his throat. "I noticed your scar. I can tell it's something that happened recently because it's still pink, but I'm not going to ask, and you don't have to tell me either."

I don't know why, but the gentleness in his words undid me. The tears slipped down my cheeks and I bowed my head, letting them fall in dark splotches on the sand.

"Would you like me to hold you for a minute? I won't try to kiss you."

My throat tightened as I attempted to cut off the flow of tears. I didn't feel embarrassed or angry at myself for crying in front of Jon—and that was a good feeling. My emotions had been stacked neatly away in the corner closet of my heart, buried by the work of planning twelve weddings since the first weeks after my recovery. Lorea and I had been completely booked, and I had reveled in the exertion because it kept me from focusing on my wounded heart.

I looked over at Jon. He opened his arms. With a sniff, I leaned into them and let his embrace cover the torrent of emotions whirling through me. It felt good to be held, caressed, and safe for the moment. The ocean continued its steady pounding of the shores, and I listened to its soothing sounds. I wasn't this person—the girl who cried on the guy's shoulder—a guy I hardly knew. I had to get a hold of myself, but my seams were unraveling.

"Last summer, I thought I was falling in love. My boyfriend tried to kill me, which is why dating hasn't been that appealing lately," I mumbled against his chest.

Jon tensed, probably trying to think of what to say, so I hurried to continue. "I don't know if you heard about Sylvia

Rockfort last year and how her wedding planner was almost killed."

"Wait, that was you?" He lowered his head. "The guy who murdered your other client and then went after you?"

"Except the news didn't tell you that his first victim—my client—was also my best friend."

The lines around his eyes tightened as he pulled me close. "That's terrible. I'm so sorry."

I allowed some of my fear to dissipate and let myself be comforted by him. "I thought I was doing okay, but I've been working so much and maybe haven't dealt with everything like I should have." I thought about the two counseling sessions I'd made it to because of Detective Ford's insistence—well his and Lorea's, added to my whole family. The sessions helped, but I'd been so busy that I hadn't returned. "So I have some trust issues that are pretty much a part of who I am now."

"I'm sorry I tried to rush things." He pulled his head back to look at me. "I couldn't help myself, though. You'll only be here for another week."

"Were you thinking of proposing by Monday to keep me on Kauai?"

His face reddened, and I poked him. He tightened his embrace. "No, but I actually have plans for the future which may or may not include a permanent move to the mainland."

I lifted my head. "Really? Why?"

"The same kind of thing Kyle is doing. He asked if I'd be interested in working with him—keeps telling me how great the soil is in Idaho."

I wondered how much he knew about his brother working near Sun Valley. Malia had confided that he was working to start his own business away from the GMO, but that his father would be furious with his decision. Maybe this was Kyle's way of trying to appease his father. If Jon took charge of the operations, it would keep the peace. But that would mean— "You're moving to Idaho?"

"I'm not sure, but I told him I would at least come and work with him for a few months. If it doesn't suit me, then I thought I'd help him hire someone else."

"And you'd come back to Kauai?"

"Well, I'd still split my time between here and Nebraska—you can't ignore the corn belt of the Midwest."

I sifted through what Jon was saying—that I might see him after this week in Hawaii. It made me nervous. I was only in this for a couple dates, but suddenly there was a possibility for much more. *Calm down*, I thought to myself, *this is only a picnic.*

"Don't worry, Adri. I just met you. I'm not going to push you. You're definitely as amazing and beautiful as Malia described, but I would never try to force your trust. Let's have fun, okay?"

I nodded.

He took my hand and helped me up from the sand, but still held me in his protective embrace. "No worries." Jon kissed the top of my head and then released me. "Ready to head back?"

I pulled my big toe through the sand, thinking how to phrase what I wanted to say. I breathed in and looked up at Jon. "I want you to know that I'm not like this. I don't just unload on guys on the first date. I'm really sorry." He held up his hand, but I clutched his fingers. "But I think I needed to tell someone. I haven't talked about what happened very much, so thank you for listening."

His eyes softened and he glanced at my mouth. "And now I want to kiss you again, so we'd better go."

For a second I thought about giving in to that part of me that wanted to be held and kissed, but I didn't trust my own heart. It had led me astray, and I was forever marked by the experience. I squeezed Jon's hand and then let it go.

Chapter 6

AUTHENTIC HAWAIIAN SHAVE ICE

Ingredients:
Strawberry Syrup:
1 1/2 cups diced fresh strawberries (or blend up whole berries)
2 tbsps freshly squeezed lime juice (1 lime)
3/4 cup water
3/4 cup white granulated sugar

Pineapple Syrup:
1 1/2 cups diced fresh pineapple
2 tbsps freshly squeezed lime juice (1 lime)
3/4 cup water
3/4 cup white granulated sugar

Ice
Macadamia nut ice cream or your preferred flavor

1. *To make the strawberry syrup, combine the strawberries, lime juice, water, and sugar in a small saucepan. Bring the mixture to a boil, then cook over medium heat for 5 minutes. After removing the pan from the heat, leave the fruit in the syrup while it cools to room temperature. Then, after it cools completely, strain the mixture through a fine mesh sieve into a small pitcher or squeeze bottle.*
2. *In a separate saucepan, repeat the process from Step 1 with the pineapple. (*Cook pineapple for about 10 minutes.)*
3. *If desired put one scoop of ice cream in the bottom of each bowl. Finely shave ice into bowls or cups, then pour syrup over the ice.*

Courtesy of www.mashedpotatoesandcrafts.com

We repacked everything, now covered with sand, and headed to where we'd left the bikes. I admired the bits of broken seashells scattered along the beach and a few pieces of driftwood as we walked in comfortable silence.

A dark shell caught my eye, and I bent to pick it up. Black and white lines ran down the contours of the shell. "This one's pretty." I held it up for Jon to see.

"It's rare to find an unbroken shell, but this beach actually has a few." He studied the shell and handed it back to me.

Beachcombing in Hawaii was against the law—I had read that in my blue ultimate guidebook of Kauai—but I didn't think holding onto a chipped shell would land me in jail. The problem was I didn't have anywhere to put it. "I'd like to keep this one."

"Here." Jon unzipped a side pocket on the backpack.

"Thanks." I dropped the shell into the pack.

Jon readjusted the backpack and then took my hand. As our fingers intertwined, a pleasant warmth spread across my cheeks. We crested the hill, and I turned to see the ocean. Jon released my hand abruptly.

"Hey!" He hurried toward where we'd left the bikes and stopped short. They were gone. "I locked them up—together." Jon looked toward the bike path angrily. "Someone would have to take them apart to steal them."

Vehicles couldn't get on the bike path, so if someone actually stole the bikes they would have to carry them. It didn't seem likely. I turned in a circle and caught sight of a gleam of metal near some shrubs. The dry grass crunched underfoot as I jogged over to the bush. "They're right here."

"What?" Jon ran over and lifted the bikes up, examining the locks, which were still in place. "That's strange," he said. "I wonder if someone did try to steal them."

"But isn't that where we left them?"

"No, look at the grass over here. You can see where the bikes flattened it." He pointed at the indentation, then pulled the bikes from the bush and began unlocking them. "A lot of people just wind the lock through the tire and onto a branch, but I locked the bikes together."

He had wound one lock through the front tire and frame of the bike across to the other bike's frame and vice versa with the second lock. A couple minutes later with Jon muttering under his breath about thieves, he had the bikes ready to go. "Everything looks okay. You ready?"

"Thanks again, Jon, O mighty protector of vintage bicycles." I touched his cheek. He grabbed my hand, tickling my sides until I squealed. When he let go, I grabbed my bike and pedaled onto the path. I had a head start for about three seconds before I heard the dinging of the little bell behind me. I shrieked and pedaled faster. Jon laughed as he raced to catch up.

"Those skinny white legs are no match for mine, you know," he said coming up beside me.

"You'd better watch it, mister, insulting my pearly whites."

"I wasn't talking about your teeth, but you do have a great smile."

I reached out to try to smack him, but he veered away with a chuckle. We rode that way teasing back and forth for the next ten minutes, until Jon pointed toward the ocean. "Let's stop at this dock. It's kind of cool. We missed it on the way. I got blinded by the reflection off your legs."

"That, or you were too busy checking out my backside."

His raised his eyebrows. "Who me?"

We followed the paved trail off the main path to a pavilion overlooking the desiccated remains of a large dock. The path led all the way to the edge of the cliff and a gated viewing area, so I began to brake as I rode down the hill.

One minute I was gazing out at the rugged beauty of the ocean, the next I was tumbling over the top of my handlebars screaming. The momentum pushed me forward, and that combined with the downhill slope brought me right to the edge of the cliff. My feet skidded on the red dirt, but I couldn't stop. I grabbed at the grasses and rocks, trying to find something to keep me from falling. Just as I was about to go over the edge, Jon gripped my arm and I jolted to a stop.

A searing pain went through my right shoulder and I cried out.

"Hold on. I've got you," Jon yelled.

I reached over with my left arm and clasped his hand. My feet dangled for a second, but I kicked forward until I found a base for one foot. "My shoulder!" I cried as Jon pulled on my right arm, the pain scorching through my body.

He stopped pulling, and before I knew what had happened, he'd flipped me over and dragged me up to the top on my back. The rocks bit into my skin, and I winced as pain again shot through my arm.

I turned my head to see how in the world I'd gone from riding my bike to cliff-jumping in two seconds. The front tire had come off my bike. The tire had rolled to a stop at the railing in front of the dock. Waves slapped against the dock and the roar of the ocean reverberated in my ears.

"Are you okay?" Jon knelt next to me, carefully brushing the dirt from my arms. "I thought you were going to go right over the edge."

"Me too." I closed my eyes, trying to ignore the throbbing in my arm, legs, and back. A stinging sensation across my legs indicated I had some great abrasions.

"Are you in a lot of pain? Your legs are all scratched up."

"Guess they won't be white anymore." I leaned over and saw the angry red scrapes. I sucked in a breath through my teeth and squeezed my eyes shut. "Man, this stings."

"You know I was just teasing." Jon said in a mock serious tone. "You don't have to go to drastic measures to change. I think you're beautiful."

I laughed and opened my eyes. Jon hovered over me and I focused on the concern I saw in his face. "Thanks. And thanks for saving me."

"I'm sorry about your shoulder. We'd better get some ice on it as soon as we get back. And those scrapes are nasty. Do you need to go to a doctor?"

"No, I'll be fine." I moved my shoulder slightly and cringed, but I concentrated on the movement, deciding that it was something akin to a sprain.

"Here, let's get you out of the sun." Jon helped me over to the pavilion. I grimaced with every movement chaffing against my road rash. He helped me sit and handed me a water bottle.

While I sat in the shade, Jon gathered up my bike parts and leaned them against the picnic table. Then he called the rental shop and explained the problem. A few minutes later, he sat beside me. "They said they are on their way to pick up the bikes and they can give us a ride back."

My shoulders slumped. "I was having such a good time."

"Hey, don't worry. It's been a great day, just a little more eventful than we bargained for." He watched me, studying my face. "You didn't hit your head, did you?"

"No, I executed a perfect flip." I picked out another piece of dirt from the scrape on my knee and glared at the scratches on my arms. "Good thing I don't have to be in the pictures."

"You'll be in them, just not all of them," Jon said.

"Would it be okay if we walked back?"

Jon shook his head. "I know your arm is hurting you, and you're tired, but let's wait for someone to pick us up. Tell you what. When we get back, I'll treat you to some famous Hawaiian Shave Ice from Hee Fat General Store."

I didn't want to give in, but my body ached from the impact with the hard red soil. Walking for three more miles definitely wouldn't help my injuries. "That sounds good."

It turned out that we had to walk down the path a little ways to the next beach to meet our rescue pickup, but the movement helped get my mind off the nagging thought I couldn't banish. How did my bike tire come off? Parts like that don't just work loose. Jon said the bikes had been moved. Had someone tampered with my bike?

"Do you think someone was trying to get the wheel off to take the bike?" I asked Jon.

"That wouldn't make sense. Any fool could see it was chained to the frame as well."

When we returned to the bike shop, the owner greeted us and offered us a refund. Jon refused, and I told the owner I was fine.

He frowned. "We're very sorry about this. I just don't know how it happened."

"You and me both," I said.

"Are you sure someone didn't tamper with the bikes while they were left unattended?"

"They had been moved, but they were locked securely, so I don't know." Jon motioned to the bikes behind the counter. "Do you think the screw just came loose?"

The man shook his head. "Those were some of our newer models, but even if it was older, those parts don't just come loose." He studied me for a moment. "Are you sure you're okay?"

I glanced at my shoulder. "A bit sore but I still enjoyed the day."

"Let me get you some ice." The owner went into another room and returned with a baggie of ice.

"Thank you. This will help." I held the bag on my shoulder and winced.

Jon put his hand on my waist as we exited the bike shop. "I know just the thing to take your mind off your battle scars."

I flinched as he helped me into the car and my leg brushed the seat. "You're going to slather me in numbing cream?"

"No, remember? I'm going to treat you to an authentic Hawaiian treat."

The Hee Fat General Store was also in Kapa'a, so it took us less than five minutes to drive to the shop filled with wonderful souvenirs and a shave ice counter in the back. There were six people in line, so it allowed me plenty of time to stare at the dozens of flavors available.

I leaned into Jon. "So this is kind of like snow cones except they put a scoop of ice cream with it?"

Jon scoffed. "That is the ultimate insult to shave ice. It's nothing like a snow cone—closer to Italian ice."

I poked him in the ribs. "You're serious about your treats, huh?"

"Oh yeah." He helped me re-adjust the ice on my wounded shoulder.

He smelled like the ocean mixed with a citrus scent, maybe lime, and I allowed myself to relax and breathe him in. A second later I felt him staring at me and turned to meet the question in his eyes. "Feeling okay?"

I nodded and he gave me a quick squeeze as we stepped toward the counter. I listened to Jon order coconut ice cream topped with shave ice in the Hawaiian Sunrise flavor which included strawberry, mango, and pineapple syrups. I opted for a scoop of macadamia nut ice cream and my shave ice was flavored with mango, guava, and lychee. We sat on a bench in front of the store, and I let the sweet concoction melt on my tongue.

"What do you think?" Jon asked before he shoveled in another mouthful.

"Delicious." The ice was shaved so thin, it reminded me of gelato, and I loved the interesting new flavor of lychee—the employee told me it tasted like a combination of pear and grapes. I had to agree.

Jon finished his shave ice in record time, then leaned his head back against the wall and closed his eyes. I studied him, sifting through our experiences of the day. He had almost kissed me, teased me mercilessly, and saved my life—not bad for a first date. Part of me still wondered about that almost-kiss, but the rest of me was frustrated with my breakdown on the beach. Although my heart did feel a bit lighter, I still didn't like crying in front of people.

Jon peered at me beneath his lashes. "Am I that good looking? 'Cause I can feel you staring at me."

I rolled my eyes and turned back to my treat. "I was just thinking about our first date."

He chuckled. "Worried what might happen on the second?"

"Nope. Are you still up for helping me track down that secretary?" I asked.

His brow furrowed. "I don't know if we'll have much luck with that if my dad hasn't found her. But yes, I'll help you get the files you need."

"Thanks, Jon, for listening today, for understanding, for . . . everything."

He tapped his foot against the sidewalk. "About that second date."

I held my hand up. "Hold it, buddy. Let's see how you come through on your promises first."

"I guess we'll just have to extend the first date a little longer then." He chuckled. "C'mon. I have something for you."

"Oh?" My stomach flipped, and I ordered myself to quit acting like a giddy teenager, but the way he looked at me when he spoke made fireworks spark through my heart. I glanced at his mouth and bit my lip as he held out his hand with his penetrating gaze. The sugar had taken the edge off my scrapes, and his tanned body was looking much too appealing.

We got in the car and headed back to the southern region of Kauai. "It's back at the hotel," he said.

My eyes widened and I tried to cover my reaction, but too late. Jon laughed. "The front desk is holding it for me, and don't worry, it's not a room key."

I punched him—but not too hard. He pretended it hurt and laughed some more. Jon kept doing that—making me feel comfortable then twisting up my insides, making me blush and act like a schoolgirl. I kind of liked him, maybe a tiny bit more than I wanted to at the moment.

When we pulled up to the hotel, he opened my door for me and walked me past the front desk out to the wide deck overlooking the ocean. "Hey, would you like me to talk to someone about that psycho lady?"

I thought about Mrs. Harper. The plans were set now, so maybe she would leave me alone. "Thanks, but I don't want to stir the pot."

"Are you sure?"

I nodded. "I'll let you know if I change my mind, though."

"Okay then. I'll be right back," Jon said and jogged toward the entryway.

I watched him go and then turned back toward the deck. The waves rolled in, crashing against the beach with the rhythm and sound that I had loved since the first time I visited the ocean at age twelve. The sounds of the waves had lulled me to sleep many nights as I listened to a recording of the tide moving in and gulls crying. But nothing could compare to the raw beauty of the ocean up close.

My concentration shifted and the back of my neck tingled with the sense that someone was staring at me. I turned around, but Jon hadn't returned. There were several people milling about, talking, laughing, and getting ready to check out the swimming pools facing the beach. I let my gaze wander around the perimeter of the balcony, but I didn't see anything out of the ordinary. Then I shifted to look at the water again and stiffened when I made eye contact with a man standing in my direct line of sight. He stared, unblinking, and fear clutched at my throat. It was the same muscled Polynesian man I had encountered earlier, and as I stared at him he lifted his hand to his heart, tapped it twice, and then narrowed his eyes.

I took a step back and bumped into someone. "I'm sorry." I turned to apologize to a young woman behind me. When I faced forward again, the man was gone. I stood there for a few minutes, searching the crowds of people, but I couldn't see him or his light blue shirt decorated with the black outline of the hibiscus flower. It was nothing. Maybe he was just flirting—no harm done. I told myself it was okay, but I didn't feel better.

A few minutes later Jon returned, carrying a gorgeous plumeria lei. "Adri, are you still hurting? You look a little pale."

I opened my mouth to tell him about the man I'd seen, and then pressed my lips together. What if he thought I was over-reacting? And then I decided not to tell him because he would want to soothe me, tell me nothing was wrong, and that was not what I wanted to hear at the moment. "Just a little tired."

"This is for you." Jon held out the lei. "Beautiful flowers for a beautiful woman."

It looked different from the one he'd given Malia and I upon our arrival. The flowers were twice as thick on the strand. Jon placed it over my head and leaned in to kiss my cheek. He hesitated for half a second, all I needed to do was turn my head and my mouth would meet his, but I waited a nanosecond too long in my indecision and he pulled back.

"This is lovely. Thank you." The heady scent made me inhale deeply, and before I could stop myself, I sighed.

Jon didn't seem to notice. He studied me with some kind of knowing expression moving across his face, his mouth turning up slightly.

"I've had a great day." I embraced him, careful not to smash the flowers. "There are a few things I need to do—Malia's bridal shower is the day after tomorrow."

He nodded. "That's right, I remember Monday is a busy day for everyone. Sorry to keep you. I was just trying to see how long I could prolong the first date."

For a moment I thought he might invite me to dinner, and as much as I wanted to, I couldn't. My body ached and I needed to rest. "Thanks for today."

"Looks like you could probably use a nap and more ice," Jon said. He glanced at my shoulder, and the dull ache seemed to increase with the attention.

"That might be a good idea." I stepped forward, and he walked with me to the elevators. I didn't want him to accompany me all the way to my room, so I put my hand on his arm and looked up at him. "Thanks for everything, especially the flowers." I motioned to my lei. "I'll see you later, okay?"

"I'll call you as soon as I find something so we can plan date number two." He motioned to the lei he'd given me. "Keep that in the fridge in your room in this sack." He handed me a plastic sack. "And you can wear it tomorrow if you want."

"Good to know." I didn't say anything about tomorrow. Jon knew I had work to do, but it sounded like he was going to try to squeeze into my schedule if he could, and at the moment that sounded fine with me.

Chapter 7

HOW TO STORE YOUR HAWAIIAN LEI

Place flower lei inside a clear plastic bag and tie off. Refrigerate lei in between wearing and flowers will last up to three days before browning. When flowers start to wilt, hang lei to dry to enjoy the last of the unforgettable plumeria scent.

Courtesy of www.mashedpotatoesandcrafts.com

My room had a large, dark wood-framed mirror hanging above the dressers. I stood in front of the mirror, admiring my lei for a minute and reliving the afternoon with Jon. A flutter of excitement about Jon's attraction teased my middle, but then I frowned. I was doing exactly what I told myself I wasn't going to do—get involved with another guy. Without warning, Luke's face flashed through my mind, and I sucked in a breath as I remembered that he was supposed to arrive sometime today. A blast of mixed emotions regarding Luke, and then Jon, made me slump into my chair. Lorea hadn't let up on the fact that I still owed Luke a date for saving my life last summer, but Luke hadn't badgered me. He'd honored my request for space and time to heal, checking in on me occasionally.

My original hostile feelings toward him and his profession as a divorce lawyer had changed, but I didn't like the way my heart was already beating faster as I pictured his rare smile and blue eyes.

With a shake of my head, I rose from the chair and removed my lei. Holding it close to my face, I breathed in the scent. Then I positioned the plumeria flowers on the top of the desk and grabbed my camera. My mom would be thrilled with all the pictures I was taking for our blog.

I glanced at my watch—it was almost five-thirty, which meant that in Idaho it was nine-thirty. It was a perfect time to webcam my mom and show her the leis while they were still fresh.

Our conversation was brief, but I filled her in on some of my activities. I left out the parts about how I almost died on my bike ride. And I definitely didn't say anything about my adventure in snorkeling from yesterday. Mom urged me to have fun, relax, and take lots of pictures.

After signing off with Mom, I carefully stored my lei in the fridge and grabbed my planner. Malia's family was flying in tonight for her bridal shower on Monday. The party would be a success, because the resort staff was helping me put together a spa gift package for each guest with certificates for massages, facials, manicures, and pedicures. These party favors were supposed to include some special monogrammed items with the Tri-C logo, but I didn't know if we would get them in time for the bridal shower.

I never left things until the last minute, but the new logo design had just been completed last week, and Neil had asked if we could wait and then do a rush order on a few things. I didn't think Kyle really liked the idea of his father pushing the Tri-C influence during a wedding, but when he said Neil never missed an opportunity to market, Malia had disagreed, saying that he was simply proud of what their company stood for. The undercurrent of tension made sense now that Jon had confided in me his own plans to visit Idaho's farmlands. Perhaps the pressure from Neil was too great for his sons.

I drummed my fingers on the desktop as I thought about each element of Malia's bridal shower. The party would definitely top any bridal shower I'd done so far, because Malia didn't know that her family had combined it into a sweet bachelorette party.

Malia had been adamant that she didn't want a bachelorette party because in her words, "I don't want to deal with the unsavory traditions surrounding that kind of party."

I decided to call the maid of honor, Jenica, to see if she needed help with any of the preparations. She answered on the second ring.

"Aloha," she said.

"Hi, Jenica. It's Adri. I'm calling to see if you needed help with any of the final preparations for Malia's party on Monday."

"Oh, thanks for checking. I think I've got it all figured out. This is going to be marvelous," she gushed. "I found a fire dancer who was available for a surprise visit later that night."

"Uh, I don't remember anything about a fire dancer. In the middle of the day?" I flipped through my notes, wondering where Jenica had taken off with our carefully laid plans.

"Technically he's not just a fire dancer, but a bachelorette party isn't a party unless there's a little dancing. You should see this guy's abs. Wowzer."

"Jenica, did you forget that Malia specifically requested not to have a bachelorette party for the very reason you just described?" I planted both my feet on the ground and sat up in my chair to take a cleansing breath. "As the maid of honor, it's important that you remember Malia's wishes and make this about her, not about what other people would want."

"I'm sure Malia will be fine. This is Hawaii. Can't we indulge in the culture a little?" Jenica's voice had a snappy tone to it that I didn't appreciate.

"I think it's important to remember what Malia wants."

"How about you do your job and I'll do mine." Jenica's voice rose a notch and I cringed.

"Sounds like a good idea. I'll talk to you later." I ended the call before I said anything I would regret.

I stared at the phone, thinking about Malia and her request for sweet parties only. It would upset her if Jenica didn't honor her wishes, but I wasn't sure how I could interfere as Jenica was one of her best friends. After gnawing on my bottom lip for a minute, I thought of someone who might help.

My heart sped up as I dialed Heather's cell number. I didn't want Malia's future mother-in-law to think I was a meddler, but I had a feeling that she wouldn't stand for Jenica's plans.

"Adri, how are you doing?" Heather answered with a cheerful tone.

"I'm good, but I'm calling for a little advice." I swallowed my nerves and waited for her to respond. I really didn't know Heather that well, but she seemed kind and also had a take-charge attitude.

"Okay, I'll try to help," Heather said.

I briefly described Jenica's plans and how they were exactly what Malia didn't want. Heather listened and then she sighed.

"When I met Jenica, I wondered how on earth someone like her could be Malia's best friend," Heather paused. "Sorry, that's not very nice, but I have an idea that will help. Why don't you give me Jenica's phone number? I'll call her and offer to help with the party, confirming bookings, etc."

"Um, okay." I scrolled through my phone for the number, switching Heather to speaker phone. "I'm not following how that solves the problem."

Heather chuckled. "That might be for the best. When the booking for the fire dancer gets cancelled, you can claim innocence."

"Oh, I see. I doubt she'll believe me though." I rolled my tongue over my teeth as understanding of Heather's plans came clear. Jenica would be spitting fire, but I would risk her wrath if it would keep Malia's genuine smile in place. "Are you sure you're okay with that?"

"What good is a mother-in-law if she can't meddle a little, right?" Heather laughed and the tension eased out of my shoulders.

"Thanks for helping me on this."

"Any time."

I said goodbye, biting my lip as I considered the implications of getting Heather involved with Jenica, but then I thought of Malia and reconsidered my guilty conscience. I wouldn't think about it anymore and hope for the best.

I returned my attention to the rest of my notes. The caterer was all set, and the hotel had several cabanas reserved on the beach for the party. I closed my planner with a snap. My stomach grumbled, but I didn't want a big meal. I settled for a granola bar, dark chocolate, and an apple. After eating, I scooted onto the bed, curling around a soft down pillow. It had been a long day, and my shoulder was throbbing again. I dozed until a rap at my door brought me back to consciousness.

As I got up, I winced at the stiffness in my joints, especially my shoulder. The peephole showed no one at my door, so I opened it a crack. I squinted and stepped halfway into the hall. I looked up and down the hall, then my gaze landed on a pink piece of paper at my feet. I bent down and snatched the paper as I stepped back into my room. The paper crinkled as I unfolded it and I read the printed note.

We are more important than any wedding, but we are willing to make some concessions for your acceptance of a new time for the luau. We appreciate that you have come to your senses and are willing to accept that often we must be accommodating to those with greater needs than our own.

Your prompt reply is requested.

Mrs. Amelia Harper, Director

By the time I finished reading, my heart pounded and the back of my neck burned with anger. The woman was out of her high-heeled mind if she thought I would respond to her condescending request. Evidently, she wasn't going to leave me alone. I walked over to my desk and pushed a button on the white telephone base.

"Yes, would you please connect me to Chelsea at the concierge table?"

"One moment, please," the operator said.

"This is Chelsea. How may I help you?"

"Chelsea, this is Adri. I'm just checking to make sure that everything is as we had arranged this morning. No other changes, correct?"

Chelsea cleared her throat. "Uh, yes. I apologize but Mrs. Harper has been difficult to deal with. We're doing our best to accommodate both parties."

"I have a written contract that you need to uphold, and I won't tolerate any more threats from Mrs. Harper. Please relay to her that if I get so much as an eyebrow raised in my direction, I won't notify security, I'll call the local police and report harassment."

"Yes, I understand Adri, but if you could consider her terms, they might be satisfactory."

"I'm tired and this is the end of our conversation. Good bye." I thought about slamming the phone down, but remembered my training and set it down with mock gentleness.

Before I boiled over, I flipped open my laptop and searched for anything on Mrs. Amelia Harper. Unfortunately, all I had to go on was her name. I didn't know where she was from or who she worked for, so the search brought up dozens of Amelia Harpers with nothing suspicious enough to pinpoint who I might be dealing with. The women were either too young or too old to be the same Amelia I'd encountered and most of the others appeared harmless. There were no glaring headlines about a criminal named Amelia Harper. I closed my laptop. There were other ways to find answers to my questions.

I grabbed a robe and headed for a long, hot shower. Something strange was going on with the notorious Mrs. Harper. I couldn't ignore her any longer. Tomorrow was Sunday—my day off. After a good night's rest there would be plenty of time to do some snooping, and if I couldn't find what I was looking for, Jon was willing to help me.

The adrenaline and anger from too many frustrations zapped the tired bug out of my system. I was still exhausted, but every part of me felt too wired to sleep. I towel dried my hair and let it hang loose down my back, the ends still seeping moisture. My body called out for something comfortable, so I pulled on a gauzy turquoise skirt and a white blouse with a pair of silver flip-flops and headed out for a walk under the stars.

Gusts of ocean breeze blew against the empty hammocks secured to the palm trees. When I stepped off the darkened path onto a patch of sand illuminated by light, a tiny brown lizard skittered across. The corners of my mouth lifted slightly as I watched the two inch lizard hide in the grass. Kauai's beauty and diversity snapped me out of my funk.

Inhaling slowly, I let the soft scent of plumeria overtake me and rub out the incident with Jenica and the indirect confrontation I'd had with Mrs. Harper.

The wind blew one hammock almost sideways but its mate stayed in place. I squinted and leaned forward. The other hammock was occupied by a man. I wondered if he was asleep. I didn't want to disturb him so I turned to step back on the path.

"I saw you, Adri. You don't have to hide."

I froze as I recognized Luke Stetson's voice—the clear tenor cut through the night. I turned, but the spotlight made it difficult to see. "Luke?"

"Yep. I got in a couple hours ago—couldn't resist coming down to listen to the ocean."

A mixture of relief and anxiety moved through me as I stepped to the edge of the path. "Sleeping off some jetlag?"

"Nah, stuffed myself full of coconut shrimp. I needed a place to stretch out." He lifted his arms over his head and groaned as he sat up. He wore khaki cargo shorts with a light green graphic tee. I noticed his flip-flops in the sand near the hammock. I'd never seen Luke this relaxed before.

"The food here is delicious. I tried my first Hawaiian shave ice today."

Luke lifted his eyebrows. "Yeah, I heard all about your date from Malia."

I tried to cover my surprise. Awkward didn't begin to define the conversation we were heading into, but I didn't know how to sidestep it. "The Connelly family has been very kind to show me around the island."

"Jon in particular, I'm guessing," Luke said.

I decided to be straightforward. "Yes, he took me on the bike trails along the coast today."

"Malia says you're like two peas in a pod." He said this in a teasing falsetto.

"Not really. It was just a date." I tried to keep my voice casual.

"And you ended up nearly killing yourself, right?"

I couldn't hide the surprise at how much intel he'd already gathered since arriving. "What, am I under surveillance?"

"When Malia gets excited about something she babbles, and Jon is her future brother-in-law, so it makes sense he would share details about his date with the hot wedding planner."

I blushed. "It was a close call. I'm still a little sore, and I'll have some great bruises to show off tomorrow. Want to hear the whole exciting story?"

Luke chuckled, but before he could wave me off, I launched into the details of how the wheel came off my bicycle and Jon and I wondered if it had been tampered with. I told Luke how the bikes had been moved, but were still locked up tight. "I guess it might have been better if the bikes were stolen, since I ended up nearly cliff-diving, and we didn't get to finish the ride back."

"That's a lot to deal with, Adri. Are you sure you're okay?"

Luke had a way of piercing my outer shell and getting to my heart too quickly. "I'm fine."

"So you like the Connellys? Malia is going to be okay?" he asked.

"They seem to be a wonderful family. Malia and Kyle remind me why I chose this profession. They're so in love."

Luke rolled his eyes, just as I expected. "Kyle seems nice enough, but I don't trust Jon." He rubbed at the stubble on his face.

"Is that jealousy I hear in your voice?" I cocked my head. "Jon asked me on a date. He lives here—hence, no future dates."

"Still, I don't know about him." Luke shook his head. "Have you heard about the class action lawsuit going against their company? The school district is suing because so many of the students and teachers were getting sick from environmental hazards."

"I knew the locals didn't like the GMOs but I hadn't heard that."

"It's big time. Never happened before. I think your buddy might even be sweating a bit." Luke stretched his feet down to the sand and stood, the hammock swaying behind him.

The information I had about Kyle starting his own business and breaking away from the family business seemed even more relevant now. He must have known about the lawsuit. I wondered if that was motivating his plans. Jon had also expressed interest in checking out things in Idaho. Perhaps he was ready to move away from trouble as well.

"The Connellys seem genuine. They're wealthy, but down to earth. Neil isn't the sole owner of Tri-C Enterprises. Maybe there are some conflicts between the owners."

"Just as long as Malia and Kyle don't get caught up in it," Luke muttered. "She needs her happily ever after, and even though I told her those don't exist outside fairy tales, she insists that her life will be different." He rubbed his eyes with the back of his hand.

I studied him, sifting through the varying emotions he'd just portrayed. He cared a lot about his cousin. Luke did his best to help people, but he was also a cynic. In our brief conversation, I'd already caught his anti-wedding vibe several times, and as usual, it left me confused as to whether it was a front or how he really felt. Was he that bitter about his own past?

"I still don't understand why you came." I ventured closer to the hammock.

He snorted. "Thanks for the warm welcome."

I touched his forearm, giving it a light squeeze. "No, that's not what I meant. It's good to see you here—I'm just surprised."

Luke cleared his throat. "Malia asked me to give her away. You know she doesn't have any brothers."

The news floored me. I knew that Malia's father had passed away a few years ago and that she didn't have any brothers, but I didn't know Luke would be giving her away. She'd been somewhat vague on that detail, at one time suggesting that Neil might be walking her down the aisle to meet her groom. I understood now that she wasn't sure Luke would really show. "I didn't realize you two were that close."

"We've always been close, but really, I think she wanted to force me to take a vacation." He pulled his toes through the sand. "After my wife died . . ." He pressed his lips together. "Malia has worried over me a lot. She and Dana were good friends. And when Malia begs, she gets her way." He smiled, but I wondered if it was just to reassure me since he'd mentioned his late wife. He cleared his throat. "I'm not sure how to say this."

"Well, you haven't been hesitant about anything else tonight. Why stop now?" He *was* jealous about Jon, but I wasn't sure how I felt about that.

Luke shook his head. He studied me for a second and then shrugged. "Don't you think it's strange that you had an accident with your bike and Jon was there to save you?"

I wrinkled my nose. "Why is that strange? Should he have let me fall off the edge of the cliff?"

"No, I mean you said that he locked the bikes up so securely. Why would anyone bother messing with them?" Luke leaned back against the palm tree, studying me.

"I don't know. People do strange stuff all the time."

Luke continued to stare at me, and I couldn't read his expression. "Or maybe someone was trying to give you a warning."

"What kind of a warning? Don't ride your vintage bicycle to Donkey Beach?"

"It just seems strange." Luke rubbed his chin. "Malia was the one who first brought it up, but she didn't think Jon would go to those kind of lengths to impress you."

"Luke, he didn't have anything to do with it. Accidents happen."

"Like that woman you found out on Tunnels?"

I flinched and took a step back as her face came to mind again. It made sense that Luke knew about the body, but I hadn't brought it up for obvious reasons.

"I'm sorry, I think my brain is fried right now. Malia talked nonstop from the airport to here and through dinner. I basically know every move everyone has made since they've been here." He took a step toward me. "It made me worried for you when Malia told me how you were the one that found that woman. And then when she told me about your accident. I didn't like it. They probably don't see how much that could affect you, but I do."

My chest tightened as the images I'd been pushing away floated back into focus—the woman's green eyes, her arm moving back and forth. I sucked in a breath, the harsh reminder of a young life taken settling on my chest.

"Sorry, I didn't mean to upset you." Luke pushed at the hammock and it swung back and forth behind him, brushing his legs. "I'd better get to bed." He moved to walk past me.

I grabbed his hand before he could leave and pulled my thoughts into focus. "Luke, I'm glad you could come. And I don't mind you watching out for me. Don't be afraid to tell me something if you think it's important."

Luke patted my hand and nodded. "Okay, I think you need to be careful. I worry about you even when you tell me everything is fine. Do you want me to walk you back up to the hotel?"

"No thanks. I'll just be a few more minutes. I promise to be careful," I said, removing my hand from his arm. "Good night."

After he had walked down the lighted pathway, I stepped into the darkness again and looked up at the stars twinkling. The ocean's constant movement was soothing, and it made me realize just how tired I was. I retraced my steps back to my room and prepared for bed. As I fluffed my pillow, I thought about what Luke had suggested, that someone had tampered with my bike.

My skin chilled. Mrs. Harper came to mind, but that seemed ludicrous. She wasn't an all-powerful mobster or something, was she? I brushed Luke's speculation off, but later I had a bad taste in my mouth when I thought about how Jon had taken an extra-long time to lock up the bikes. Would he have orchestrated something like that to get close to me? Of course, if someone did tamper with the bike, they expected the wheel to come off much sooner than it had—it was pure luck that I happened to be riding downhill toward the edge of the ocean cliff when it finally disengaged.

I groaned. It was exhaustion and stiff muscles making me think crazy thoughts. The bike accident was just that—an accident. But as I closed my eyes and fought for sleep, I couldn't ignore the warning bells going off in the back of my mind.

Chapter 8

HAWAIIAN OMELET

Whisk 3 eggs with 1 Tbsp. water and pour into heated sauté pan. Let eggs cook for about 30 seconds. Layer diced ham, shredded cheese, pecans, and diced pineapples over egg mixture. Cook for one minute, then using spatula, fold half the egg mixture over the other half to create omelet. Cook on medium-low heat for about one minute. Flip over and cook until done, one-two minutes.

Serve garnished with fresh pineapple and basil leaf.

Courtesy of www.mashedpotatoesandcrafts.com

Even though I'd planned to be up early, I skipped the sunrise Sunday morning and stayed in bed for a few extra luxurious moments, moving my stiff muscles slowly. My mind whirred with questions about every person I'd come into contact with since arriving. When I thought of Jon Connelly, his easy grin came to mind. I liked his playful personality. I'd had a lot of fun with him, and even though I wasn't happy that I'd broken down in front of him, it had provided a connection between us that meant more than teasing and flirting.

The cleansing release of sharing my past with someone had helped me to see how far I'd really come. Most of the past six months had been filled with me working to exhaustion, trying to convince myself that I was stronger than every weak moment I curled up in bed, trying to stop the night terrors from haunting me.

I sat up and let my bare feet dangle over the edge of the bed, brushing the carpet. I slipped through the sliding glass door on the balcony and lowered myself into the wicker chair. The waves rolled relentlessly toward the shore. The ocean was powerful. Well, so was I. *Adri, you're stronger than you think,* Jon had told me yesterday. I straightened and breathed in the salty air. He was right. I was stronger, and I could handle what life had given me. It was time for me to let go of my fears and figure some things out. Mixed feelings about Luke twirled in the back of my mind. I knew I'd have to do something about them, but I wasn't sure how at the moment. Right now, it was enough for me to say that I was strong enough to deal with my problems.

The next person I thought of was the green-eyed woman chained under the water at Tunnels Beach. She'd haunted my thoughts ever since I discovered her arm waving in the current, as if signaling me to find her. Who was she? And why did someone kill her? Even though I'd made my best effort not to dwell on her, an emotional pull kept me thinking about the body. She'd seemed young—perhaps not too much older than me. Her whole life was still in front of her and someone had snatched it away. I wanted to know why—I needed answers.

Something itched at my memory of that day. There *was* something I should know, a missing detail that would answer a question. I closed my eyes and listened to the surf and allowed my memory to take me back. Removing the fear and anxiety, I reminded myself of my own personal strengths. If there was something I could do to help this woman, I needed to take the chance. I went through everything in my mind, struggling with the emotion connected to the memory. After a few minutes, I sighed in frustration. There was something on the fringes of my memory, but I couldn't access it. At least I'd decided not to be afraid of the murdered woman. Maybe whatever was locked away would be triggered by something else, and I'd finally be at peace.

A clatter of dishes in the hallway interrupted the investigation into my mind's secret compartments. Time for me to get going. I showered and pulled on another maxi dress. This one had a pattern of purple hibiscus flowers on a creamy yellow background, and the fabric was soft against my skin. I took a minute to tame the curls in my hair before hurrying out the door.

I didn't see anyone I knew at breakfast, but I wasn't familiar with everyone in the wedding party. Malia's mother and her siblings had arrived last night, and the last of the guests would fly in later that morning. It was a happy time, and I was grateful to be a part of it. I noticed that fresh fruit seemed to be the norm for breakfast. The sweet taste of pineapple and crunchy pecans added a unique flavor to an otherwise ordinary ham and cheese omelet. I savored each bite of my breakfast. With a belly full of good food, I was prepared to study the next person on my list: Mrs. Amelia Harper.

With purpose, I strode toward the concierge desk. Chelsea wasn't working today because it was Sunday, and I hoped that would be in my favor. A young man with thick black hair and a freshly-shaved face sat in front of a computer, clicking through screens. He wore the signature hotel uniform and looked up as I approached.

"Good morning. Can I help you?" he asked.

My eyes flicked to his name tag. "Yes, Pua. I have a few questions I need help answering." I was proud of myself for not butchering his name. Even though I couldn't speak many words, I'd taken time to study up on the Hawaiian language. The basis of only twelve letters in the alphabet made it easy to remember that it was most important to pay attention to all of the vowels.

Pua nodded. "Have a seat, and let's see what I can do."

I paused for a moment to collect my thoughts. I had to word my question so as not to arouse suspicion and still get the information I needed. "I'm Adri Pyper, wedding planner for the Wright/Connelly wedding. I've been working with Mrs. Harper this weekend." I hesitated, noting how Pua flinched when I spoke her name. I smiled sweetly. "We had some booking conflicts, so I've spoken with her and received some correspondence as well, but I can't remember to which man I was supposed to deliver my message. Can you direct me?"

Pua licked his lips, probably deciding how to answer my question without divulging private information. "You say you're supposed to talk with someone from PFI?"

"Yes, that's right." I didn't miss a beat. "But I don't have a name. One of the other concierge's pointed him out to me yesterday, but I'm afraid I've seen too many faces since then."

Pua looked behind me, his gaze flitting from one end of the room to the other. "I'm not sure where Mitt is, but Teo is right over by that column. He must be on surveillance." Pua didn't point, instead he looked to the right behind me. I turned, following the direction of his focus. It took all my will power not to widen my eyes when I saw the same Polynesian man who had gestured to me yesterday in a threatening way. I turned, averting my eyes from his penetrating study.

"I see him. I remember him now." I tapped my fingers on the countertop as my mind raced. I needed to pump Pua for more information, but I wasn't sure what else to ask.

"I wouldn't contact Mrs. Harper directly without talking to Teo first. I saw a few police officers approach her today and Teo about got himself arrested."

"Really?" I smoothed out the surprise in my face. "Thanks for the warning. She hasn't been very pleasant to deal with so far, but I've tried my best."

Pua blinked rapidly. He was nervous about what he'd just said, but I couldn't miss this opportunity. "I talked to some police officers too, but I don't know if they found what they were looking for."

"They questioned you, too?" Pua seemed concerned.

"I had some information about a case they are working on," I ventured.

"Hmm, I got the idea that the officers were here today to issue a warning to PFI, but I've been wrong before. Kauai has had a lot of troubles with these rallies." Pua pursed his lips. "I apologize. I probably shouldn't have told you that. I trust you'll be discreet."

"Of course." I concentrated on making my face impassive while my head was pinging with the information he'd just unwittingly shared. I decided to change tactics. "Should I be worried if they've threatened me concerning the booking conflicts we've been having?"

Pua's face darkened with anger. "Unfortunately, that seems to come with the PFI territory. I don't agree with how they've been given free rein over the hotel, but I can't do anything about it. Chelsea is head of the concierge department."

I extended my hand again covering my surprise. I had no idea that Chelsea headed the department. "Thank you for your help. I really appreciate it. I've never been in a situation like this before."

He shook my hand with a solid grip, his large hand engulfing mine. "We'll see what the next few days bring, but you shouldn't have any more trouble."

The wedding luau was Saturday, almost a week away. That seemed like plenty of time for more trouble to brew. The fact that Chelsea had more control than I first realized gave me an uneasy feeling. I exited the lobby on the far side from Teo. I had no intention of speaking to him, but I did have every intention of calling Detective Ford in Idaho. Tony Ford was my brother Wesley's best friend and had always been protective of me. Since he lived in the town next to me, it was easy for him to keep an eye on me. Hopefully he could help answer a few questions.

The maid was just leaving my room when I returned.

"Mahalo," I thanked her in a low voice.

She smiled and bobbed her head as I entered. The room was pristine. It would be nice to have someone to clean my own home every day. The thought made me miss my assistant, Lorea. She was mildly messy and always cursing how much she had to clean. The dress business we had started last summer was doing well and it kept Lorea plenty busy. I needed to give her a call as soon as I sorted through all the information in my brain. Chatting with Pua had turned out much better than I'd expected.

I booted up my computer and sipped on a coconut water while I jotted down notes. As soon as I connected to the Internet, I Googled PFI in conjunction with Amelia Harper's name. Searching was difficult when dealing with an acronym, because the search returned several different companies and organizations and none of them linked with Mrs. Harper's name. After clicking through acronym finders, prison fellowships, and pellet fuel companies, my mouse hovered over something that made sense. I clicked on Pure Foodists International and was brought to a site with bold statements on the purity of food and a movement against GMOs. Bingo.

A little more research confirmed what I already knew from the Connellys. Kauai was the heartland of several major GMO companies, each with their own test plots securely guarded and posted with no trespassing signs. I'd seen them previously when the Connellys had taken us up to Wailua Falls. Neil had pointed out several test plots. To me it had looked like ordinary farmland, but as I listened to his explanations, I recognized that the plants were in several different stages of growth. There was corn in a seedling stage in one plot and fully developed plants in another area. Neil had explained how each plot was used to test the biotechnology the company was working on.

I refocused on Pure Foodists International. They claimed that certain companies were overrunning the best farmland by creating their own personal Frankenstein seeds, stripping the soil, destroying the land, and poisoning surrounding properties with their chemical experimentations. PFI claimed that the food sources of the United States were in a downward spiral as a direct consequence of the unethical practices of these GMOs.

A little hunting had me smiling in pride over my investigative skills. PFI had planned a secret rally to combat the attack on pure food. They planned to descend on the farming areas with banners raised and if necessary, force. Reading between the lines, it was easy to conceive such fevered antagonism turning mere threats into something much worse.

If a person wanted to take part in this rally, they had to go through several points of contact to join the membership of PFI and be invited. It only took me a few seconds to debate whether I would write such an email requesting more information. I used a different email account that didn't give away my name and infused as much self-righteous food-protective tone in my note as I could muster.

After I sent it off, I dialed Lorea's number.

"Adri, how are you? Is Hawaii everything you hoped it would be?" Her voice sounded more cheerful than usual.

"Actually, yes. I still wish you could be here."

"I know, but how often does a girl get the chance to make her sister's wedding gown, right?"

"How did it turn out? Did Terese love it?"

Lorea let out a happy sigh. "She loved it. Everything was perfect."

"You sound happy. I'm glad. You know, Terese's wedding's over. You could still catch a flight here. I have my own room." Logistically, I knew it couldn't happen because Lorea was covering for me and the six weddings we had planned in June, but I wanted her to know just how much I missed her company.

"Tempting, but some wedding planner I know overbooked her summer so she could drown in her work and then took off for Hawaii."

The usual snap had returned to Lorea's voice, and I found myself smiling. "So tell me, who did you end up taking to Terese's wedding?"

I heard another dreamy sigh and laughed because it was so atypical of Lorea. Coming to work for me had been a struggle because she was such a cynic about romantic fairy tale weddings and love. She'd been burned at some point and her family and I had tried our best to get her back into the dating game. Terese had finally won out for a single date because she insisted that Lorea couldn't attend her wedding alone.

"Lorea? Aren't you going to tell me?" I asked. "It must have been good, don't think I missed that sigh."

She chuckled. "Just for that, I'm keeping you in suspense."

"It was Colton, wasn't it?" I referred to the cute deliveryman that had been flirting with Lorea over the past several months but never had the nerve to ask her out.

"Nope, it wasn't him. Now, if you'll excuse me, I have an appointment with Jessie in a few minutes, and I have to finish pinning this hem."

"Okay, but I'm not letting you off the hook," I warned. "Next time we talk you have to tell me."

"I will, maybe," Lorea hedged.

"I'll just call Terese and find out if you don't tell me."

"Adri, that's not fair," Lorea whined.

I laughed. "Have fun with Jessie. She's such a sweetheart. I think her wedding will be so much fun to plan." I thought of the delightful young lady who planned to marry her true love in September. A feeling of homesickness nudged me, maybe a side effect of too much worry on the island. "Take care of yourself and thanks for working so hard."

"No problem."

I ended the call. I had meant to tell Lorea so much more about what was going on in Kauai, but she was delightfully distracted with something that had my curiosity burning. At the same time I was thrilled with the possibility that she might have had a good experience with her wedding date.

Glancing back at my notes on PFI, Mrs. Harper, the hotel, and Kauai's GMOs, I decided that I would let Lorea live in her little fairy tale and not worry her over the prospect of Pure Foodist rallies, mystery, and murder.

Chapter 9

COCONUT SHRIMP

Fresh, deveined shrimp are best for this recipe.
2 cups vegetable oil
1 cup bread crumbs
1 cup unsweetened shredded coconut
1 pound medium shrimp, peeled and deveined
Kosher salt and freshly ground black pepper, to taste
1/2 cup all-purpose flour
2 large eggs, beaten
Heat vegetable oil in a large skillet or Dutch oven over medium high heat.

In a large bowl, combine bread crumbs and shredded coconut; set aside.

Season shrimp with salt and pepper, to taste. Working one at a time, dredge shrimp in the flour, dip into the eggs, then dredge in the coconut mixture, pressing to coat.

Working in batches, add shrimp to the Dutch oven and fry until evenly golden brown and crispy, about 2-3 minutes. Transfer to a paper towel-lined plate.

Serve immediately with dipping sauce. For dipping sauce, use orange marmalade, mustard, and horseradish mixed to taste or use a sweet chili sauce.

Courtesy of www.mashedpotatoesandcrafts.com

I tried calling Tony next and ended up leaving him a message. In as few words as possible, I told him what happened at Tunnels and asked if he could find anything about the woman's identity or how I should approach the police in Kauai with the same question. I ended with strict instructions not to tell Wes anything about me finding the woman's body.

My phone vibrated with a text message as soon as I ended the call.

My lips twitched when I saw the name Jon Connelly.

Jon: Wanna go for a Sunday afternoon drive?

Me: That sounds nice.

Jon: Can I pick you up at 2?

Me: Sounds great.

My hair was a thick mass of curls that I pinned up to keep my neck cool. I swiped on some peach lip gloss and shimmery bronze eye shadow. I tidied up my clothing and waited for Jon to arrive. He knocked on the door at 2:02, and I scolded myself at how much I had anticipated his arrival. I opened the door and all scolding thoughts fled from my mind.

"I see you have shoes on today. You must be ready." Jon's flirtatious smirk made his eyes crinkle. He wore khaki cargo shorts with a green polo shirt and sandals. He looked like he'd stepped off the pages of a Hawaiian travel brochure, and he was here to see *me.*

"I *am* ready. Thanks for inviting me."

"Malia's family is all over at the house, so I thought I'd escape for a while." He put his hand on the small of my back as we exited the lobby.

"I have a little surprise planned for this date." He opened the door to his convertible and lingered for a moment, smiling down at me.

"As long as it doesn't involve bicycles, I think I'm excited."

He chuckled but didn't say more as we pulled north of the parking lot and our attention turned to the island breezing by us. The trees reminded me of Dr. Seuss illustrations in *Scrambled Eggs Super!*, and I wondered briefly if the author had visited Hawaii. Jon pointed at the landscape. "Those are Norfolk pine trees. I've always liked how they look—each limb sort of separate from the other."

I nodded, thinking of the characters in the Dr. Seuss book hiking rugged mountains and climbing trees to find special eggs in tall, odd-shaped trees. The Norfolk pine branches were spindly, not full and bushy like the blue spruce pines I was used to seeing in the Sawtooth Mountains in Idaho. The mountains of Kauai rising up around us created a beautiful contrast to the ocean below.

"How is everything going with the wedding plans?" Jon asked.

"Pretty good. Most everything was done before we got to the island, but Malia didn't have her veil picked out yet when we left. I hope she's found something that will work."

"I doubt Kyle will even notice a veil, he's so whipped."

"I don't always see that in all of my clients," I said. "The weddings are so much more fun to plan when the couple is smitten with each other."

Jon shook his head. "Are you saying I shouldn't be teasing my brother so much?"

"Only if he really deserves it." When we pulled off at the Lihue airport exit, I glanced at Jon, but he just raised his eyebrows with a grin. He turned onto a road with signs marking the Lihue heliport, and I sucked in a breath. "No way. Are you taking me on a helicopter ride?"

"I should've blindfolded you," he replied.

I did my best to contain the squeal of excitement bubbling up in my chest. "I can't believe it. Really?"

"Yes, it's the best way to see the island."

"This is going to be so amazing. I've heard about these rides," I said. "Thanks."

"Kauai is like a whole different island when viewed from the air."

He parked the car and hopped out to get my door. After we checked in and received safety instructions and rules, Jon took my hand and we followed the tour manager out to the helipad. The whir of chopper blades from several tours taking off greeted us as we walked closer to the helipad.

We climbed inside a yellow helicopter with the doors off for better viewing and donned a pair of bulky headsets. The pilot gave a few extra instructions and checked that we were buckled in securely before starting the rotors.

My stomach rose up with the beating chopper blades, and I took in a deep breath as we leveled out and headed farther inland. Sitting next to the open doorway was unnerving and I found myself clutching the sides of my seat when the helicopter tilted to the right. Jon caught my eye and laughed when he caught me studying the parachute packs.

"I've never had to use one of those," he said.

"Let's keep it that way," I said. I concentrated on the details the pilot narrated for us, and tried to relax as we flew over the island. The gorgeous scenery helped, and the tension rolled off my body as I experienced my first helicopter ride. "Everything is so green and vibrant." I pointed to the lush forest sweeping ahead of us.

"A bit different than Idaho, right?" Jon said.

His voice came through my headset fairly well but there was a bit of interference so I had to strain to hear. "We're in the desert, but the farmers definitely help green up the landscape." The patchwork of farms reminded me of my hometown, except these farming plots weren't surrounded by desert. The ocean and beaches encroached on their borders, making the crops bold in color from the fertile soil.

"Look over there." Jon pointed out of my side of the helicopter. "Our test plots are southeast of us."

I leaned forward and turned my head toward the area he was pointing at. Rectangles and squares in multiple hues of brown and green created a geometric portrait.

"Hey, see that spot over there with all the vehicles?" Jon asked. "I'm pretty sure that's one of our new test plots." His voice held a note of concern, and I turned to look at him.

"What's wrong?"

"Maybe it's nothing," he said. "But there's quite a bit of activity down there. I thought Kyle had it all blocked off because we have a new test crop of our nutrient seed." He looked past me, and shook his head. "I'm probably just looking in the wrong spot. It's hard to tell from this vantage point."

I nodded and followed his gaze. "Hopefully it's a different field. It looks like a patchwork quilt from here. I don't know how you can tell which one is yours."

"You're right." Jon smiled. "We have a pretty large parcel of property there. My dad has been pointing out the landmarks to Kyle and I since we were kids."

The helicopter turned gradually and headed west. We left behind houses and buildings and flew closer to the mountains. The pilot pointed out a few sights, but he had indicated that he'd give us plenty of time for peaceful viewing as well during the tour.

"He's going to fly over Waimea Canyon now. Have you heard of it?" Jon asked.

"I saw some pictures of that in my guidebook. It said something about being the Grand Canyon of Hawaii." I wished I'd snagged my guidebook with its dog-eared pages and highlighted reminders of things I wanted to do. Of course, I didn't want to take my eyes off the scenery before me to look at a book. I'd remember to check it later.

Jon didn't say anything as the helicopter climbed alongside the mountain and then soared over the red gash that was Waimea Canyon. When I caught sight of the canyon, I understood his silence was respectful of the beauty before us. I sat in awe at the incredible depth of colors in the landscape. Hardy trees thrived in the dark red soil variegated with different shades of orange and rust. For a moment, it seemed as if we'd entered a different country because the canyon was so unexpected in contrast to the beaches of Kauai.

"This is fantastic." I turned and caught Jon watching me. "It reminds me a little of the Snake River Canyon back home. There's a pretty great vantage spot in Twin Falls."

"Yeah, I was surprised the first time I saw this side of the island. Almost like a desert compared to the rest of Kauai." He motioned to the scenery before us, vivid with no doors on the helicopter to block the view. "It does remind me of the Grand Canyon."

"I've never been to the Grand Canyon, but if it's anything like Waimea, I guess I'd better plan a trip."

"You've never been?" Jon asked. "But it's not that far from you, is it?"

I shrugged. "Far enough that my travels haven't taken me past it."

"You'll have to remedy that. I think you'd like it." Jon motioned to the gorgeous panorama in front of us. "Of course, this has its own unique appeal. And there's more to come. We'll be flying up to the Wai'ale'ale Crater and then along the Na Pali coastline." Jon pointed in the direction of the ocean beyond the mountainous terrain. "It's one of the most beautiful places in the world. We were right next to it at Tunnels Beach the other day."

The pilot navigated through the narrow causeway of red cliffs in a gradual climb upwards. As we went farther up, the mountainside turned green and lush, and I saw heavy clouds hanging above the crater. The pilot kept us below the fog, but I felt the increase in humidity rushing through the open doors. My breath caught as we circled around the crater and flew lower. Everything was green or bright white with the lush vegetation and gushing waterfalls adorning every crevice of the verdant crater.

"Wai'ale'ale is the wettest spot on earth," the pilot said. "It rains here almost every day of the year averaging over 426 inches a year."

Mist clung to the tops of the mountains, so thick in some places that I couldn't see the peaks. I'd never seen anything like it before and even though I knew a picture couldn't do it justice, I snapped several. Describing this to Lorea and my family wouldn't be enough; they needed to see it for themselves. Gratitude swelled within me for this beautiful piece of earth I was witnessing.

"Jon, thank you for this. It's unbelievable."

He took my hand while we both gazed out at the untouched beauty before us. A few moments later, the landscape changed again as the pilot flew through the mountain pass along the Na Pali coastline. We traveled along the jagged rock faces of cliffs stretching upwards several thousand feet. Below us, the shoreline was absent of beaches. The helicopter flew in low. The craggy rocks jutting out into the ocean reminded me of a giant's toes stretching along the surf.

There was no sign of human interference on the northwest side of the island. Not a single road gashed the mountainside, and the shoreline appeared almost alien in its contrasting beauty of lava rock overgrown with flowering bushes surrounded by Kauai's signature reddish sand.

We ascended the cliffs and Jon squeezed my hand. "Look over here." He pointed out his side of the helicopter.

"This area is referred to as the Cathedrals," the pilot said.

I could see why. The steep mountain pushed against the heavy clouds in jagged slopes that looked somewhat like a cathedral's spires. I wanted to memorize the scene before me. We circled around the Cathedrals and after a few more minutes, the pilot headed east along the route that would take us back to Lihue.

Soaring over the breathtaking island of Kauai from a helicopter was something I hadn't even put on my bucket list—it was so far out of my price range. I leaned back in my seat and wondered if this would be how life with the Connelly's would go? Everything elite. Once-in-a-lifetime experiences becoming everyday occurrences? Perhaps that was part of the reason Malia was so happy she and Kyle were living in Idaho. There was definitely something to be said for normal life in the middle class.

I thought of Luke with his laid-back presence. Even though he drove a Harley, he wasn't ostentatious. He had to be doing well for himself with the amount of divorces I'd heard about lately in the Sun Valley/Ketchum area, but he didn't seem like the type to overindulge.

Or maybe I was just comparing him to Jon. Money had never been what attracted me to a guy, but it was still important to consider because I'd obviously been raised in a different atmosphere than the Connellys. What did I want? Even as I reveled in the thrill of the helicopter ride that had cost Jon three-hundred dollars apiece, I knew the answer to my question.

More times than I could count, an evening sunset in Rupert, Idaho had taken my breath away. My vantage point had been from a dirt dike by the irrigation ditch around my parent's home or sitting on the back of a four-wheeler in the middle of a field, listening to the shush-shush of sprinklers watering the potatoes. The sun kissed the horizon and turned into a fiery ball streaking red, pink, and purple across the sky. If I closed my eyes now against the beauty of Kauai, I would see that desert sunset.

I would always be a down-home country girl. Simple things brought joy to my life. That didn't mean that there weren't plenty of big-ticket items on my bucket list, but there were plenty of things I could do without. This helicopter ride definitely should have been on my list, though. Kauai held its own simple beauties, and the quiet island had a rural feel with plenty to offer any type of explorer. The Connellys were lucky to live in such a gorgeous place. I smiled at my circular thinking as we approached the helipad and Jon gave my fingers another gentle squeeze.

We disembarked and had our picture taken in front of the helicopter. Jon linked arms with me, laughing at my wobbly legs, and we headed back to the car.

"If we leave now, I think the timing will be perfect for the last part of my surprise."

"There's more?"

He nodded. "And you didn't even need to use the parachute. I'm glad you didn't try to bail on me today."

"Hey, that wasn't my fault. I'm really not accident prone."

"I think we'll have to go on a few more dates for you to prove that," Jon replied, helping me into the car.

I smiled and buckled my seatbelt, not responding to his veiled request about more dates. Luke was always in the background of my thoughts, and I wished I knew what it was about him that made me hesitant to start dating someone else. As we coasted down the mountain, I relaxed, feeling the cool breeze against my skin. Jon pulled up next to a whitewashed building called The Shrimp Station.

"This isn't the surprise. This is just dinner. These guys make the best coconut shrimp on the island."

"Malia said I had to try some while I was here."

Jon and I sat outside under a canopy at a wooden picnic table, and ate crunchy shrimp battered with flakes of coconut. I wasn't a huge seafood fan, but I admitted that they were delicious. I laughed when Jon licked his fingers and stretched his arms above his head.

"My mom gets after me for eating here too much. She's kind of a health nut," he said.

"I don't blame you. These are delicious."

I finished off my shrimp and remembered how Luke had mentioned eating coconut shrimp last night. It was irritating that he kept crossing my mind, especially when Jon was right here. I dabbed my lips with a napkin and forced Luke's steel blue eyes from my memory. Instead, I focused on the laugh lines around the blue-green eyes in front of me. Jon was a welcome distraction for my stressed-out heart. I took his hand as we walked back to the car and a smile crept across his face.

Almost a half hour later, the sun had turned a brilliant coral hue as it approached the surface of the water. Jon parked behind a long line of cars, all of them flanking a low stone wall on the shoreline. He jumped out of the car and got my door again, something I appreciated.

"You're about to experience sunset on the wall."

There were probably a dozen or more people sitting, facing the ocean, laughing and talking. Jon found a spot for us, and I sat with my legs dangling over the edge of the rocks. As he sat beside me, I saw a turtle splash through a wave. "Oh, look! Sea turtles."

Jon swung his feet back and forth from the wall. "That's why I picked this spot. They're always here."

The surf rolled in, and several times I saw the round bodies of the sea turtles as they rode the waves, bobbing up and down on the surface. A few minutes later, my focus shifted to the blazing glory of the sun sinking into the water. Jon pulled me closer and I leaned into him. I'd already experienced an ocean sunset with him at the Beach House restaurant, but this one seemed even better. It was as if I could reach out and touch the sun.

"You're right. This is a great surprise." I hummed a few lines of a Hawaiian song I'd heard earlier in the day.

Jon didn't respond he just stared at me until I asked, "Penny for your thoughts?"

"You really are a rare beauty," Jon said. "Your eyes are such a deep brown. I love that chocolate color with your blonde hair." He smoothed a strand of hair behind my ear.

I felt self-conscious with the way he was looking at me— really seeing me. So I surprised myself when my arms wrapped around his waist. "I think this date pretty much knocks out any I've ever experienced."

He draped his arm around me, and I relaxed into him. We sat there for a minute staring out at the ocean. He shifted his head, and his lips brushed my temple. His closeness created a swarm of butterflies in my stomach—happy, sparkly butterflies that had my lips tingling.

I turned my face and smiled at him. As he leaned forward, I ducked my head and took his hand. I wanted to kiss him, but my meditation this morning had helped me understand the depth of my own strength. If I kissed him, I wanted to be sure it was what I really wanted, not what the sparks flying between us demanded. Normally, sparks dictated all things romantic for me, but my ex-boyfriend had kind of ruined that for me.

Jon didn't say anything about me dodging the kiss, and he didn't seem upset, either, which boosted him up a few more points in my book. After the sun had set, Jon helped me up from the wall. "It's great to have such good company, Adri."

He took my hand, and it made me want to kiss him even more. He wanted to be close to me, but he was honoring my wishes. As we walked, he swung our hands back and forth in a rhythm that was reminiscent of grade-school buddies. I giggled.

"What's the joke?"

"No joke. I just think you're charming, that's all."

His eyes crinkled with laugh lines. "I've heard a princess call her prince that, you know."

I didn't say anything to that as he tucked me into his car, but my cheeks were warm. We sang to a reggae tune on the way back to the hotel, and I thought about how I must be the luckiest wedding planner in the world.

The red light of the hotel phone was beeping when I got back to my room, and I had about six voice messages on my cell. The red light was annoying so I pushed a button to hear that message first.

"Adrielle, dear. We know that you're the wedding planner for Kyle Connelly and Malia Wright. Don't think for a minute that our carefully laid plans include the son of Tri-C Enterprises on the premises. Reschedule the wedding luau. I warned you what happens to people who don't respect my wishes."

I shook my head after listening to Mrs. Harper. Her nasal English accent was unmistakable. I kept the message, but mentally deleted her from my mind. Even though her message had me worried, I told myself there was nothing she could do to me. I wouldn't let her ruin the perfect day I'd had.

I turned my attention to the multitude of voicemails on my cell and groaned when I saw they were all from the maid of honor. Heather must have followed through on her plans, but not without Jenica discovering the interference.

After flinching at the screeching quality in her voice on the first message ranting about my controlling behavior and messing up her plans, I deleted the rest without listening. Taking a few cleansing breaths, I stood, consulted my planner for the room numbers of each of the wedding guests and headed to room 407. I caught myself clenching my hands into fists on the elevator and forced myself to relax.

Jenica swung the door open with a smug look on her face, and I hoped she hadn't done something that I couldn't fix. "Hello, Adri. Did you get my messages?"

"I did and I'm not sure what is going on or why you are so angry." She opened her mouth to speak, but I held up my hand. "Jenica, who's getting married this Saturday?"

She narrowed her eyes. "'Malia, of course."

"Then I shouldn't need to say anything more, but I will. *Malia* is getting married on Saturday. Her bridal shower and bachelorette party is tomorrow. I'm not sure what you are planning, but Malia didn't want anything suggestive at the party. The man you were telling me about is very different from the fire dancers performing at the luau for the wedding breakfast. Malia made a special request concerning her bridal shower, and it is my job to make sure that the bride is happy. That's also the maid of honor's job, but maybe you forgot."

"Well, you're just as snobbish as I thought you were," Jenica spat.

"Say whatever you like, Jenica, but what is most important is to honor the bride's wishes."

She opened her mouth and closed it again, reminding me of some of the fish I'd seen while snorkeling. "Fine!" She moved to close her door, but I stopped her.

"Fine, meaning what?"

"Fine, have it your way. We won't have any fun. We'll be just as prudish as you want us to be."

"Thank you. I'm hoping that tomorrow will be what Malia hoped for."

"Oh, you little witch," Jenica shrieked before slamming the door in my face.

"That went well," I mumbled to myself as I walked back to the elevator. I had said more than I should have, but I was so stunned at how horrible Jenica was acting compared to sweet Malia, my mouth had taken over my brain. I'd have to hope that Jenica wouldn't do something rash in retaliation since she obviously didn't suspect Heather at all. As a wedding planner, I usually wouldn't dream of enlisting help to override someone's plans, but not many of my clients were of the same caliber as Malia and her paradise wedding.

Chapter 10

BRIDAL SHOWER FAVOR, HAWAIIAN STYLE

Using ribbon, tie a bottle of finger nail polish to a pair of flip-flops with a personalized note from the bride.
Example:
I'd flip without friends like you.
Thanks from the bottom of my toes!

Courtesy of www.mashedpotatoesandcrafts.com

Tony called me back the next morning.

"Adri, I can't believe you found trouble on your first day in Hawaii."

"Technically, it was the second, but yeah, I'm lucky like that." I walked over to the patio door and pulled it open, letting the fresh ocean air permeate my hotel room.

"Are you okay?"

"Yes, I'm fine."

"No, I mean it. Are you doing okay? That's a scary thing—seeing a body." Tony's concern was sincere, and I felt bad for worrying him.

"I'm doing great. The family I'm working with here is fabulous. They're taking good care of me. I didn't want to bother you. There are just some things that I can't get out of my head. I want to know who that woman was. Can you help me?"

"That's the thing." Tony paused. "I probably could make some calls, but unless I have a good reason they're not going to give me information in an ongoing murder investigation."

"Dang."

"But you can ask them. That would be totally natural. Don't worry that it makes you look suspicious. The police will understand that you're concerned after being the one to find the body. Call up the investigating officer and tell him your concerns. If he can release her identity, he will."

"Okay. It's just, every time I think about that woman chained under the ocean, I think that there's something else I should remember but I don't know what it is." Even while talking with Tony, her face swam before my vision almost pleading with me to figure out what I was missing.

"You could tell them that. Again, that's normal. You were probably in shock after finding her, right?"

"Kind of." Tony knew me so well. He would predict that I went into shock and hated being vulnerable in that kind of a situation. "Please don't tell Wes. I haven't told my parents yet because they don't need to worry. I'm not in any danger."

"I won't tell any of your family."

"Thanks, Tony. Sorry to bother you."

"You're not bothering me." He sounded cheerful. "I saw Lorea the other day. You left her with plenty of work, but I think she misses her best friend a lot."

"I miss her too."

"Well, take care of yourself."

"I will."

After I ended the call, I thought about the obvious note of happiness in Tony's voice. Could he be Lorea's mystery date? I shook my head. That was too hard to fathom, unless it was some kind of favor to keep Lorea from having to find another person to go out with.

I texted Lorea:

Are you going to tell me who your date was?

She replied about five minutes later:

Maybe, when you tell me what you're going to do about Luke.

I grumbled. She knew just how to needle me, but I wouldn't let her get the best of me. I sent her a picture of Jon and me in front of the helicopter with a subject line: Luke's busy.

My phone pinged with the alarm I'd set for breakfast. I needed to eat and make sure everything would be ready for Malia's bridal shower. I hurried to get ready for the day, showering and dressing in yellow capris and a white and black striped top. I walked down to a lovely buffet table set with tropical fruit, oatmeal, granola, pancakes, and scrambled eggs.

I filled a bowl with fruit and another with oatmeal and a sprinkling of granola and looked for a place to eat on the veranda. There was a light breeze that carried the scent of the ocean. I settled in for a nice view of the beach as I ate. Not five minutes later, a shadow fell over my table. I looked up to see Luke carrying two plates of food.

"Mind if I sit with you?"

"Not at all, just don't block my view."

Luke chose the chair next to mine. "It is a nice view," he said, carefully arranging his plates. He took a bite of pineapple and leaned back in his chair. "So what's on your agenda for today?"

"Malia's bridal shower." I downed my glass of orange juice, not realizing how worried I still was about what the maid of honor might end up pulling. "She wanted it simple, so I've tried my best to keep it that way."

"I'm sure it will be perfect." His eyes wandered over to mine. "Any other plans today?"

"I don't think so."

"You're not doing something with Jon?"

I shook my head. "Why so many questions about Jon? He's just showing me around the island."

He shoveled in a mouthful of pancakes and chewed slowly. "I met him last night. He mentioned he'd taken you on a helicopter tour. I got the feeling he's a player."

"What do you mean?"

"He seemed pretty friendly with Malia's sisters. He looked like a pro."

"Oh, so you're jealous of Jon because he knows how to get a girl's attention?" I lifted an eyebrow.

"You know what I mean." Luke took another bite. "He can mess around with some other girl. You don't need to be hurt again."

Even though my defenses were raised, I paused because I heard what Luke was really saying. He knew exactly what I'd been through in the last two years. Maybe it was the Hawaiian air, but instead of getting angry like I usually did, I reached out and took his hand. "Thanks for watching out for me."

His eyes widened and I couldn't keep from laughing at his obvious surprise to my reaction. "I'm sorry. I'm not trying to be overprotective."

I rolled my eyes. "If you say so."

He squeezed my hand and looked into my eyes. "You know, I haven't asked you for a while about that date, but I'm still interested if you are."

"I am." I couldn't tell if he was asking me out or talking about the future.

He licked his lips and his cheeks darkened. Was he blushing? "Do you think maybe you'd have time to do something while we're here?"

His anxiety was endearing and my heart picked up tempo as I considered the loaded question. This wasn't the first time Luke had asked me on a date. Last time I'd refused, but there had been extenuating circumstances, and one had to take into account that he was a successful attorney specializing in divorce. Our interests weren't exactly in line, but last summer I'd seen a side of him that no one else in the Sun Valley area had seen.

"I might. It's hard to know, with the scheduling changes and last-minute things I'm doing to prep for the wedding, but Malia keeps insisting I take some time for myself."

"So I just need to arrange it through Malia?"

He laughed when I narrowed my eyes. "You have my number."

"What about this afternoon after the bridal shower?"

I opened my mouth to say no because I wasn't sure how long the shower would last, but then I hesitated.

Luke's hand still covered mine. He glanced at his fingers grazing my knuckles. "If you'll give me a chance, I'll be on my best behavior."

I lifted an eyebrow. "You mean you'll can the cynic for an hour?"

He nodded and figuratively zipped his lips.

"Well, this afternoon might just work. What time were you thinking?"

"How about I'll be ready when you're ready?" Luke moved his hand from mine.

"Okay. I'm guessing it'll be a little after three."

Luke nodded and then leaned forward, studying me. "Are you stressing about something?"

His attentiveness caught me off guard. I didn't want to voice my opinion of his cousin's maid of honor so I blurted out one of the worries that was currently front and center. "I'm having a tough time getting the rest of the wedding favors ordered because Neil's personal assistant quit, and they can't find the files." I thought it was strange that Tri-C was having such a difficult time getting into Charly's computer. It made me wonder if there was more to the story.

"Hmm, that is strange," Luke said. "Why wouldn't the files be on Neil's computer or Jon's for that matter?"

"Exactly." He'd just validated my thoughts. I guess I wasn't over-analyzing things and I didn't want him thinking about Jon again, so I changed the subject. "I'm not going to worry about it though. Tell me what you have in mind for our date."

"Okay." Luke drummed his fingers on the table, considering me. "I guess I'd better tell you in case you're too chicken to try."

I tilted my head. "I'm not afraid of much."

"Paddleboarding," Luke said. "You've heard of it?"

I clapped my hands together. "Yes, I really wanted to try it out. Are you sure we'll have enough time before sunset?"

"I checked and three hours is plenty of time."

I tapped my watch. "Now I can't wait for the bridal shower to be over."

"This feels nice. You seem genuinely excited to spend some time with me." Luke had cleaned up both of his plates, and he leaned back in his chair.

"It is kind of weird, huh? I feel like maybe I should yell at you, or call you some names, just to keep things normal." The first time Luke visited my wedding shop came to mind, and I cringed at the memory. The divorce attorney flirting with the wedding planner hadn't gone over so well with me.

Luke laughed and shook his head. He stared out at the ocean. He seemed to be miles away, and I wondered what he was thinking about. There was something different about him here in Kauai. Probably just the fact that he appeared so relaxed. I watched him, trying to pinpoint what had caught my attention. He turned to me. "Enjoying my profile?" he teased.

"Just thinking that I haven't seen you this relaxed. It's nice."

"Are you calling me uptight?" He chuckled. "Just kidding. You probably *haven't* seen me like this before. It's this place. I can't help it."

"Well, it's nice to see a different side of you. I hope you can enjoy your time here."

"You too, and remember what I said about Jon. I'm not trying to interfere, just be careful."

"You sound like my dad."

"Okay, I'll shut up now."

"That's a good idea." I brushed off my capris and stood. "It was nice to eat breakfast with you, but I've got to run."

"Me too, but I'll be running on the beach." Luke stood and waved as he walked toward the elevators. "I'll see you later."

I waved back, trying to talk myself out of the way my middle tingled when he said he'd see me later. Luke and I usually seemed to rub each other the wrong way. He often said things that caused me to bristle, and I had a hard time biting back retorts. But as I watched him walk away, I found myself admiring his tall physique and dark hair. It was kind of nice to have someone worry over me who really understood. With a sigh, I headed back to my room to brush my teeth again before getting to work.

The hotel staff had everything in order for the bridal shower, so after checking on the luncheon and giving the chef the final head count, I headed back to my room. I met Mrs. Harper on the way.

She was flanked by Teo and her other henchman, who I assumed was Mitt. Today she wore a gray business suit with pink cuffs, a pink beaded necklace, and gaudy pink diamonds in her ears. She'd overdone the rouge and her cheeks looked too pink, but then again, her entire persona was a pink nightmare.

"How fortunate to bump into you Miss Pyper. I was concerned that you hadn't answered me. Teo assured me that you got the message. I thought your manners were better than that."

"I'm not discussing this. Please don't approach me again. I will have no further contact with you." I stepped to the side, but Teo stepped in front of me.

"I don't want to have to use unnecessary force," Mrs. Harper intoned. "But it can be arranged."

I looked from Teo to Mrs. Harper. "You're insane. I'm going to my room. Get out of my way."

"Not until you change the time for your luau. I have an agreement with the hotel, and I'm not going to take no for an answer." She flicked her hand toward Teo. He took another step toward me.

I screamed. It kind of hurt my throat—I probably should have used my stomach muscles to support the shriek but something in me snapped. "Help! Security! Help me!"

Mrs. Harper blanched, and when Teo looked to her for the next command, I dodged out of his reach and ran for my room. Several hotel guests had witnessed the scene, and a few called after me, but I kept running. The elevator was just closing as I approached and I dashed inside, startling the young couple leaning against the back wall. When I reached my room, I was out of breath, and the adrenaline pumping through my veins made me want to keep sprinting. The door slammed shut behind me. It probably wasn't the best idea to escape to my room alone. What if they broke in and attacked me?

While sliding the extra lock in place on the door, I punched 9-1-1 into my phone. I didn't care if Mrs. Harper and her thugs were mostly bluffing. It was time to put a stop to their aggressive tactics.

I explained to the operator that I was being harassed and was scared for my safety. She said that she would send someone over right away. I ended the call and fell back on my bed, covering my face with my hands. A tremor passed through my body as I struggled to slow my breathing from the fight or flight response I'd just experienced.

I was surprised when I opened my door fifteen minutes later to see Officer Kinau standing there. His dark blue uniform looked freshly pressed, and I noticed the concern in his eyes. "Is everything okay?"

My breath came out in a huff. "It isn't actually, but I hope you can help me."

He nodded. "I heard the report and offered to come over because I wanted to check on you anyway, see how you were doing. Why don't we go down to the lobby? The staff is concerned, and I'd like to take your statement."

"Okay, let me just get my sandals." I stuffed my feet into the leather straps but then I remembered the message. "First, you should hear the message Mrs. Harper left for me." I pushed the message button and watched Officer Kinau as we both listened.

His brow furrowed and he took a few notes. When the message ended, he held up his hand. "Save that message. I'm glad you thought to have me listen to it. Are there any more?"

"No."

"Okay, let's head to the lobby."

As we walked, I related the incident with psycho woman and her thugs to Officer Kinau. He asked me a few questions about my run-ins with Mrs. Harper and then assured me that he would issue a warning for no further contact from them.

When we reached the front desk, Officer Kinau talked to a few members of the hotel staff. Some of them had witnessed the incident and corroborated my statement. I couldn't really press charges because all Mrs. Harper had done was threaten me, but Officer Kinau assured me that they weren't taking the situation lightly. I made sure to mention PFI and that they had planned some kind of rally which was why I was being targeted.

"That is serious," Officer Kinau said. "We try to keep an eye on these organizations but they're pretty secretive."

"They know that the owner of Tri-C is involved with this wedding because it's his son, Kyle Connelly, who will be married Saturday," I explained. "I don't know if that's why they're being so aggressive."

He adjusted the volume on his radio when it started chattering. "Could be. We'll have a talk with the hotel security staff. It's best to steer clear of those people, but if they do try to approach you again, please call us immediately."

"Oh, I definitely will do that." I pressed my lips together. I wouldn't let Mrs. Harper ruin my reputation as a wedding planner.

Officer Kinau rubbed a hand through his short black hair. "Have you remembered anything else regarding the woman you found at Tunnels?"

"No, I haven't." My insides churned with questions that I wanted to ask, so I voiced the most pressing one. "What about her identity?"

He shook his head. "We're close on that. We'll see if I get a chance to tell you before the media gets hold of the info."

"Oh, okay then." I made a mental note to check the news later on.

"You mentioned that there was something you might have seen but couldn't recall at the time." Officer Kinau looked at me, his gaze intent. "Has anything come together since Friday?"

"Sorry, but no. I'm beginning to think that maybe it was nothing." I folded my arms and then worried that the gesture looked defensive so I let my hands rest at my sides. "I mean, I want to remember and it seems important, but then there's nothing that really stands out."

Officer Kinau pulled out a card. "Even if you think of something that appears to be unrelated, don't hesitate to call and run it by me. Sometimes it's the little things that point us in the right direction."

I took the card even though I still had the one he'd given me Friday at the beach. "Thank you. I'll do that."

He stepped back, glancing at the hotel staff moving about. "Take care of yourself, Ms. Pyper."

I nodded and watched him walk toward the security desk. I secretly wished that he was on his way to arrest Mrs. Harper. But I wasn't going to wait around for them to find her or her henchmen.

By then it was almost noon. I had about twenty minutes to decompress and get ready for Malia's bridal shower. Was every day here going to be this crazy? Putting a hand over my heart, I took a deep breath reminding myself that I could be strong. After I touched up my makeup, I sent up a silent prayer for safety and exited my room. Thankfully I met up with Malia and her family and walked with them down to the beach.

Her bridal shower was scheduled to start at one o'clock, so we were a few minutes early. The resort's food service had prepared chocolate dipped strawberries, fresh pineapple, and a delicious chicken salad for the luncheon. There were fourteen women in attendance, and everyone appeared to be in the mood to celebrate. Malia hugged Jenica and when the maid of honor glared at me I just waved and smiled back. I hadn't heard anything else about a bachelorette party or fire dancers. I'd have to thank Heather again for her help.

Most of the women seemed relaxed, and everyone enjoyed their food. It was my first time in a beachside cabana and the atmosphere was perfect. Malia was flanked by her mother on one side and her future mother-in-law on the other. The three chatted easily. It was nice that Malia didn't need to worry about mother-in-law jokes because she seemed to have a good relationship with Heather.

Jenica had a little game prepared where each guest held a seashell up to her ear and then whispered some marriage wisdom they had "heard" from the ocean. Malia blushed dark red a few times, and everyone laughed and begged her to share the advice, but she refused.

There was also a photo book that Malia's mother had made and passed around for everyone to sign and include more words of advice. When the book was placed in my lap, I glanced at some of the sage wisdom imparted, along with the common pieces of advice I'd heard many times as a wedding planner. I tapped the pen on my cheek, thinking of something unique I could add as a single person who hadn't had much luck with relationships. Finally I decided on something that Malia would appreciate and wrote in careful script:

Always give him the benefit of the doubt and look for the best in his intentions. Laugh together and remember why you fell in love with him.

I passed the book to the next guest, wondering what kind of advice people would give a wedding planner when she was ready to take her vows. Marriage had always been a dream of mine but it couldn't be forced. I decided not to dwell on my past. My mother definitely did enough worrying for the both of us. With a glance at Malia, my worries fled. Her happiness was contagious and everyone seemed to be in a good mood.

The best part was when Malia handed out favors for the party. She held a wicker basket and bounced up and down on her toes. "I wanted to thank all of you for celebrating this special time with me so I put together a little something special with the help of the hotel."

I grinned because I knew what was coming and these ladies were going to be pretty excited. Malia handed each guest a small drawstring bag made of silk in the same beautiful coral shade that she'd picked for her wedding colors. A card printed on a sea foam green paper reminded me of her accent color, and I was impressed by what a great eye she had for details. Each card was attached to a pair of flip-flops.

I gave Malia a knowing smile when she handed me the favor, and she nodded. I pulled on the drawstrings and saw two bottles of finger nail polish clinking together. One bottle was coral and the other was silver with flecks of glitter. While

I examined the polish, I heard excited voices so I hurried to read the attached card on my silver flip-flops. On the front of the card it said:

I'd flip without friends like you.

Thanks from the bottom of my toes!

On the inside of the card, Malia had printed up a rhyme and signed each one.

For friends of the dearest kind

A gift from Malia you'll find

In the resort spa today!

Enjoy a deluxe wedding guest package at the spa, any day during your stay.

With love and thanks from the happy bride-to-be,

Malia

Everyone looked happy. Malia hugged her friends and family and the chatter grew louder as the women laughed and made plans for the premier spa services at the resort. The bridal shower had been a success. I stood to check on a few things and was pleased to see the service rendered at our little beachside bridal shower. Malia hugged me a few minutes later.

"Adri, thank you so much. That was so wonderful. Wasn't it great to see how happy everyone is about their *little* gift?"

I nodded. "They were pretty excited. I am too. I'm just so glad it worked out."

"A few of us are going down to schedule right now," Malia said. "Do you want to come along?"

"Actually I have some things I need to do first, but thank you." I opted not to mention my date with Luke. Malia would be just as thrilled over me dating her cousin as she was with the dates I'd been on with her future brother-in-law, but I didn't want the extra attention. "I'll make sure I get my massage scheduled."

"Okay, I hope you're planning time for fun in that little book of yours."

I laughed. "I am." I felt a tad guilty. Maybe I shouldn't be going on a date with Luke. There was surely some work that I could do, and I had just been out with Jon yesterday.

Most of the guests had left, but I lingered for a few more minutes and walked along the beach. The crashing of the waves drowned out the conversations of other people so it made me feel almost like I was alone staring out over the vast ocean. I thought about what Malia had said—making time for fun—and decided that I wouldn't chicken out from my earlier decision— I would go on the date with Luke. How many people could say their first date was in Hawaii?

Then I thought of Jon. My first date with Malia's future brother-in-law had also been in Hawaii. I recalled advice from my friends to date a few different men this time around and not feel like I had to commit to anything serious yet. It made me feel better when I thought about the possibility of dating both Luke and Jon. I found myself looking forward to another chance at seeing Jon, and I wondered if part of that was my own hesitancy about feeling anything for Luke.

A breeze tousled my hair, and I turned to head back to the hotel. Breathing in the salty air, I smiled. I had a date to get ready for.

I was halfway back to the hotel when someone called my name. Turning, I saw Heather wave and quicken her step to catch up with me.

"Adri, I'm so glad you're still here. I wanted to tell you what a wonderful job you're doing with all the wedding celebrations."

"Well, thank you. I'm enjoying it." I looked past Heather to see if someone was with her but didn't recognize anyone from the bridal shower. "And thanks again for your help with Jenica. She must have thought I did it or put you up to it. She definitely didn't suspect you."

"But it's nice to have deniability." Heather raised an eyebrow.

"I agree."

Heather smiled. "I had a few minutes so I thought I'd walk the grounds. Are you heading to the spa?"

"No, not right now. But Malia did try to talk me into it. She keeps insisting that I need to have fun here too."

"This is a magnificent place, and you should soak up every minute." Heather rolled her shoulders. "Malia said she'd schedule a massage for me, and I'm definitely looking forward to it."

"That does sound nice. I'm not sure what spa treatment I'll try first, but anything that involves being pampered is fine with me." I started walking, and Heather fell into step beside me.

After a few beats of silence, Heather glanced at me. "I don't want to bring up bad feelings, but are you doing okay after finding that woman?"

My throat tightened. I didn't really want to think about that, but I also didn't want Heather worrying. "Yes. I mean, I feel terrible about it all, that poor woman being murdered." I shuddered.

"I kept hoping it wouldn't be murder." Heather cringed. "It is awful."

"It sounds like that's what the police think too. I keep wondering who she was."

"Have the police been in contact with you again?"

Mrs. Harper and her henchmen came to mind, and I thought about confessing that the police had been in contact with me for a different reason, but I didn't want to upset Heather. "No, but they did tell me if I thought of anything else to give them a call."

"Anything else? Like what?" Heather tilted her head slightly, her expression full of concern.

"There was something about the body—I don't know—I just keep feeling like I should remember something, but I don't." I shrugged. "I guess it was just the shock."

Heather patted my arm. "You're probably right. I'm sorry that you had to start out your trip with a bad experience."

"It's okay. I'm staying busy, so that helps."

"I hear Jon is trying to keep you busy as well." Heather smiled at me.

My cheeks warmed with her attention. "Jon has been very nice. You have a great family. You should be proud."

Something passed over her face and her eyes grew shiny with moisture. "Thank you. It's been a stressful time, but I think everyone has been more than gracious."

I squeezed her hand. "Malia and Kyle are going to have a beautiful wedding."

She sighed. "It's all come up so fast after months of planning, but I do believe they will be happy together."

We had made it to the spa entrance, and I reached to open the glass door for her, but Heather stopped me. "I hope you'll take time for yourself and enjoy this beautiful island. Let me know if there's anything I can do to help."

"Thanks, I will."

It almost seemed as if she wanted to say more, but someone opened the door from the inside and ushered Heather into the warm beauty of the spa. My attention shifted to first-date preparations with a divorce attorney, and I hurried toward my room with a skip in my step.

Chapter 11

EASY HOMEMADE RUB FOR MUSCLE ACHES

2-3 tbsps coconut oil and 7-10 drops of wintergreen, peppermint, white fir, and/or lavender essential oil.

Mix and store in cosmetic jar or other airtight container.

Coconut oil melts at room temperature, for best results store in refrigerator until ready to use. Scoop out a small amount and massage into skin.

Courtesy of www.mashedpotatoesandcrafts.com

Luke and I practiced on the paddle boards we'd soon be riding next to the Hanalei River. Luke wobbled and grabbed my arm and we both stepped off our board onto the platform.

"Sorry." He shook his head as he stepped back on the board. "Hopefully my balance will improve."

"You'd better not do that on the water," I replied. "I'm going to keep my distance for safety's sake."

Luke held out his paddle and tapped me on the backside. "It wouldn't take much to make a splash."

I held up my paddle in return. "Watch it, Mr. Stetson."

We both laughed and turned our attention back to Tommy. He walked around our group of about ten would-be paddleboarders, giving tips on stance and how to enjoy the ride. When he finished, he helped us down into the water with a few more instructions.

"You'll be paddling down the Hanalei River, following it as it empties into the Hanalei Bay." He pointed downstream. "Be careful when you enter the ocean. It's a whole new set of skills to navigate the boards on the waves."

"What's the best way to hold the paddle if we want to try surfing?" Luke asked.

"You can use it to aid your balance," Tommy replied. "Just keep paddling and stay out of the choppy waves." He held up his paddle. "Keep your distance from the other surfers and ride the wave in, letting the blade of the paddle skim the surface of the water."

I lifted my eyebrows as Luke copied the move. "You are so going to biff it."

"Hey, you might be surprised at my athletic prowess." Luke hefted his board, and we walked to the edge of the man-made canal that connected riders to the Hanalei River. He wore a carved seashell necklace on a thin strand of twine. The white shell rested just below his collarbone. Luke's broad chest was bare and incredibly toned for someone who spent a ton of time creating divorce papers—not that I was looking too hard at the way his delts flexed when he practiced paddling through the air.

My fingers tingled from clutching my paddle so tight, and I took a deep breath as we pushed off from the shore. We started in a kneeling position, moving carefully along the canal until it emptied into the river. Then with a little squeal, I managed to stand up and keep my balance, holding the paddle in front of me and swiping through the shallow river near the bank.

Luke stood right after me, wobbling slightly until he planted his feet in the stance Tommy had demonstrated. "I can't believe I'm finally on a date with Adrielle Pyper, wedding planner extraordinaire."

I rolled my eyes and chuckled. "You are privileged, you know."

He laughed. "Really though, thanks for coming with me. This is pretty awesome." He rubbed his hand across the back of his neck, his fingers brushing the black curly hair dampened by humidity.

"My older brother Wesley would love this." I motioned to the jungle of trees, vines, and flowers overhanging the riverbanks.

"I always wished I had a brother, but it was just my two sisters and me," Luke said.

"And I always wished for a sister. Wes and I used to fight a lot when we were younger, but now we're best friends, and he got me a sister when he married Jenna."

From the riverbank, a rooster crowed, and Luke and I laughed. Luke switched his paddle over and directed his board closer to mine. The river moved slowly and we floated on the lazy current, paddling leisurely as we passed houses with private boat docks, red bougainvillea bushes, and trees that blocked the view of anything beyond the banks.

"So, tell me something about how you grew up." I reached my paddle out and tapped the back of Luke's board.

He hesitated, eyeing me as if trying to decide where to start. "I was born in Colorado, lived there until I was eleven and then we started moving east. My dad owned a carpet cleaning business and did other odd jobs on the side."

Luke stared ahead as he spoke. "He wasn't a very good businessman. Every time he made too many enemies in a town, we'd move on. When I was fifteen, my parents divorced and my sisters and I stayed with my mom in North Carolina. We were happy kids, despite the circumstances."

"I'm sorry. That must have been hard."

Luke shrugged. "Not really. When you don't know any different, you don't realize what you're missing out on. Dad died two years ago. I'd tried to keep in touch with him, but he just didn't care to have much of a relationship. Mom still lives in North Carolina near the Great Smoky Mountains."

I listened to Luke's story. His words evoked a profound sadness and disappointment in his father. The relationship that my dad had with Wesley was what made the two such good farmers and fathers.

"I'm sorry that things weren't better between you and your dad. I can't imagine what that must have been like."

"You know, I loved my dad." Luke let his paddle skim along the water and his voice dropped a notch. "I just don't want to be like him."

"You're not."

It was quiet on the river for the moment. A few kayakers were up ahead of us and the rest of the paddleboarders from our group were spread out, some behind and some out of sight down the river. He tipped his head back and I followed his gaze to the helicopter flying past. "Sometimes it feels like I am. I ran when Dana died—left everything and started fresh in Ketchum. I worry if I made the right decision."

"I ran too. After Briette died, nothing made sense anymore." Her memory didn't hurt like it used to when I spoke of the past. "It was like the whole world went flat, and the only way I could get my bearings was to go back home."

"I know what you mean," Luke responded. "Only I ran about as far away from home as I could get."

"Are you happy?"

Luke paddled on his left side, mulling over the question. "I think so."

"Then don't worry—that's what my dad tells me." I smiled at Luke. He wasn't wearing his glasses, and his dark blue eyes reminded me of the ocean up ahead.

"I am a little worried about entering Hanalei Bay." Luke pointed to where the river met the ocean. "Looks like some of our classmates are trying out the water."

There was quite a bit more activity as we entered the bay. Several people were wet from falling off of their board. Even as the current changed and my board wobbled, I saw a guy about Luke's age splash into the water. I concentrated on paddling to maneuver my board into the oncoming waves. They were quiet waves, rolling into the bay and losing most of their force by the time they rubbed up against the beach. That's probably why I wasn't worried when I should have been.

"Wow, this is different than the river," Luke said and knelt down just as a wave rolled into his board.

I didn't react quickly enough and the seemingly tiny wave pushed my board up and knocked me off balance. With arms flailing I entered the salty water of Hanalei Bay.

The water was only about five feet deep this close to shore, so I stood and wiped my dripping face with wet hands. That reminded me that my hands were empty. Where was my paddle?

"Nice day for a swim." Luke called as another wave lapped against my board. He held up my paddle. "Need a hand?"

"The water feels great," I said. "You should jump in too."

"Oh, so you jumped in, huh?" Luke smiled. "I must need my glasses 'cause from here it looked like a pretty decent fall."

"You're right," I paused. "You do need your glasses." I climbed on my board and sat upright as if I was in a kayak. Our instructor had showed us the method of paddling while sitting, and I decided to try it until I mastered the waves.

We meandered along the shoreline watching surfers and other paddleboarders. A Coast Guard cutter trolled on the outskirts of the bay, its dark gray hull sometimes blending in with the surf. Several sailboats were anchored farther out in the bay. Luke wanted to try surfing, so I told him I'd watch to see if he decided to "jump" in the ocean. I laughed when he did just that to escape a wave that was larger than he expected.

He finally rode one mini-wave to shore and I cheered for him. "You did it!"

"That was cool." Luke grinned. "And look at you. You're doing great."

"I think I got the hang of this." While he'd been trying to catch waves, I'd practiced paddling into several waves, going back and forth along a section of the beach.

"I'm going to be sore tomorrow." Luke rolled his shoulders back and sat down on his board.

"Definitely. I think I discovered a few new muscles today." I paddled next to him and followed suit, sitting on my board carefully. "But it is worth it. This is awesome."

"Agreed." Luke held my gaze, his smile deepening.

My insides fluttered. "You really are a nice guy, no matter what Lorea says."

"See, now I know you're teasing because Lorea likes me now." He chuckled. "Better watch out, Adri. You can't hide behind the man-hater anymore."

"Well, that's true because I think she's giving up on the whole ban against dating. She's acting all twitterpated this week about a date she took to her sister's wedding."

"Really?" Luke narrowed his eyes. "I'll have to give her a talking-to." He tried to keep a straight face, but we both started laughing.

My stomach growled loud enough that I think Luke heard it above the waves. He stood back on his board. "I'm ready to head back and get something to eat. How about you?"

"That sounds good." As I pulled myself to a standing position, Luke swiped his paddle so a sheet of water caught me from the waist down.

I squealed and leaped for his board, knocking him into the water. Luke grabbed me as he toppled over and held onto me as a wave pushed us toward the ocean floor. We emerged and he still didn't let go, his hands firmly on my waist. "Don't you dare dunk me," I sputtered, grabbing his shoulders.

"I'd never," Luke said. "I'm just hanging on to my beautiful date."

Even though we were playing, it felt different being this close to him. I resisted the urge to put my arms around his neck, instead keeping my hands on the tops of his shoulders. "Thank you," I said. The words sounded much more intimate than I'd planned. I told myself that the warmth along the back of my neck was probably sunburn, not me flushing like a schoolgirl over Luke Stetson.

The water glided past us ,and he reached out an arm and grabbed hold of my board. "Here you go."

He helped lift me up, and I tried not to feel self-conscious about his closeness as I scrambled onto the board. The way he kept smiling made me wonder what he was thinking.

We joked with each other and enjoyed a leisurely pace back up the river against the current. The time went by fast, and soon we were docking our boards and climbing back onto dry land. Luke had picked up sandwiches which we ate under the canopy of trees. Neither of us tried too hard to disguise the appetite we'd worked up. I caught him looking at me a few times, and I'm sure he noticed my attentions on him. I didn't want to compare and contrast Luke and Jon—I just wanted to enjoy the long-awaited date with Luke, but I couldn't ignore the happy jolt zinging through my chest each time he smiled at me.

He walked me to my room back at the hotel. "That was one of the best dates I've been on."

"Yeah, I think you have an unfair advantage whenever the date is set in Kauai, because that was perfect." I said.

"Thanks for coming." Luke leaned in for a hug.

"Thank you," I mumbled against his shoulder.

He pulled back, but kept his hands on my arms. "Hopefully these girly muscles will feel okay tomorrow."

"I'm stronger than I look you know." I resisted the urge to copy his motion and squeeze his biceps.

"Oh, I know," he said. "That's definitely true." He rubbed my arm with his right hand. "Good night, Adri."

"See you tomorrow." I stepped into my room, my hand touching the warm spot on my arm where he'd just held me.

I sat on my bed and let out a happy sigh. I really liked Luke, but as soon as that thought entered my mind, it was chased by images of Jon Connelly. I shook my head. I wouldn't ruin a perfect date by over-analyzing things. There was certainly enough going on that I could easily shift my concentration, so that's what I did.

I checked my email and found a letter from PFI declining my request for more information. The organization stated that they wouldn't be allowing any new members in until after the rally to protect the privacy of others involved.

I decided it was exactly the reason I needed to call Officer Kinau. It would give me a good opening into my other questions.

When he answered, I told him briefly about how I had tried to gain more information about PFI and their ensuing rally.

"Yes, I'm aware of that. Kauai's police force is on alert. Your information at least helps solidify the leads we have that say the rally will be happening this week."

A nervous tremor tingled up my spine. I hoped that nothing would interfere with Malia and Kyle's happy day. "There's something else I wanted to talk to you about."

"How can I help?"

"Were you able to identify the woman I discovered?"

"We were, but unfortunately we haven't been able to contact her next of kin, so I can't release that info."

"Oh, I was hoping to know who she was. I thought maybe it would help me. There's something that keeps bugging me, like I should know something or remember something about that day, but it's right on the edge of my memory." The pen I had ready to record the woman's name sat idly in my fingertips. I frowned and twirled it around before dropping it on my notepad.

"Well, I'll call you as soon as we're clear to do so." Voices and radio static grumbled in the background. "Maybe try letting go on that memory. Sometimes the harder we try to force ourselves to remember, the more elusive the memory becomes."

"That's a good idea." I hung up, sitting back and thinking about what he'd said. Letting go of the itch in the back of my brain was easier said than done, but I'd do my best to relax and quit thinking about problems I couldn't solve.

Chapter 12

PHOTO TIP

Turn the flash off your camera and utilize natural light to get the best images with natural color. Try to capture candid moments of people when they aren't posing for the camera. You'll often find hidden gems when subjects are truly relaxed.

Courtesy of www.mashedpotatoesandcrafts.com

The resort was taking care of most of the setup for Malia's wedding, but I needed a few more personal touches. Tuesday morning, Malia agreed to take me to the Connelly's beach house to see if we could find Kyle's old photo album.

The traffic was slow-going on the Ala Kinoiki Highway toward Koloa, but island driving was always at a slower pace. She pulled off the road onto a private drive that led to the house. The house was painted dark green with brown shutters and wasn't overly large. It surprised me that it wasn't a mansion, and then I remembered that this was the Connelly's second home and because it was a beach house, it was probably worth over a million dollars.

"So this is where Jon lives," I said as we walked up to the front door.

"Pretty lucky, eh?" Malia unlocked the door and we stepped inside.

The foyer was lined with multi-colored tiles. I caught the scent of plumeria and looked behind me to appreciate the yellow blooms on the tree in their front yard. "Very lucky."

"Did Jon tell you he's thinking of moving to Idaho?" Malia asked with a glimmer in her eye.

"Yes. How do you think Neil feels about that?"

"Well, when he finds out, I think he'll be upset, but what can he do?" Malia lifted one shoulder.

"Is that what Kyle thinks?"

Malia walked into the front room and began examining a large built-in bookshelf. "Kyle recommended that Jon not tell his dad because of all the grief Neil gave Kyle when he broached the subject of moving to the mainland to work."

"I'm glad that Kyle stood up to his dad so he could come and sweep you off your feet." I knelt next to Malia and brushed my fingers over the books stacked on the shelf.

Malia grinned. "Me, too. I think we're going to have a great life together, because Kyle's first priority is me, not money."

It was the first hint of anything negative I'd heard from Malia regarding her in-laws, but not unjustified. The Connellys weren't snooty, but they also didn't understand what it meant to live the median lifestyle. I supposed it was hard for someone with that kind of cash flow to grasp, and possibly why Kyle and now Jon would meet with resistance when it came to leaving the family company.

"Here it is," Malia said. She pulled out a large blue binder with Kyle's name written on the spine. She flipped it open, revealing photos of the Connellys. I recognized Jon's toothy grin in a grade school picture with Kyle. Malia and I laughed at a few of the photos from Kyle's "awkward" phase. A picture of Jon and Kyle on the beach reminded me of our date.

"Hey, I just remembered that Jon still has my ring from our bike ride the other day," I said. "Maybe I'll call him and see if it's in his room. He had it in a pocket of his swim shorts."

"Or just go on up and get it," Malia said. "I'm sure he wouldn't mind."

I already had my phone out, dialing Jon's number but it went straight to voicemail. "Hmm, no answer."

"I know he wouldn't mind." Malia pointed at the stairs. "His room is the first one on the left upstairs."

"Okay, I'll be right back." I jogged up the stairs, thinking I'd have to text Jon and ask permission later.

There were three doors along the hallway upstairs. I figured one of them was probably Kyle's and the other was a bathroom. Jon's door wasn't shut tight, so I pushed it open and it stopped halfway against a pile of clothes and gym shoes. Shaking my head, I walked inside and took a moment to survey his living space. I rubbed the back of my neck. This was prying. I checked the doorway in hesitation, but when I thought of Jon's easy smile, I relaxed. He wouldn't mind, even if I teased him about having a messy room.

If I remembered right, he had been wearing blue swim trunks when we went to Donkey Beach. I scanned the room, hoping the trunks would be left out with his other clothes. There were a couple piles by his bed and another pile that looked incongruous sitting atop his bed that had been neatly made. I didn't really want to dig through his clothes, so I hesitated, wondering if I should wait until I could talk to him.

I glanced in his closet, noting the two suitcases and a gym bag with snorkel gear hanging out the side. A diving belt with a flashlight, knife, and other tools hung next to the gear. The desk in the corner was made of a gleaming dark wood that appeared almost black. I walked closer to admire the construction and noticed his blue shorts hanging on the chair in front of the desk.

Lifting them carefully, I glanced behind me hoping Jon wouldn't be too upset if he found out. I unzipped the side pocket, and reached inside. My fingers explored the folds of material until I clasped my ring. As I pulled out my hand, the lining of the pocket followed me and deposited something on the floor with a clank. I set my ring on the desk before bending down to retrieve the golden circle that had been in Jon's pocket.

My heart stuttered as I stared at the bracelet in my hand. The metal band was yellow-gold and had a mother of pearl background flanking the logo of Tri-C Enterprises. Bile burned the back of my throat and I struggled to breathe as I remembered where I had seen it before. The dead woman. I had been totally freaked out by her arm moving in the water as if in a wave, but something had been nagging me about that day—some detail I had noticed.

It was this bracelet. The image came back to me clearly now. Her hand moving with the current and the gold around her wrist. Of course, I hadn't recognized the new company logo but the construction of the bracelet was too familiar to be ignored. The secretary had sent me one mock-up of the logo and a picture of this bracelet that would be given out to all wedding guests. Jon was supposed to be helping me track down the images and find out where the secretary had placed the orders for the bracelets to be made. What was he doing with one in his pocket?

My mouth went dry as a million thoughts raced through my brain. Was the dead woman connected to the company? She must be to have been wearing the bracelet with the new logo that no one outside of the family had seen. But no, this couldn't be the same one. It must be one that Jon found—and kept in his swim shorts? I kept trying to think of a way around the scenario that had been presented to me, but every explanation I came up with was lame.

Then I remembered the missing assistant who had quit with access to the new logo locked on her computer. Her name was Charly. I covered my mouth and shook my head. I didn't like the scenario fitting together in my mind. No, it couldn't be her. All of the Connellys would have recognized and identified her—wouldn't they?

I started to put the bracelet back in his shorts, but then I gripped it in my hand and slid it into my own pocket. I couldn't just leave it in Jon's shorts—not until I figured out what was going on. The police would know. I could show them the bracelet and ask if one had been found on the body. With a shudder, I nixed that plan. It would make me look suspicious and I would probably end up getting arrested—Jon too.

A better idea would be to do some sleuthing on my own. I had the rest of the day to figure things out, and I owed it to Jon to ask him first. Maybe it wasn't the same bracelet, just one that reminded me of what I'd seen. I wouldn't let my mind go where logic kept taking it—if Jon had taken this bracelet from a dead woman, it meant he knew who she was and might have something to do with her murder.

"Adri, did you find it?" Malia's voice floated up the stairs.

I snatched my ring and jammed it onto my finger, then I froze. If I took the ring, I would have to mention to Jon that I had retrieved it from his board shorts and then he would know about the bracelet immediately. Pulling the ring off my finger, I dropped it into his pocket and zipped it closed. It was the only way to buy me time to figure things out. Jon wouldn't know that I had taken the bracelet—he might think he misplaced it. I needed to answer Malia before she came upstairs. "Um—didn't find it in the first pair of shorts. Maybe I didn't remember right."

"Do you want me to help you?" she asked.

What I wanted was more time to search Jon's room. How could I do so with Malia waiting at the bottom of the stairs? I hurried out into the hallway and poked my head around the staircase. "It's okay. I'll meet you outside. I'll leave him a note. I just need to use the bathroom, and then I'll be right out."

Malia nodded. "Okay, see you in a few."

Noting the time on my watch, I reentered Jon's room. Hopefully I could find something to ease the worry gnawing at my insides. First, I looked for some paper to leave him a note. Malia probably wondered what was up with that—who writes notes when you can just text? The door shut downstairs, and I glanced at my watch again.

I found a crumpled ad for pizza and smoothed it out on Jon's desk. Grabbing a pen, I scrawled out a note:

Hi Jon,
Tried to find my ring, no luck.
Let me know if you still have it.
Thanks,
Adri

I left the note on his desk and kicked his board shorts under his bed, then threw a towel on top of them. My insides quivered, but I continued to search his room. His desk was neat and mostly empty, except for his laptop. I thought about turning it on, but since I was already on the verge of a heart attack just being in his room, I decided that would have to wait—it was probably password protected anyway.

I pulled open his drawers—they weren't neat, but there was nothing in them but clothes. What was I looking for anyway?

"Hey, Malia said you were up here." Jon's voice came from his doorway.

I jumped. "You scared me."

Jon looked confused. "What are you doing?"

My face flushed and I swallowed past the thickness in my throat. "I'm sorry. I was looking for my ring."

"Your ring?" He took a step forward into the room. "Oh, that's right. The one you gave me Saturday at the beach."

"I didn't mean to be nosy, but I thought your board shorts would be easy to spot." I motioned to his cluttered room. "Didn't peg you for a Mr. Messy."

"Hey, I'm not that messy." He held up his hands and then closed his closet door.

I made a clicking sound with my tongue. "You know what they say about boys who don't clean their room."

"What?"

I shrugged. "I don't know." With a toe, I kicked at a pile of laundry beside his bed.

He laughed and pulled me into his arms. "I missed seeing you yesterday. How'd the bridal shower go?"

Part of me wanted to relax into his embrace, but the weight of the bracelet in my pocket seemed to increase with each passing second. Jon was acting totally normal, but what would he do when he found his shorts and noticed the bracelet was missing? Would he suspect me? I had to keep things light and distract him.

I hugged him and then stepped away. "It was nice. I just had to put out a few fires and steer clear of the monster bridesmaid."

Jon laughed. "That bad, huh?"

I nodded and swallowed. "Well, Malia's waiting. We should go."

"Let me get your ring first. I'm sure my shorts are in here. I thought I left them hanging on my chair."

My leg muscles tightened, freezing me in place. I wasn't prepared. I wanted to just ask him about the bracelet, but I was afraid. What if he lied to me?

Jon leaned over his desk and picked up the piece of paper I'd scribbled on. "You left me a love note?"

"It's not a love note."

"What's this little heart supposed to mean, then?" He tapped the paper and held it in front of my face.

I flushed again. "Habit?"

"Oh, so you're saying you have a habit of sneaking into guy's rooms and leaving little love notes?"

"Nope." I twisted my hair with my hands and attempted a playful smile.

"Nope? Is that Idaho lingo?"

I grinned. "Habit."

He took a step closer and touched my arm. "You know what they say about girls who sneak into boy's rooms?" he whispered.

"What?"

"I don't know." The lighthearted teasing air vanished from his voice as he studied my face.

If I didn't act normal, he would suspect me for sure. But I wasn't going to kiss him. I'd already kissed one murderer in my lifetime, and it was one too many. I commanded my mind to stop. Jon was not a murderer. There was nothing uncomfortable about the way he held me or looked at me. Maybe I should trust him and ask him why he had the bracelet. Perhaps he'd picked it up from Tri-C in his efforts to help me locate the company logo. There was probably a simple explanation, but I faltered as Jon's fingers grazed my chin.

Luke's words came to mind about how Jon was just a player. I bit my lip. How well did I really know Jon? I couldn't trust my own judgment, and that's what angered me the most. I'd always had great instincts and a knack for reading people, but ever since the scar on my chest changed my life, I'd been questioning myself on everything.

And here I was standing close to another man whom I didn't really know. But I wanted to be held.

I leaned my head against his chest. "I still have trust issues."

"Maybe a kiss would help? You know, test the chemistry."

"I'm pretty sure the chemistry is there, but I wonder how much is organic and how much is practiced." I stepped out of his embrace.

It was Jon's turn to blush. "Well, I'm thirty-two. I've had girlfriends, if that's what you mean."

"I just don't want to be played."

Jon stepped back, but kept eye contact. "That hurts."

"I know, but can you honestly tell me that you weren't hoping I was maybe an easy catch when you first met me?" As soon as I said it, my neck prickled with heat. Being straightforward carried certain risks, and I hoped I hadn't just crossed an invisible line.

"I can honestly tell you I never viewed you that way." Jon's shoulders drooped. "Sure you're hot, but I'm not a player."

I clenched my fists. "Show me a man who would admit that he's a player."

Jon huffed and tipped his head back before answering. "Unfortunately, I could introduce you to several. But that's not me. Ask Kyle. He's my brother, he'd tell you."

I stepped back and folded my arms. The distance cleared my head somewhat. Jon wasn't fighting back. He seemed disappointed in my accusation, and his response sounded sincere.

"Adri, I told you I'm coming to Idaho." Jon held out his hands as he spoke. "There could be a future for us if you wanted to pursue it."

If he had said that only ten minutes earlier, I would've been happy and hopeful. Why did I have to go snooping in his room and ruin everything? Jon was part of Tri-C and would likely have something to do with the design, but keeping the bracelet in his board shorts was suspicious.

He leaned forward, touching my arms lightly. "I'm sorry. I didn't mean to make you uncomfortable."

There it was—the genuine kindness I saw in his face. The way that topaz ring around his blue eyes pulled me in was dangerous. I swallowed. What would happen if I voiced my suspicions? "Jon, I—"

"Ah-ha!" He interrupted me and stepped around the pile of clothes, snatching up his board shorts from under the bed. "Found 'em."

Sweat beads formed at the nape of my neck as I watched him unzip the pocket and search inside. His brow furrowed slightly, and he hesitated for half a second. If I hadn't been watching for it, I might not have noticed because the next second he pulled out my ring with a grin. "This what you were looking for?"

My face heated, and I held out my hand in a cupped position. He dropped it into my palm then turned and rummaged in the pocket again. He was probably searching for the bracelet. Would he suspect me when he couldn't find it? I needed to say something—anything——to change the subject. "Thanks."

He dropped his shorts and turned to me. "No prob."

"I mean, for being patient with me. I didn't intend to be rude."

Jon lifted his chin. "Oh? So it's natural for you to accuse all your dates as players."

That stung and my shoulders stiffened. "I'm just trying to protect myself."

"I wish you'd let me help with that." Jon leaned against his bed and gave me a playful pout.

The corners of my mouth turned up slightly. "Maybe."

He reached for my hand, and I let him take it. "We'd better go. Malia is going to be teasing us like crazy, and I haven't even kissed you."

I watched Jon carefully. He didn't seem preoccupied, unless it was with me. The way he took every opportunity to be close to me dropped my defenses down a notch. When I slipped my hand into my pocket and brushed the bracelet with my fingertips, my defenses slipped back in to place. I needed some answers, but first I had to find someone trustworthy to help me with my questions.

Chapter 13

PROGRESSIVE PHOTO DISPLAY BACKGROUND

Create a great conversation piece and wonderful gift for the bride and groom by gathering photos from childhood, dating and courtship, and engagement photos. Either arrange photos digitally or have them printed and adhered to foamcore or large 14 x 16 inch frames.

Courtesy of www.mashedpotatoesandcrafts.com

The lobby of the Hyatt continued to impress me, no matter how many times I walked through it. After Malia dropped me off, I paused to get my bearings and allow some of the adrenaline to burn off while I decided what to do next. I stopped at one of the huge marble columns and looked out toward a gathering of people on the veranda. Chelsea was talking to Pua—the other concierge who'd unwittingly helped me—and the conversation didn't look happy. He was stoic, but the muscles in Chelsea's jaw clenched as she spoke and then she gripped something in her hand and slapped it onto his outstretched palm a second later. She spun on her heel, and I moved quickly to the other side of the mezzanine as she stomped back to the row of computers flanking the back wall.

The wrinkle in my forehead tightened as I scrutinized the situation. Smoothing my hand across my forehead, I watched them both for a few more moments before returning to my room. The anger in Chelsea's step had been evident. I hoped that it meant she was going to bat for me instead of thinking up other ways to rearrange Malia's wedding schedule. Perhaps she was in trouble for helping Mrs. Harper, who ultimately brought the police to the hotel because of her associations with PFI.

The turquoise and purple floral design on my planning binder reminded me of why I was in Hawaii. Mrs. Harper would not ruin Malia and Kyle's special day because I wasn't going to let her mess with my plans. I let my fingers trace over the silver embossed title, *Adrielle Pyper's Dream Weddings: Where happily ever after is your destination.* I had achieved my dream of running a successful wedding planning business. My happily ever after wasn't exactly where I wanted it to be yet—I still yearned for the kind of love I saw in so many of the couples I worked with—but it would happen. At age twenty-six, I still had time, but since my nephew's birth in

December, it was getting harder not to notice the ticking of the clock.

With a shake of my head, I pushed out my daydreams and concentrated on what needed to be done next on my list. The bracelet and the swirling questions regarding Jon threatened to take over all of my plans. I needed a breather from my suspicions. Burying myself in Malia and Kyle's wedding plans was the best therapy. The Connellys had planned another outing for tomorrow at Secret Beach. I planned to go along and snap some candid photos of the wedding party to place in a fun digital collage Lorea was helping me with for the reception.

For every wedding I planned, I created a handmade gift for the couple. It was a unique touch that all of the newlyweds had appreciated, and I loved coming up with new ideas. For Malia and Jon, the gift was a bit more time-intensive than some I'd done in the past, but Malia would be happily surprised when she saw the presentation.

I was in the process of creating three large collages as the backdrop of the guest book table. One had photos of Malia and Jon as children and teenagers, and as soon as we finished scanning in more of his pictures, that would be complete. The second was complete, filled with pictures of the happy couple during the two years they had spent dating and engaged. The third was to be filled with Hawaii and everything leading up to the wedding day. They would be printed as a poster and then affixed to foamcore for stability. The final touch would be to hang the display with ribbon from a latticework. Lorea and I were proud of the idea, and Malia didn't even know the extent of what we were doing with the photos she'd been helping me collect. It would be a perfect addition to her wedding décor, and a nice way for me to give the couple their wedding gift.

Malia had scanned in several photos from the family albums she'd looked through and sent me some zipped files of those photos along with more recent ones of the family. There were dozens of pictures to go through, and I sorted them into different folders. A few of the pictures had people that I didn't recognize with the Connellys. I wondered if they were relatives or work associates. I filed those into a folder with a question mark—I'd go back to them if I thought I needed more for the collage. Jon and Kyle sported cheesy grins in several of the photos. I found myself smiling as I flicked through the digital record of the Connelly brother's antics.

After I sorted through the last few photos, I fiddled around with the layouts and adjusted some of the pictures I'd taken since arriving in Kauai. I typed up a few notes and emailed the files to Lorea. Photoshop was not my forte; lucky for me I worked with someone who had a knack for it. Lorea would get everything finished in plenty of time for me to send it to the printer.

With that project completed, my mind returned to the questions I had surrounding Jon and the bracelet I'd found. It made me sick with worry, so I snatched up the next thing I could find to focus on. My blog needed some attention, so I logged onto MashedPotatoesandCrafts.com and began writing a post about Hawaii. The next piece of wedding planning advice was already in the queue, so I checked in with my contributors to make sure they had everything they needed for our schedule of posts. When I started the blog about the same time I opened my shop, it had been merely a hobby. Indulging in crafts had long been a passion of mine and my mother's, so it was natural to create something that embodied my favorite things. With the explosion of Pinterest on the crafting scene, and the other social media connections I had, my little site had turned into a community of crafters with a penchant for spuds. Every comment I read made me happy. The sponsors I worked with made it possible for me to keep the site running and still do my day job. I felt extremely blessed to be experiencing the small joys of my life each day.

I leaned back in my chair and closed my eyes. I was in Hawaii, executing a well-planned wedding, and even though everything hadn't worked out perfectly, and I still had a lot of work to do, I needed to take time to revel in my surroundings. Closing my laptop, I stood and stretched. The knock at the door, however, startled me. I glanced at my suitcase where I had stowed the bracelet, wondering again if I should have just left it in Jon's shorts.

There would be time to study it out later. I didn't want to think about the body or why I thought the bracelet had something to do with the poor woman and Tri-C. I walked softly toward the door to check the peephole. Relief spread through my core. For once, Luke was just the distraction I needed. Usually when my thoughts circled around him, I ended up focusing on the complicated feelings I experienced whenever we were together, but at that moment he was rescuing me from the mystery of the gold bracelet. I hesitated a nanosecond, deciding on whether I should confide in him about my worries. With a shake of my head I swung the door open. "Hello."

"Hi. How are you today?" he asked.

"It's been a pretty good day so far." I stepped aside and motioned with my right hand. "Do you want to come in?"

"Uh, thanks." He stepped inside and let the door shut behind him. He looked good in dark brown cargo shorts and a white V-neck shirt. His rimless glasses framed dark blue eyes that often appeared stormy, but at the moment Luke's gaze wasn't as confident as I was used to. He cleared his throat. "I stopped by in the hopes that you might have time to go on another date with me."

I kept my face expressionless to hide my surprise. Yesterday's date with Luke had been a blast. Maybe he really did like me if he was asking me out again so soon. I had a feeling he was trying to keep me away from Jon, and for once I didn't mind.

"What kind of a date?"

"The Pu'u o Kila lookout," Luke answered. "I promise it won't take long, and you definitely don't want to miss it." His expression was hopeful.

"Can't say I've heard of it." I hesitated and looked at my laptop and the pages spread about my desk. "I was just thinking that I needed to take a break from all this inside work."

"So you'll come?" His face lit up, and my stomach did a little flip.

I waited for my brain to catch up with my heart. "Yes, I'll come. Is what I'm wearing okay?" I motioned to my mint green capris and the cream blouse I wore.

Luke nodded and looked down at my feet. "I meant to give you a heads up, but if my timing's perfect, let's capitalize on it. You look great, except you'll need tennis shoes and a jacket."

I noticed that he had a pair of running shoes on. "Where's your jacket?"

"In the rental car." He thumbed behind him. "It might rain, and you could get a little dirty, so if you need to change I can come back in a few."

"No, I think this should be fine. I don't own anything that doesn't wash well."

Luke nodded. "I've been warned about the red dirt though."

"Me too. That's why I brought these." I said as I slipped on an old pair of sneakers. "The official guidebook recommended bringing a pair of *trashable* sneakers."

"I didn't get that memo," he said.

I made a tsking sound. "Sounds like lawyer boy didn't do his homework."

Luke chuckled and the sound lightened my mood even more. "You ready?" he asked.

"Yep." On the way out the door, I grabbed the guidebook and stuffed it into a bag with a jacket and a rain poncho.

While Luke pulled out onto the road and headed in a westerly direction, I consulted my guidebook and looked up the Pu'u o Kila lookout.

"What are you looking for?" Luke asked.

"I want to know the insider information on where you're taking me." I continued scanning the index. "But I don't know how to spell the name. Do you?"

He shrugged. "I try not to butcher the names, but by the way people cringe when I asked for directions, I'm not doing too well. This place is on all the top ten lists."

"How'd you hear about it?"

He looked over at me. "I talked to a few locals. They all recommended the same spot when I asked them where to take a beautiful woman on a date if she liked a bit of hiking but really needed a place to feel the peace of the island."

"You did not," I said.

Luke's mouth quirked up on one side. "I may not have said those exact words but that's kind of the way people described Pu'u o Kila."

"Aha! I found it." I gave him a triumphant grin and flipped to the page indicated. At the same time I realized that Luke was taking me in the same direction as Waimea Canyon. The sight of the canyon from the helicopter tour had been amazing. That day with Jon had been carefree and fun. Now my suspicions and worries clouded my thoughts concerning him. I'd left in a hurry after he found me in his room, but I wondered if he was thinking about me.

"Maybe I shouldn't let you ruin the surprise." Luke reached for my book, but I leaned toward the window and quickly read the information. "It says it's one of the greatest views in the Pacific."

"Really?"

I continued reading, getting more excited by the description. "This says that the Pu'u o Kila lookout puts you above the Kalalau Valley so you can see the Na Pali coastline. That was one of my favorite parts of the helicopter ride."

Luke hesitated when I mentioned my date with Jon, but he recovered quickly. "Sounds like I picked a winner then."

I relaxed into my seat. He was taking me to the exact same place that Jon had taken me, except that we were driving. "It will be neat to see the area from a different viewpoint."

"I think you'll like it." Luke moved the steering wheel slowly through the steep upward climb.

I watched him drive and took in my surroundings as we chatted about Malia and Kyle and how they would get along in Idaho compared to the paradise of Hawaii. Luke seemed relaxed, and I found myself studying him, the way his dark hair curled at the nape of his neck and the shadow of stubble that still hadn't disappeared from his chin.

We'd met under interesting circumstances and kind of had a rocky start, but our paddleboarding date had given me the opportunity to get to know Luke a little better. The details he'd shared about his childhood and his father gave me new insight into his quiet nature. When we first met, he'd been difficult to read and standoffish, so I couldn't get a good handle on what he was thinking. I didn't mean to, but I found myself comparing him to Jon's fun-loving personality and the way he teased and cajoled everyone around him. Luke was definitely more serious, but his smile had a way of ratcheting up my heart rate. The depth of feeling I always noticed in his eyes made me want to work harder to really get to know him.

About thirty minutes later, we reached the peak and the parking lot of the lookout on a small plateau. Luke helped me from the car and as we walked toward the signs indicating the vantage point, I pulled on my jacket. Mist hung in the air and a blanket of clouds hovered in the east.

"We're right close to the Wai'ale'ale Falls." He pointed to the bank of clouds. "Listen and you'll hear the helicopters. It looks different from the ground up, doesn't it?"

I let my gaze follow the line of mountains and travel across the horizon. The growth on the mountain was thick with flowers, trees, and shrubs. The vegetation was interrupted by waterfalls cropping up from recent rains. It was the most beautiful vista I'd ever seen, but I didn't dare speak because the silence around us felt sacred. It seemed the soul of Kauai beat right here in the valley looking out at the Na Pali coastline. Every shade of green imaginable had been used in the Creator's palette. As we stood there at the edge of the mountain, a few of the sun's rays broke through the clouds and shimmered to the ocean below, the light tilting as it traveled through the heavy humidity in the air.

My eyes filled with tears that I blinked away, but when I glanced at Luke, I saw moisture on his lashes. He reached out and took my hand as we continued to experience the glorious canvas before us. And in that moment, I knew that Luke had been here before with his wife. He had pretended that he hadn't been, probably because he never broached the painful subject willingly. Her name was Dana. Luke had mentioned that last fall before he had closed up the subject again.

Standing this close to him almost seemed like I was intruding, but the way my heart connected with the beauty before me overpowered any conscious thought. My fingers intertwined with his, and at the same time a gust of wind blew against me, rocking me back from the face of the cliff. Luke reached out to stop my fall and just as quickly the wind was gone, replaced with a silence so profound that I thought I heard the roar of the ocean from at least a mile away. Luke held me in his arms, and I wrapped mine around his waist and leaned my head against his chest.

Something powerful was going on with my heart. My emotions bubbled to the surface. I let out a breath, allowing them to be whisked away by the feather light shift in the breeze. He looked at me and I whispered, "Thank you." Luke nodded and lowered his face toward mine. As I stood there in his arms, I focused on every good thing I knew about Luke. He was real. He would never hurt me. His wife had died from Hodgkin's disease and losing her had broken his heart, but in an attempt to salvage his life, he'd moved to Sun Valley, Idaho from North Carolina and set up his practice. We'd danced around the idea of dating for over half a year, and he'd been patient with me as I took my time to heal, and to mourn Briette's death in a new way after discovering her killer.

Luke's breath warmed my cheek as he moved closer. He was going to kiss me, and I didn't know if I should stop him or not. All thought had left my mind when I stood and experienced the rapture of witnessing beauty undefiled in the Kalalau Valley. I let my eyes close just as laughter cut through the silence. Luke tensed, and I opened my eyes again to see what had ruined our perfect moment. He turned his head to look at the newcomers. A family with several teenagers drifted past us with waves, greetings, and more laughter. I found myself smiling despite the keen disappointment of having our moment interrupted.

Luke shifted but kept his arm around me as we both looked out toward the Na Pali coastline again. "Would you like to go for a little hike?" he asked as he stepped away from the cliff's edge.

I nodded.

He led the way along a path cut through the red dirt toward a better vantage point of the Wai'ale'ale Crater. Swollen clouds hung over the crater, eclipsing the view of most of the falls and trickling down the verdant slopes. We talked about anything but the moment we'd shared, maybe we were both thinking about what might have happened if that group hadn't arrived. Laughter had stolen my first kiss with Luke, and I felt silly that it bothered me so much. What about Jon?

Rain started to fall in a light drizzle, so we donned our ponchos and headed back toward the parking lot.

"Can we look one more time?" I pointed at the Na Pali coastline. Luke nodded and took my hand. The sight was beautiful still, and changed with the sun hiding behind the clouds and the lighting subdued through the haze of moisture. I glanced at Luke and decided to be bold. "Did you come here with Dana?" I asked in a voice just above a whisper.

Luke flinched. "Yes."

I waited to see if he would say anymore, but he held perfectly still, his hand a dead weight holding my own.

"I'm glad she got to see this." I turned to see his reaction to my words.

He swallowed. "She said God painted this for us."

"I agree."

Luke stepped back, letting go of my hand. "We'd better go before we get drenched." He took a step to the side to see if I would follow. I struggled to keep the disappointment from showing on my face and stepped away from the cliff. I walked toward the car with quick steps. The rain was coming harder now, creating tiny rivulets along the red path like tears flowing toward the Wai'ale'ale Crater. My own eyes stung with the few tears that had escaped. Luke still held onto so much pain. I wished that I could help him let go.

When we got to the car, he helped me remove my poncho and then shook it out before stuffing it in a bag. He turned the heat on high, and I held my hands in front of the vent, warming my fingertips. Luke sat in the car and readjusted his seat, leaning his head back and closing his eyes.

"Thanks for sharing this with me," I said. "I can see it was difficult for you, but I want you to know that it means a lot to me."

He shook his head. "I don't know what I was thinking." He frowned and the frustration seemed to emanate from him.

"What's wrong?" I studied his face, trying to decide if he was angry at me or himself.

"Nothing." He leaned forward and rested his head in his hands. "I just thought that it would feel different."

"Luke, what you just shared with me was the single most beautiful part of the world I've ever witnessed. I could stand there all day and soak in that peace."

He didn't say anything. I wondered if it was because he was too overcome with memories of his wife. "I want to tell you something," I whispered. "I've opened the door to my pain and taken a look inside. It hurts. A lot. But I did it anyway." I put my hand on his arm, wishing that I could embrace him or switch some lever to help him release the sorrow he held onto. "I finally realized that I was holding onto the pain as a way to protect myself."

He lifted his head a fraction of an inch, and I tilted mine to meet his gaze. "What do you mean?"

"I think you're doing the same thing." I looked into his dark blue eyes. "Would Dana really want you to lock your heart away? To be unhappy and cynical for the rest of your life?"

"You don't know Dana. Don't act like you do."

"I didn't say I knew her. I asked you—the person who knew her best—what she would want you to do. I'm sorry if that makes you uncomfortable, but if you can't answer that question honestly, then I don't know why I'm even wasting my breath talking to you." The last sentence snapped out, harsher than it should have but I didn't take it back.

His eyes narrowed, and he faced forward putting the car into drive. I folded my arms tightly across my chest as he pulled out onto the road and headed down the canyon. "I'm doing the best I can, Adri." Luke glanced at me and then focused on the road.

I chewed on my lip, trying to think of the right words to say. "No, I don't think you are. I think that your best is much better than this half-dead kind of living you're doing now. I'm not trying to say it doesn't hurt to lose someone you love, or that you'll ever really get over it. But this is not your best effort at living—you can do better."

Luke pursed his lips, but didn't answer. I fell asleep on the drive home, dreaming of flying out over the Na Pali coast and tugging at Luke's hand, trying to get him to take flight with me.

Chapter 14

PINEAPPLE UPSIDE DOWN CAKE

1/4 cup butter or margarine
1 cup packed brown sugar
1 can (20 oz) pineapple slices in juice, drained, juice reserved
1 jar (6 oz) maraschino cherries without stems, drained
1 box yellow cake mix
Tip* Use ½ cup reserved pineapple juice and ½ cup water instead of just water in the cake mix.

Heat oven to 350°F. In 13x9-inch pan, melt butter in oven. Sprinkle brown sugar evenly over butter. Arrange pineapple slices on brown sugar. Place cherry in center of each pineapple slice, and spread remaining cherries around slices; press gently into brown sugar.

Add enough water to reserved pineapple juice to measure 1 cup. Make cake batter as directed on box, substituting pineapple juice mixture for the water. Pour batter over pineapple and cherries.

Bake about 45 minutes. Immediately run knife around side of pan to loosen cake. Place heatproof serving plate upside down onto pan; turn plate and pan over. Leave pan over cake 5 minutes so brown sugar topping can drizzle over cake; remove pan. Cool 30 minutes. Serve warm with fresh whipped cream or vanilla ice cream.

Courtesy of www.mashedpotatoesandcrafts.com

When we arrived at the hotel, I didn't wait for Luke to get my door. He was still brooding, so I thanked him and then hurried toward my room. I didn't even look behind to see if he followed me, even though I really wanted to. He needed space. We had both said some hard things, and I didn't want to fight with him, or make him feel worse about the situation.

Anger and disappointment tapped at my heart, reminding me that it was best left caged and protected. Every time I put myself in a vulnerable situation, I ended up hurt. As I thought about it more, I understood exactly why Luke behaved the way he did. I slumped onto the loveseat in my room and held my arms tight across my chest. Hunger pains squeezed my stomach, reminding me that I hadn't eaten. Luke probably had planned something and then axed that after our blowup at the lookout.

Even though I wasn't in the mood to play nice, I tried to see the situation from his point of view. He'd taken me to that place for a reason. It was sacred to him, and he wanted to share it with me, but the emotions had been too great for him to handle. Since he was a man—at least that was the excuse I gave him—he'd lashed out when the feelings became too real. Luke didn't know how to deal with all the memories of his wife that had probably come to the surface while looking out at the Na Pali coastline.

Goosebumps popped out on my arms, and I swiped a hand across my eyes. I'd caught a glimpse of the real Luke today, before he'd shoved that version of himself in a corner. What would it be like to spend time with the tender and caring Luke who had loved his wife so deeply? With a sigh, I rose from the love seat. I couldn't help Luke until he decided to help himself, and I wasn't sure what needed to happen for him to decide life was worth the risk to enjoy, instead of just enduring.

The hunger pains hadn't ceased, so I decided to head out to see what some of the hotel restaurants had to offer. I scanned the dining room for signs of PFI activists and Chelsea, but the hotel was relatively quiet. Tuesday night probably wasn't usually a busy night for them. That made it easier for me to find a quiet booth in the restaurant where I ordered soup and a sandwich. By the time I'd eaten, I was more at ease. I'd sent up several prayers in Luke's behalf and reminded myself that I needed to be forgiving and understanding of his loss. But another part of me was still disgruntled about the bit of hope that clung to the gates of my heart, wishing that Luke would give me a reason to open them for good.

I walked through the lobby in a semi-daze with a belly full of yummy pineapple upside down cake. When the waitress offered me a slice of the moist cake just as I was finishing my meal, I couldn't resist the fresh Hawaiian pineapple amidst the warm yellow cake with brown sugar bits dotting the sides. Another slice would have been perfectly sinful, but I was tempted to return to the restaurant and bury my dating woes in brown sugar and pineapple. I paused to look back at the restaurant and then continued walking toward my room, and bumped into Malia.

"Adri, I've been looking all over for you. There's a problem with my veil. I left it in the lobby while I was hunting for you." Malia tugged on my hand and I followed her to the lobby. "What have you been up to?"

"Oh, just eating the most divine pineapple upside down cake on the island and wishing I could eat the whole cake."

"Uh-oh." Malia stopped and looked closely into my eyes. "What's stressing you out?"

I waved my hand. "Nothing really. You know how I get worked up over the details. Now what's the problem with your veil?"

Malia groaned. "Everything. I looked at so many veils before ordering this one and it's still not right. I'm hoping that you can help me fix it."

"Um, okay." Malia had struggled to pick out a veil that fit perfectly with her dress. Lorea had offered to make one for her, but in the end she'd ordered one from another bridal boutique out of Chicago.

Malia approached the concierge desk, which thankfully was absent of Chelsea at the moment. She pulled a garment bag from the desk and unzipped it, removing a bright swath of white silk and rayon. A wreath of rhinestones was attached to the veil. Malia held it up and frowned. "It's all wrong for my dress."

"It's a beautiful veil, but you're right," I said. "It doesn't go with your dress." Malia's dress was simple and sleek, form-fitting with a no-nonsense train attached to the back. What made it stand out was the intricate embroidery on the bodice. I pictured her dress in my mind, concentrating on its beautiful simplicity. The veil had several layers and it would overpower the dress. "You need something softer, simpler."

"I'm trying not to panic. I said I wouldn't be that kind of bride." Malia took hold of my hand and squeezed. "I don't need to panic, right?"

I chuckled. "You don't need to panic. We'll figure something out. Let me take the veil. I can webcam Lorea. Maybe we can even remodel this one. The main problem is it's too big in contrast to your dress."

"Thank you!" Malia hugged me. "I knew you'd be able to help."

"Don't thank me yet, but don't panic either. We've got three days."

"Remember I'm getting some bridal pictures done on Thursday."

I forced myself to smile instead of grimace. "Oh, that's right. A little more pressure, but Lorea is a genius. Let's see what we can come up with."

"I'm going to stop by a couple shops here, but I'm not super hopeful," Malia said. "I don't want it to be cheesy, but I'd like something that's indicative of the island."

"That might be more difficult." I had sudden visions of hibiscus flowers smeared across the bright red and yellow shirts and colorful mumus I'd seen all over the island. "I'll call you if I think of anything."

Malia waved as she hurried out the front of the hotel. I looked at the veil in my hand, wondering what I'd just gotten myself into.

Within twenty minutes, I had connected with Lorea via the Internet and filled her in on the dilemma. I held up the veil in front of my computer and let her study every angle, while I mentioned what Malia had requested.

Lorea smoothed her short black hair and one of her eyebrows slanted upwards as she studied the layers of material. She cleared her throat and leaned forward. "You need plumeria, not the yellow one. The reddish-purple one."

"Plumeria? How is that going to fix the veil?"

"Didn't you say Jon gave you a lei?"

"Yes, but—"

"Remove one of the flowers," Lorea interrupted. "We're going to do a mock-up for Malia."

"Okay." I hesitated for half a second, wondering what Lorea had planned. The lei was in the fridge, so I carefully removed it and pulled it from the plastic bag. Muttering under my breath, I detached one of the fragrant blossoms from the string and held it up to the computer for Lorea to see.

"Perfect. Now I want you to show me the layers of the veil and I'm going to tell you where to snip the threads. Ready?"

My sewing kit was ready. No certified wedding planner should be without an emergency sewing kit. Under Lorea's supervision, I was able to pick out the threads joining three of the five layers of the veil. The material flowed noiselessly onto the bed as I rearranged the remaining two layers, a soft white blend of silk and rayon.

"Now clip the flower onto the left side of the veil, right next to the material." Lorea motioned from the computer screen, and I wished for the hundredth time that she was on site. My fingers fumbled with the delicate plumeria, and I held it carefully while I pushed a straight pin through the fragrant blossom.

I held the veil up and examined my handiwork. Under Lorea's tutelage, the veil looked completely different. "Lorea, you are amazing."

Lorea's dark eyes sparkled. "Aren't you glad I'm not a kokolo?" She laughed as she referred to the word "dummy" in her native Basque tongue.

I laughed. "You're brilliant, definitely not a kokolo, but you already know that." I grabbed my cell phone and took a picture of the veil to send to Malia. "I think this just might work."

Lorea's face moved in and out of focus on my computer screen. "Tell her that she could do a cluster of three plumeria instead of the one."

"That would be gorgeous." I snapped a few more pictures and sent them to Malia. After taking off the extra layers of fabric, the veil was lightweight and simple. The flowers were the special island touch she needed without overpowering the simplicity of the sheer white material. "I'm sorry she didn't go with you in the first place."

Lorea shrugged. "I think maybe she needed to figure out what she wanted. Speaking of, you have some reporting to do."

"What?" I infused my voice with innocence.

"You've mentioned Jon a few times, and I know Luke is there, so what's the deal?"

I slumped into the chair and rested my cheek in my hand with a sigh. "It's complicated."

"Girl, you have a knack for making things complicated."

She was teasing, but I still straightened and gave her the evil eye. "Says my very single friend."

Lorea rolled her eyes. "Remember, I went on a date."

"Wait—you still haven't told me? Who was it?"

"Uh, uh, uh." Lorea shook her finger at me. "I'm not giving you one single detail until you tell me what is up in Kauai." She lowered her lashes and added, "And maybe not even then."

The events at Pu'u o Kila still burned in my chest. "I got into an argument with Luke."

Now it was Lorea's turn to sigh. "You two need to kiss and get it over with."

"Whatever. Luke buried his heart with his wife."

"Ouch. Okay, so it sounds like more than just an argument." She fiddled with the Basque cross or *Lauburu* she wore around her neck. Lorea always did that when she was worrying over something.

"I just can't get through his baggage, and I'm not sure I want to." My heart hitched as I spoke the words that had been swirling around my mind. If only I knew what I wanted. Luke was complicated. Jon was simple, or at least he appeared to be.

"What about Jon then?"

"I have trust issues."

"I won't argue with that." Lorea's voice was soft. "You don't have to rush anything, but will you please have fun for me? I'm working my head off here."

"I'm sorry. I shouldn't complain. This island is paradise. Jon is fun and he knows about my past, so he's treading carefully, while making sure I know that he wants to kiss me."

"So kiss a little. You're in Hawaii. Find a beach and a sunset and let him kiss you if Luke won't."

"You're hilarious." I laughed and leaned back in my chair.

"Yes, and I have an appointment, so I've gotta run." She glanced to her left. "I'll expect a full report though. Get busy."

"I will." I signed off thinking that once again, Lorea had escaped the truth. I still didn't know who her mystery date was. My phone pinged with a text from Malia. She was thrilled and would stop by soon to see the veil in person. Lorea would be happy. I thought of that word, happy. It was time for me to take charge of my happiness. My heart was lonely. I thought of Luke again and felt a pang of regret as he drifted into the background of Jon's attentions. I wasn't anywhere near love, but even "like" was more complicated than I was equipped to deal with. At the same time, I had a yearning to share that sunset kiss Lorea had commanded me to enjoy.

When I thought about kissing Jon, a gold bracelet came to mind that curbed my daydream. I'd been so busy, there hadn't been time to find any information. The bracelet was tucked in an interior pocket of my suitcase, and although it beckoned to me like some kind of magic ring, I couldn't bring myself to look at it again. The mystery opened up too many possibilities. I'd tried my best all day to ignore those possibilities, but one question kept resurfacing. Why did Jon have a bracelet in his swim trunks?

I shook my head and leaned back on the pillows, closing my eyes. There would be no sleep until I allowed myself to sort through my questions. With calming breaths, I let my mind go to that dark and scary underwater experience from just days earlier. In an instant the woman's green eyes floated in my mind. I shuddered but kept myself in the memory, mentally examining her body. Her hand floated in the water, the fingers slender and graceful. There had been a bracelet, and I thought it was gold, but maybe it wasn't the same kind I'd found in Jon's pocket. Maybe my brain had just connected the first thing that triggered that part of my memory.

I sat up and rubbed my eyes. There must be a simple explanation, and I wouldn't jump to conclusions. Finding the bracelet had helped me to remember that I'd seen one on the woman's arm, but it didn't necessarily mean it was the same exact one. Officer Kinau had asked me to call him if I remembered anything at all from that day but when I thought about reporting my memory of the bracelet, it seemed weak and suspicious. Until I talked to Jon and asked him my questions, it didn't seem right to say anything to the police.

The Connelly family all seemed approachable, especially Heather, but there was no way I could share my suspicions. It probably wasn't a good idea to share the memory of the woman wearing a gold bracelet that was triggered because I found an identical one in her son's swim shorts. I groaned. It would be nice to talk to someone, but not until I understood what the bracelet had to do with Jon.

It was time for a distraction. I pulled out my laptop and propped myself up on a pile of pillows on my bed. The door to my balcony was slightly ajar and the curtain swayed with the ocean breeze. It was a beautiful setting, and I wanted to concentrate on something less stressful for a few moments. The progressive photo display was almost complete. All I needed to do was go through the last batch of photos that Malia had emailed me.

I unzipped the file and waited for the pictures to load. There was probably about fifty more pictures in this batch to sort through. I selected a few that I thought might finish off the holes in my collage and attached those in an email to Lorea. I'd asked Malia for a few photos that showed Kyle working at Tri-C and she'd obliged with about a dozen new pictures.

There was a silver-haired man and a woman with auburn hair that kept showing up in some of the recent photos. They appeared to be related to Tri-C so I filed those with a note to find out if the people were important to Kyle. I didn't want to add a photo to their wedding present if it included someone that Kyle didn't really care for.

After I sorted through the last few photos, I leaned back against the headboard and closed my eyes. Images of Kyle, Jon, Neil, and Heather remained in the forefront of my mind. With a sigh, I closed my laptop and plugged it in to charge up the battery. My mind still churned with questions, but I told myself that I would see Jon tomorrow and take the first opportunity I found to ask him about the bracelet. Until then I commanded my inquisitive side to be quiet so I could get some much needed rest.

Chapter 15

COCONUT WATER SMOOTHIE

Puree two handfuls of spinach with one cup filtered water and one cup coconut water. Add one cup blueberries, handful of almonds, ½ frozen banana, and blend until smooth. Serve garnished with fresh mint leaves. Kids love this purple smoothie!

Courtesy of www.mashedpotatoesandcrafts.com

On Wednesday we left early for another outing with the wedding party. I'd stashed the bracelet, and my argument with Luke, back at the hotel. Putting on my best smile, I was fully prepared to enjoy myself. It would be a little tricky because today both Jon and Luke would be there. I wasn't sure how to act because Jon was nice and even if Luke drove me crazy, I still cared about him. Treating them both like good friends was probably the best scenario for now.

Jon was charming, and greeted me with a kiss on my cheek. I noticed that Luke tried to hang back, but one of the Connelly cousins sidled up next to him. By the way she laughed and flipped her dark hair, I guessed she would do her best job to flirt. Good luck.

Ignoring Luke, I climbed in a different vehicle with Jon, Malia, and Kyle. We chatted and laughed as we rode together toward Secret Beach. After parking off the road, we grabbed our gear and headed for the sand. It was a short walk to Secret Beach, named thus because it was only accessible by walking down a path of sparse trees about a quarter mile from the road. I stifled a laugh at the perfect Hawaiian surfer stereotype in front of me. A guy with shaggy blond hair rode a rickety bicycle with his bare feet while holding a green surfboard under his arm. He stopped on the trail ahead of us and stashed his bicycle in the grassy undergrowth. He continued barefoot toward the beach.

"Does Secret Beach have good surfing?"

Jon followed my gaze. "Better in the summer, but that guy looks like he knows what he's doing."

As we approached the beach the vegetation tapered off, and I saw a few spindly-legged roosters strutting around the underbrush.

"There are so many chickens running wild here."

Jon chuckled. "It reminds me of my favorite joke."

"What's that?"

He cocked his left eyebrow. "Why did the chicken cross the road?"

I started laughing.

"Wait, I haven't even given the punch line yet."

"Okay, why?"

Jon paused and then grinned. "Because he lived in Kauai."

"Now that is definitely a knee-slapper." I shook my head and gave him a courtesy laugh.

"Hey, I came up with that on my own."

I patted his arm. "You're a comedian, Jon."

"Don't get him started," Kyle interrupted. "He'll be telling knock-knock jokes next."

Malia giggled as Jon protested. "Hey, you laughed the first time I told you."

She patted his other arm. "Don't worry Jon, I think you're cute." She turned to Kyle. "Just like your brother."

Kyle put his arm around her and kissed her cheek. They walked ahead of us, murmuring to each other.

"Ah, young love," Jon whispered. He carefully wrapped his arm around me. "Can I whisper sweet nothings in your ear?" Then he whispered, "Sweet nothings." His breath sent a tingle down my spine and I shivered. Jon laughed. "You're ticklish, aren't you?"

Skipping ahead on the trail, I shook my head. "Not at all."

Jon dashed to catch up to me and tickled my side. I tried not to but a giggle escaped, and we both broke out onto the beach laughing.

Malia's family was already heading across the beach to the left toward the lava rocks. Her parents wanted to see the lava pools, so Neil and Heather planned this outing for the wedding guests. Luke walked ahead with Jon's cousin. I remembered her name now—Rianna. The twinge in my heart made me uncomfortable. I recognized the jealousy creeping up from seeing her flirt with him. At the same time, I noted Luke's disinterest and how he seemed disconnected from the group as a whole. He hadn't wanted to come, but Malia had cajoled him, and now I wondered if part of that insistence had come from Rianna.

"I hope Malia's parents aren't too disappointed by the lava pools. I think snorkeling is much more impressive." Jon patted the mesh snorkeling bag he had slung over his back.

"Yeah, but you're almost a native so you've already forgotten how to appreciate the everyday beauty."

I was teasing, but his expression took on a serious note as he turned to me. "You're right, maybe I have been here too long."

I understood the meaning behind his words, and more so when he took my hand and intertwined his fingers with mine. We picked our way through the rocks, and he helped me climb up onto a flat expanse of lava rock. Wind whipped my hair around my neck and in my eyes. I pushed it out and caught sight of Luke in conversation with Rianna, their heads close together. Frustrated with myself for caring, I turned to Jon. "Thanks for showing me so much of the island. This is probably the most amazing week of *work* I've ever had."

"It's been my pleasure. What else would you like to see while you're here?"

"I'd like to see more of the north shore," I said. "Swimming with a sea turtle is on my bucket list, but I don't know if I'll be able to make that happen after what happened at Tunnels."

Jon cringed and shook his shoulders. "Not many turtles at Tunnels anyway. Ke'e Beach is really gentle and there are lots of sea turtles. Maybe I could take you?"

"I'll think about it."

Jon held my hand as we moved up into view of the Secret Lava Pools. The lava rocks jutting out from the beach formed small tide pools. By the looks of the ocean wave coming toward us, this one was refilling. A few people stepped into the water that went to their knees. The bottom looked soggy to me. Releasing Jon's hand, I bent down and reached my fingers into the water. It seemed warmer and the bottom of the pool was soft, almost moss-like.

"With the tide coming in, we won't be snorkeling here today," Neil announced. "But we wanted you to be able to see how they work. Heather and I can direct you to some better snorkeling and swimming places off the beach from where the trail head comes out." He pointed in the direction from which we'd come.

I followed the group to the edge of the lava rocks. There were several cries of delight as a wave crashed against the edge of the rocks and water started flowing into the pool.

Turning to my right, I caught sight of a lighthouse. Jon came closer and talked in my ear above the noise of the ocean.

"That's the Kilauea Lighthouse." He pointed. "It's pretty old and not very big, but the view is pretty cool from up there, plus it's kind of a bird sanctuary."

"The history of lighthouses always intrigues me." I stared in that direction until the group started moving again. I had to watch my steps along the jagged rocks since my sandals didn't protect my feet, and I'd already seen a couple people stumble against each other on the uneven surfaces. I heard a wave coming in and turned my head to admire the white surf rolling toward me. Wishing I had my phone or my camera on me, I took a mental picture of the rugged beauty as the water collided with the rocks and rolled over my feet.

I felt a hand on my back and turned at the same time I was shoved headlong into the ocean. The water enveloped me before I could scream, and the force of the sea boiled around me. Was I going to be smashed into the sharp ring of lava rocks that made up the lava pools?

My head broke through the surface just as another wave tumbled toward me. I screamed and ducked down, swimming away from the rocks. With arms flailing, I pushed against the water. Pain resonated in my head, but the need to breathe was more important. I had only made it a couple strokes when a strong hand on my arm jerked me in the opposite direction. At first I resisted, and I started to open my eyes before I remembered how badly salt water stung. Another jerk on my arm reassured me that this person could probably help me. I quit fighting and swam in the direction that I was being pulled. When my face came above water, I sucked in a breath of air. My knee knocked against a rock, and I stood wiping the water out of my eyes.

"Adri, follow me." Jon took my hand and pulled me toward the shoreline. "Step over this rock, here." He was panting, and I was trying not to cry. My head seemed to be clogged with ocean water, a dull roar left me feeling disoriented, and my eyes were stinging from the salt water dripping from my hair. A few more steps and we were on the sand. Jon pulled me into his arms. "It's okay. I got you."

I struggled to hold in my tears. The worried pitch of several voices indicated the rest of our group was approaching. I squeezed Jon tighter and he winced. Startled, I pulled back. "Are you okay?" I asked, blinking away my tears and letting out a shuddering breath.

"I'm good. Are you hurt?" He held me at arm's length and checked me over.

"My leg stings." I looked at my right calf and grimaced at the angry red scratches extending down to my ankle. Blood oozed from my ankle bone. For some reason, looking at it made it hurt even worse.

"Let's sit down," Jon said. He lowered me to the sand and turned to sit beside me. I gasped when I saw the jagged tear in his rash guard on his right shoulder. I reached out carefully pulling back the fabric to reveal a six inch gash.

"Jon, you're hurt!"

He sucked in a breath. "So are you. It's never a good idea to go swimming in the lava rocks."

My ears popped at the same time the rest of our group caught up to us. So many voices and questions reverberated with the pounding in my skull. I closed my eyes until one voice separated from the rest. "Adri, open your eyes so I can look at your pupils."

It was Luke. When I opened my eyes, his face was inches from mine. My lip trembled, and I leaned forward wrapping my arms around him. He knelt in the sand in front of me and leaned over, holding me close. "Someone pushed me."

Luke moved back, still holding onto my arms. "What?"

"I didn't fall. Someone pushed me," I repeated.

"But how?" Luke studied me and then glanced at Jon sitting next to us.

Jon's expression was intent. He was probably trying to figure out what was going on between me and Luke. He shook his head. "She went in fast. I thought someone must have bumped her off balance."

Before I could explain, everyone was talking at once. Heather was commanding Kyle and Luke to help clean our wounds and bandage us up. She handed out supplies from the first aid kit Neil kept in his swim bag. Jon's injuries were worse than mine. He had cuts on his shoulder, back, legs, and arms. I had a few abrasions in the same places, with my right leg being the worst.

Neil offered me something to drink and shooed everyone else down the beach so that we could have a moment to regroup. Luke insisted on staying. He sat in the sand beside me with a worried expression on his face. "Tell me what happened."

I licked my lips, tasting salt on my tongue. "I was standing on the edge with everyone else when someone pushed me in."

Heather rubbed some salve on my arm. "You poor thing. I don't think you were pushed, but there were too many of us on that ledge. I'm sure someone just bumped you by accident." She treated my wounds carefully, and although I wanted to relax, I remembered clearly the hand on my back.

"No, someone put their hand on my back and pushed me." I turned to look at Jon and then back at Luke. "I have good balance. It wasn't just a bump."

"Why would someone push you?" Neil asked. "We're all family here."

Jon chuckled. "Not all of us, Dad. But I have to agree, why would someone push you?" He looked at me.

I paused to reconsider. Maybe it had felt like a hand but it was a bag or elbow or something else. No. I shook my head, reliving the second before I plunged into the ocean. I had definitely felt the pressure of a hand on my back.

"It's a darn good thing Jon moved so quickly," Neil said. "That is a dangerous place to go in the water when the tide's coming in."

Jon smiled at me. "Adri did great. She was already swimming when I found her, although in the wrong direction."

I nodded, remembering the sensation of being pulled upward by Jon. "Thank you for rescuing me." I reached out my hand to squeeze his. "I'm sorry you got hurt."

"No problem. I heard war wounds soften a girl's heart." He winked and I gave a shaky laugh.

"If Adri says someone pushed her into the ocean, then that's what happened," Luke interrupted. "I've known her long enough to know that she doesn't exaggerate."

Neil appraised Luke. "She's definitely a level-headed gal, but we also had about fifteen people wandering around. It seems more likely that it was an accident."

"Then why didn't anyone say they were sorry for bumping into her?" Luke demanded.

"Probably because everybody bumped into someone while we were looking at the pools," Jon said. "You seem to be making an issue out of this, when there isn't one."

"Or maybe you pushed her in so you could be the hero," Luke spat.

"Hey," Jon started, but Heather held up her hand to cut him off.

"I'm not sure accusing people is going to solve what's already happened." Heather stood and brushed the sand off her knees. "What's most important is that Adri and Jon are safe. Jon, why don't you drive Adri back to the hotel so she can clean up and rest before dinner?"

"That sounds like a good idea." Jon stood and offered me his hand at the same time Luke grabbed my elbow and helped me up from the sand.

"Are you sure you're okay?" Luke asked. He studied my face, and my heart warmed with the genuine concern I saw there.

I leaned forward and brushed his fingers with mine. "I'm sore, but I think I'll be fine."

"Do you mind if I ride back to the hotel with you guys?" Luke asked, lifting his head toward Jon.

Jon hesitated for half a second before responding. "Sure."

Luke was definitely the third wheel in the back seat of Jon's convertible on the way back, but he didn't seem to mind. Jon gripped the steering wheel tighter every time Luke leaned forward to join in the conversation. We all talked about the island, the upcoming wedding, and carefully avoided talk of angry ocean waves at the Secret Lava Pools.

By the time we reached the hotel, it seemed like the impression of someone's hand had been burned into my back. Someone *had* pushed me. The question was, why?

Chapter 16

IRONING TIPS FOR SATIN

Turn item inside out and iron with low heat or steam-shot setting on iron. If the satin is made from polyester, it is quite forgiving. Beware of antique satin as it water-stains easily. Use paper to cover small sections of satin and iron through paper on low heat.

Courtesy of www.mashedpotatoesandcrafts.com

Jon helped me limp into the hotel with Luke trailing behind us. "I'll be right back," Luke said.

"It's okay. I've got her." Jon tried to act tough, but he was in pain. Luke jogged through the lobby with purpose. I wondered where he was headed so quickly.

"Jon, you need to rest as much as I do." I stepped away from him. "I can make it from here."

"Will you come to dinner with me and the family later? Please?"

"How much later? I need a nap."

"I think they are meeting at seven." He moved his hand toward me, but winced.

"Your shoulder. You need to get some ointment on that."

Jon nodded. "Man, I hate to say it, but you're right. Are you sure you'll be okay?"

"Yes. Go take care of yourself. I'll see you later."

He leaned in and kissed my cheek. After he left, I hobbled to my room and found myself thinking about Luke's accusation. My thoughts spun as I replayed the frightening push into the ocean. I hated the feeling of insecurity and doubt welling up inside as I thought about Jon and the rest of the wedding party there. No, it couldn't be Jon. It just wasn't possible—or at least I didn't want to believe it was. Separating old fears from the present helped me to look at the situation clearly. I didn't know Jon well enough to completely exonerate him, but the thought kept trailing through my head that Jon didn't push me into the ocean, but *someone* did.

I used a cool washcloth to blot at my scrapes and sucked in a breath as the angry red scratches burned with pain. A knock on the door elicited a groan. I really needed a nap and probably some ice. I opened the door to find Luke standing there with a Ziploc bag of ice. He held it out. "Thought you could use this."

"How did you know?"

He shrugged and stepped inside. "Adri, I'm worried about you. Didn't you hit your head?"

As soon as he asked, my head started throbbing again. I touched the right side of my skull gingerly and sucked in a breath. "I think I have a goose egg. I hit my head on a rock when I went under."

"Can I take a look?"

I sat on the edge of the bed and allowed Luke to part my hair, gritting my teeth at a new flash of pain.

"There's some blood here. Hand me that washcloth."

Luke blotted at my head and even though he was trying to be gentle, the sensation made me feel nauseated. "I think I need to lie down."

"You have a bump and a small cut. I brought some antibiotic ointment. Is it okay if I rub some on your head?"

"Sure." I closed my eyes. "Where did you learn to be such a great nurse?" As soon as the words left my mouth I realized my mistake. My eyes flew open and I grabbed Luke's hand. "I'm sorry. I wasn't thinking."

But Luke didn't look angry or hurt. "It's okay." He moved back to attending to my scalp. I let go of his hand, cursing my own stupidity. Of course he was a great nurse—he'd cared for his dying wife. How long had she suffered?

"I took some courses that the hospital offered and did some private study." He dabbed my head and answered the question I hadn't voiced. "Dana was sick off and on for about three years."

My bottom lip trembled, and I formed my words in my mind before speaking. "I can tell that you're experienced. That was probably a great comfort to Dana."

"I'll let you rest now. Your pupils are dilating normally. As long as you're not feeling disoriented or confused, it's safe for you to sleep. If you can stand it, hold this ice on your head for a while." Luke handed me the bag of ice, and then pulled the comforter over me. "Can I check on you later?"

"I'd like that," I whispered. "Thank you."

I closed my eyes, feeling drained of any energy or will to stay awake. The door clicked shut somewhere, and I allowed myself to fall asleep with the faint impression of Luke's hands on my head.

I slept until two o'clock and woke up ravenous. Room service remedied that with a chilled pasta salad and breadsticks. I ate slowly, trying to ignore the throbbing in my head. When I was finished, I decided to clean myself up. It took a lot of nerve to step into the water and bathe my scratches, but after the initial stinging sensation, the warm water was therapeutic.

When I rinsed my hair, I was startled for a moment as the water draining in the shower turned pink. My head must have bled more than I thought. I lowered the shower setting again to something that didn't feel like needles on my scalp. I carefully towel-dried my hair and applied more salve to my cuts and scrapes. The ice Luke brought had melted so instead I used a chilled washcloth on my head. I heard a text message come through a few minutes later.

Luke: How are you feeling? Do you need anything?

Me: I had a nap and a shower, doing better. Thanks for your help.

Luke: Good. Please let me know if I can help.

Me: I will.

It was sweet of Luke to worry over me, and it was nice to see that softer side of him, but part of me worried that he would retreat back into his angry shell the next time we interacted. To keep my mind off Luke, I made some phone calls for Malia's wedding events.

I toggled through the news channels to see if there was any news of a missing person, but that was fruitless. Officer Kinau had said he'd let me know as soon as they could release the identity of the woman. Thinking about her reminded me of the bracelet I'd found at Jon's house. I slid off the bed and knelt beside my suitcase, retrieving the mysterious metal band and studying it.

It was gold toned with beads next to the opening that allowed it to easily bend onto the wrist. Similar to a golfing bracelet I'd seen, this one had a mother of pearl inset in the center with the Tri-C logo printed in gold and black. There wasn't anything remarkable about it, and even though it reminded me of what I'd seen underwater, I had to ask myself if it was really the same bracelet. I frowned and tucked it back into the zippered compartment of my suitcase.

There were so many questions and my suspicions were mounting toward Jon. One part of me argued that there was no way he could be involved, but the experienced side of me urged caution. When I considered my interactions with Jon, I didn't feel in any danger, but it would be wise to take some precautions just in case. He was coming to pick me up soon, and I'd be riding in a car alone with him. As soon as the thought crossed my mind, I laughed out loud. It would be pretty hard to ignore a missing wedding planner during all the upcoming celebrations.

Although I was almost certain that Jon didn't have sinister motives, it was best to play on the safe side. I sent Malia a text, letting her know that I'd be riding with Jon and pushed my suspicions aside.

Jon picked me up at six-thirty and I felt better, although a few of my bruises were a bit swollen. "How's your shoulder?"

"It's tender, but I'll be okay." He held his arm stiffly to one side. "Is your head okay?"

"Should be fine if I don't bump it on anything else."

When we arrived at the restaurant, we were greeted by the rest of the Connelly family, who expressed concern about my injuries.

"Are you sure you're feeling okay?" Neil asked. "I don't want you getting hurt worse because we're pushing you too hard."

"I'll be okay," I said. "I'm planning on getting some extra sleep tonight."

Neil shook his head and rubbed a hand over his mustache. "That's twice now that the ocean hasn't been agreeable to you. I hope it won't taint your opinion of her."

"I'll give her another chance, I think. There's too much beauty underneath to miss."

"That's true," Heather said. "Hawaii is the land of beautiful secrets well-kept."

"Well said, Jaycee dear." Neil put his arm around Heather and kissed her cheek. I looked behind me, curious as to who he was talking to, but he and his wife were already moving forward.

Jon rolled his eyes. "When they're getting along, it reminds me of when we were kids and we thought it was gross that our parents kissed."

I laughed, remembering my own parents smooching in the kitchen. I was about to ask Jon who Jaycee was, but then I figured Neil must've been referring to Heather with some sort of pet name. We followed Neil and Heather to our table. They fit into the Hawaiian aura. She had on a lemon-yellow sundress and Neil wore a tan polo shirt with dark blue hibiscus flowers printed on it—the epitome of Hawaiian fashion. He motioned to me with one hand when he reached the dining area. "Come here, Adri." Neil hefted a large box. "I have a surprise for you."

I raised my eyebrows. "Okay?"

He set the box down and opened the flaps. "These were delivered today."

My mouth fell open when I saw that the box was full of gold-toned bracelets. Neil grabbed a handful and lifted them out with a flourish. "My assistant must have ordered these before she skipped town."

I scrambled for something to say, but the words died on my lips as Neil handed me one of the bracelets.

"There's enough that every guest will get one, and we probably have a few extras. Try it on, let's see how it looks."

The bracelet slipped easily onto my wrist, but it felt as if my skin burned. I knew in that moment that, earlier, I had only been second-guessing myself. It was identical to the one I had seen on the dead woman's arm. The same one I had taken from Jon's shorts pocket and stuffed in a secret compartment of my suitcase. The logo winked at me amidst the rainbow swirls of mother of pearl encased by the gold. It was the same bracelet. The doubts I'd indulged in shattered. If these were delivered today, how did Jon have one in his pocket?

It didn't make any sense. How could that woman have a company bracelet if she wasn't part of the company? The back of my throat ached and the tips of my fingers turned cold. Neil still waited for me to speak.

I plastered on a smile. "This is perfect timing. Does that mean you have access to the logos for the other things we needed?"

"That's the other good news. My tech guy was finally able to break through Charly's password and retrieve the completed files."

I still thought it was strange that the assistant had the only copies of the files and said so. "It's odd that they weren't on your server."

Neil flinched. "You're right. We're finding a lot of things that were odd about Charly's files." He looked like he was going to say more, but pursed his lips together.

"Well, I'm just glad these came through in time." I removed the bracelet, dropping it back into the box, and tucked the flaps of the box closed. "This saved me a huge headache."

Neil's smile returned. "Glad to be of some help."

Heather walked up beside him. "Remember, we wanted to arrange the bracelets on the satin tablecloths. I hope the humidity won't make the satin wrinkle."

"I know a few tricks. I'll check with those setting up to be sure everything looks perfect."

"Malia was right. You really do have an answer for everything." Heather patted my hand as she walked after her husband.

I nodded and tucked the flaps of the box tighter so I couldn't see the golden gleam inside. I kept wishing that I had remembered wrong. There had been a bracelet on the woman's arm, like the one I had slipped onto my wrist a moment ago. I avoided eye contact while I sorted through my thoughts. There was only one way to find out for certain. I worried that asking the police might cast suspicion on me, especially if the woman was sporting the bracelet when they found her. But if my worries were correct, the police wouldn't have any information about a bracelet because someone removed it before they recovered the body.

Jon.

It was one explanation that made sense even if I didn't like it. He must have taken the bracelet from the body, but I still couldn't believe he had anything to do with her death. With a shake of my head, I made myself go down that mental pathway—the one where Jon could be a murderer. It was stupid to trust anyone, and just because Jon was kind and good-looking didn't mean anything. But what reason would he have to kill a young woman?

I needed to find out her identity. If the police would release her name, I could at least do some Googling to find out if Jon knew her. I stared at the box and thought about the trouble caused by Neil's missing assistant. What if she was the woman who had died? I shook my head. That couldn't be right. Neil would recognize his own assistant, even if she was wearing scuba gear. It bothered me, not knowing who the woman was, not knowing if the police had found the murderer. It was time to call Officer Kinau again.

Dinner was nice, but I begged Jon to take me back early, citing my headache and other injuries. Jon actually agreed that he needed more rest, and so it wasn't odd that we didn't speak much on the way back. He was tired. So was I, but I was also extremely preoccupied with reassuring myself that he wasn't a murderer.

As soon as I was settled in my room, I checked the card Officer Kinau had given me and dialed his number. When he answered, I got straight to business.

"I'm sorry to call so late, but I think I might have more information about the woman who died, but I can't be sure without knowing her identity. Is there any way that you can tell me if I promise to be discreet?"

There were three clicks of silence. "What kind of information?"

"Well, I don't want to send up flags if it's nothing. I hope you understand where I'm coming from."

"All right. I'll tell you, but only because we found someone who could be her next of kin and the media already leaked her name."

The TV in my hotel room seemed to be blinking at me—I hadn't checked the news before calling him. I held my breath, waiting for him to reveal the secret I'd been mulling over.

"Her name is Stacia Fletcher and it looks like she worked for a GMO out of Kansas."

"Okay." I hesitated. I had half-expected him to say her name was Charly. When he didn't, I wasn't sure what to say. "I'll do some checking, and then I'll call you back."

"Miss Pyper, even if you think the information is irrelevant, I'm still interested to hear what's bothering you."

I hesitated, glancing at my suitcase and then back at my clenched fist. Relaxing my fingers, I tried to calm the tremor in my voice. "Well, there is one thing. I thought I remembered something but it's hard to trust my memory when I was so freaked out. Was there any jewelry found on the woman?"

Officer Kinau cleared his throat. "No. I can double-check, but I'm pretty sure there was no jewelry. What kind of jewelry do you remember?"

"I keep thinking about a gold bracelet, but I don't know why."

"I'll check the records of her effects and let you know. I appreciate you confiding in me, Ms. Pyper. I know this is a difficult situation."

My chest tightened. I hadn't confided all of my suspicions to him, but now everything sounded like a coincidence so it seemed better to wait. "It has been scary. I just feel so bad about her."

"If you think of anything else, be sure to give me a call."

"Thank you, Officer. I'll do that."

He paused, and I wondered if he wanted to ask me something else, but then he ended the call. I set the phone down and put a hand over my heart to calm the rush of adrenaline speeding up the nervous beat. The news that the woman—Stacia Fletcher—worked for a GMO had red flags rising all over in the detective zone of my brain. It also made my suspicions of Jon seem weak and unfounded. Maybe the bracelet was from a previous order. But that still didn't explain why it would be in his swim shorts.

I turned the TV on and flipped through the channels looking for news, but I didn't see anything. After a few minutes, I turned it off and opened my laptop. I checked the

Internet news sites and found a mention of the murder at Tunnels and the body being identified as Stacia Fletcher. There were no pictures, and I had a desire to see what the woman looked like when she was alive and healthy before her life was tragically cut short.

With a few clicks of my mouse, I began searching the Internet for Stacia Fletcher linked to GMOs. Ten minutes later I found something that made my fingers tremble. It was a smaller company named Fontana Inc. and Stacia's name was highlighted on their site. I paused, thinking about the loss of a precious life. Sometimes the world felt like a very sad place. Maybe seeing her picture would give me some closure, I reasoned. Continuing the search, I linked Stacia's name with Fontana Inc. to delve deeper.

I continued to research Fontana and found that they had sites all over the United States, including a beautiful little island called Kauai. After several minutes of Googling and clicking on dead-end links, I pulled up a newspaper article. It cited the philanthropist efforts of Fontana Inc. in bringing together scientists in a united effort. There were a couple photographs with the article.

They were low-quality pictures of people in lab coats and business suits. One included a woman with red hair. I clicked on it to bring up any accompanying information and found the name of Stacia Fletcher in an article. The report didn't list the names of the people in the photo, so I couldn't be sure, but my throat went dry when I thought of the woman underwater with red hair. I studied the woman who I thought might be Stacia carefully. How did the striking woman with green eyes end up dead?

A throbbing ache started up behind my eyes. I closed my laptop and got ready for bed. I spent a few minutes on my balcony, taking in deep, cleansing breaths from the ocean and commanding my heart and mind to be still. I needed to sleep, not worry over a murder case. My body still ached, and my head was tired from the impact of lava rocks and the pull between Jon and Luke's affections.

Everything would appear clearer in the morning. I forced myself to shelve the spinning questions about the bracelet I'd found and its possible connection to Jon. Once in bed, exhaustion won out, and I was able to drift off to sleep.

I slept until just past seven and ordered in breakfast while I prepared for the day. It didn't take long for my mind to start whirring with questions and ideas. With a groan, I put away my notebook of questions and scrawling theories on the murder. As soon as I finished breakfast, I decided to distract my inquisitive brain by concentrating on the wedding gift I needed to finish for Malia and Kyle.

Lorea had resized some photos and fixed a few holes in the collage. I just needed to add a few more pictures. I opened the folder of pictures labeled with a question mark and another labeled "Extra collage pics" and began scanning to find just the right one to finish off the display. There weren't very many of Neil and Kyle, so I looked at some of the Tri-C photos to find one suitable. I clicked past some of father and son bent over plants in the test plots and moved to the photos of a group in front of the Tri-C buildings. I jerked back in my chair when the next photo popped up. It was one of the photos I'd originally left out because I didn't know everyone in the picture. One of the subjects was a young woman with red hair.

My heart rate doubled. I enlarged the picture and studied the woman. Part of her face was in shadow, but her eyes appeared to be light, possibly green. A sense of dread seeped from the picture. Had I just stumbled upon something related to the murder?

I scrolled through the history of my search from last night until I found the article with a picture of Stacia Fletcher. My hands shook and the back of my neck moistened with perspiration fueled by the adrenaline pumping through my veins. I rubbed my eyes and leaned closer to the screen of my laptop. Then I clicked back to the other window with the grainy picture of some Fontana related employees. Stacia Fletcher was featured in the picture.

I copied and pasted the two pictures to view them side-by-side. The hunch I'd developed had turned into something solid. The red-haired beauty standing next to Kyle and Neil had a striking similarity to the deceased Stacia Fletcher.

Could the dead woman be Charly Wilks, new assistant at Tri-C Enterprises? And at the same time, Stacia Fletcher, highly sought after biological engineer from Fontana Inc.? There were no other identifying pictures of Stacia on the Internet. The only proof I had was a photo with no caption and pixelated faces. But it had to be the same woman. There was no mistaking those green eyes and her cute pixie nose.

Jon had mentioned that Charly had been a new hire and that Neil thought it was a mistake—that he'd given her too much work too soon and that was why she had quit.

The information burned in the back of my throat. I needed to do something, but what? I checked the time; it was already past ten. I thought about calling Luke, but he would immediately jump to conclusions about Jon's guilt. It just didn't seem right to me. Jon was so gentle and kind. There had to be a rational explanation for all the strange coincidences that were tying neatly together into an arrow pointing at Jonathan Connelly.

About the time I started to think about the last man I thought was gentle and kind, I slammed my laptop shut.

Gripping Officer Kinau's card, I dialed his number and paced the floor in front of the loveseat. It took a couple tries, but when I finally reached him, I thought my heart would beat right out of my chest.

"This is Officer Kinau," he answered.

"Officer, this is Adrielle Pyper, I'm really worried. I just found a picture of the woman who died in some photos from the Connelly's. I'm almost positive it's Stacia. I found some pictures of her on the Internet, but I don't know how recent they are."

"Hang on. Take a breath." His voice was mellow, but I detected a note of concern.

"Okay, sorry," I said. "I just don't understand what's going on."

"Can you send me over the picture right now?"

"Yes." I sat down and opened my laptop again.

"I'll stay on the line while you do that." He spelled out his email address, and I repeated it back to him as I typed.

I had to look at every key because my hands were shaking so badly. A minute later, he cleared his throat. "That's her. What is she doing with the Connellys?"

"I think her name is Charly Wilks and that she was a secretary at Tri-C."

"Why did you think this was the same woman?" he asked

I hesitated, knowing that my next words would implicate the Connellys. "Because she's been missing since I arrived on the island."

Chapter 17

CHOCOLATE MACADAMIA HAWAIIAN TURTLES

On waxed paper, arrange one whole pecan with four halves of macadamia nuts as legs for the turtle's body. Dip pecan into homemade caramel and set on wax paper, push macadamia nuts into the caramel and allow to set up. Dip the caramel nuts in chocolate and arrange on wax paper to dry.

Alternately you can sprinkle wet chocolate turtles with finely shredded coconut.

Courtesy of www.mashedpotatoesandcrafts.com

"Can you meet me in the lobby in about thirty minutes?" Officer Kinau asked.

"Sure, I'll be waiting." I hung up and stood looking out the window. The haze over the ocean was burning off and the sun cast a warm glow on the beach. I didn't want to sit idle in my room and stew about the possibility that I'd been on a date with another murderer. Slipping on a pair of flip-flops, I grabbed a bag and put my phone and the notebook with pages full of notes and questions about the case inside and headed out. My plan was to walk to the beachfront and then circle back to the lobby in time to meet with Officer Kinau. None of my plans seemed to be working the way I wanted on this trip.

I'd just walked past the first turquoise pool outside the hotel when someone called my name. Whirling around, I saw Jon waving at me and smiling as he picked up his step to catch up with me.

All of the implications of my search from last night seemed to scream warnings at me. Big warnings about murderers and their secrets. My first impulse was to run, but I still had too many questions. I had to find out the connection between the bracelet and Jon. Maybe it was providence that he had found me before Officer Kinau arrived. My mind raced through the clues I'd pieced together—I had to tell the police everything, even if it was just a hunch, and especially if the woman had been wearing the bracelet.

Rolling back my shoulders, I stood up straight. I would confront Jon and find out what I needed to know. But first I had to shake off the anxiety attack threatening to pounce, and act normal.

"Adri, you're a speed-walker," Jon said as he approached. "I had to jog to catch up to you." He held a single pink rose in one hand and a white box in the other. "I brought you a little something to brighten your day. I hope you don't mind me interrupting your walk—you looked like you were deep in thought."

The smile I gave him was probably more like a grimace because my nerves weren't cooperating. "I have a lot on my mind this morning." I took the rose, hoping he wouldn't notice the way my hand shook. "Thank you. This is sweet." I brought it to my nose, inhaling the fragrance. "All of the flowers have a stronger scent here. It's lovely." I struggled to infuse a cheerful note into my voice and at the same time, quit babbling.

"I'm sorry. You probably were looking for some peace and quiet after yesterday's accident. I can go," Jon said.

Dang. I wasn't doing a good enough job of fooling him. I reached out and squeezed his arm. "I am still a little sore from yesterday, but I'm happy to see you. So happy to have my head above water." I leaned forward and kissed him on the cheek.

That seemed to reassure him and he held out the white box. "Maybe this will help."

I lifted the lid and studied the assortment of chocolates dotted with macadamia nuts and coconut—a Hawaiian version of the chocolate turtles I loved. "Definitely a good start." I bit into one of the chocolates and even if my stomach was already full of suspicion, I couldn't deny that the caramel, nut, and smooth chocolate tasted divine. I held out the box. "You'd better have one too."

Jon groaned. "I shouldn't 'cause I already had some at the store, but I will so you don't feel bad."

I laughed and took another bite. As I chewed, I took stock of Jon. He looked good, as usual, sporting cargo shorts, a gray t-shirt, and flip-flops. His curly hair was mussed, and he didn't seem nervous or suspicious. It made me wonder how much he really knew.

He opened his mouth to speak, but if I didn't take the chance now I might chicken out. "Jon, I need to talk to you about something important. Let's sit."

His brows quirked and his easy smile faltered, but he nodded and sat next to me in a woven beach chair. At least if he tried to kill me, I could scream for help and someone would hear. Clasping my hands together, I pushed away my dark thoughts and scolded myself for jumping to conclusions.

Jon looked out at the ocean, frowned and turned to me. "Am I still moving too fast?"

I shook my head. "No. I need to talk to you about this." I pulled a bracelet out of my pocket. Not the same one I'd found in Jon's board shorts—that one was packaged up, hidden in my suitcase.

"The company bracelets my dad ordered for everyone in the wedding party?" He shook his head. "I know it's tacky. I tried to talk him out of it." He shrugged. "Kyle said Malia was okay with it."

I turned the bracelet over slowly in my hands, not responding to his questions. With as much determination as I could infuse into my own dark brown eyes, I met Jon's gaze and spoke. "The woman at Tunnels Beach was wearing this. Do you know why?"

Jon lurched as if I'd stabbed him. His eyes widened with fear and his lips parted, but then he shook his head and groaned. He glanced at the bracelet and dropped his head into his hands. "I knew I should have said something when I recognized her."

I sat up straighter, surprised at how easily he was going to confess. My eyes darted to the grounds around us. There were a few people milling about, but it was still early in the morning and the pool remained quiet. I tucked the hair behind my ear and glanced behind us. Was he going to confess and then take me somewhere and try to kill me? I thought about going back to the lobby before continuing our conversation, but he was still talking, and he didn't look dangerous.

"I was afraid." Jon paused and bit his lip, sucking in a breath. "I'm afraid that my dad killed Charly."

My feet were rooted to the ground, the chair seemed to hold me captive as the shock drained my energy.

Jon covered my hand with his. "I don't know what to do. I recognized her. I thought my dad did too, but when the police never came to Tri-C, I figured I'd been mistaken."

I held my tongue. The police hadn't questioned Tri-C because they knew the victim as Stacia Fletcher, but I wasn't about to show my hand. Jon reached for the bracelet.

"May I?"

I nodded and dropped it into his palm. He turned it over and the mother of pearl glimmered with a rainbow of colors in the sunlight.

His shoulders slumped. "When I saw it, I panicked. I knew that Charly had worked on the design with my dad and that they'd ordered samples. That bracelet on her wrist would link her directly to Dad. I just couldn't believe that he would actually kill her over a few files, so I took the bracelet and waited. I was going to confront him and find out what was really going on, but then the police didn't identify the body. After that, my Dad said that Charly had quit abruptly, and it made everything look ten times worse."

I leaned toward him. "What files?"

Jon blinked. "Dad said Charly was trying to steal some files on the nutrient seed we've been developing. He thought that maybe she was going to sell it to a competitor. He took everything from her, even her cell phone, had IT hack into her accounts and block them all. Then he fired her, but told everyone else that she quit.

"I think Charly had stored some of the information on a server in the cloud, and they had a hard time accessing it—that's where the missing logo has been."

His eyes held a deep worry, and I found it surprising that he'd been able to act so carefree with the knowledge he was packing around. "Did you confront him?"

Jon dropped his head. "I chickened out. I didn't ask him about the dead woman. I just badgered him about Charly. He explained what Charly had been trying to do to somehow sabotage the company. I didn't say anything about the bracelet." He paused and looked at me. "I'm sorry. I should have gone to the police, but I worried that they would just arrest my dad, and what if he's innocent?"

I gripped the arms of the chair. "Are you prepared for the possibility that he might not be? Because the woman who died was Charly."

Jon stood and leaned against a palm tree. "It doesn't make sense. Why kill her if he already fired her? And why would he leave the bracelet on her?"

He had a point, but he didn't know as much as I did either. Did Neil know about Stacia Fletcher? "We need to go to the police. It won't hurt to have them question your dad and find out what is really going on. If he did kill her, that would be horrible, but letting him get away with murder would be much worse. This woman probably has a family."

Jon bowed his head. "You're right. I've just been scared. I didn't know how to approach it after I had initially talked to Dad and he didn't say anything. I kept thinking that maybe I had been mistaken. And then Kyle's wedding is almost here. I didn't want to mess up everything."

He had a point, but wedding plans aside; it was still murder we were talking about. "What about your mom? Did she recognize her?"

"I don't think my mom ever met Charly, and if she did, I doubt she'd recognize her in that condition." Jon rubbed at the stubble on his jaw. "She's been pretty upset over the whole thing, so at first I wondered if Dad had confessed to her. Then I found out she just felt bad that the police still hadn't been able to contact any of her family so they can't release her identity."

So Jon hadn't been keeping tabs on the news either. "Your dad has to talk to the police, and so do you."

He shook his head. "I don't want to ruin Kyle and Malia's wedding."

"It won't ruin anything."

Jon raised his eyebrows. "I think if the father of the groom is arrested for murder right before the wedding, it would be a pretty bad thing."

I winced. "You do have a point."

Jon moved and knelt in front of me, placing his hands on my knees. "Adri, did you think that I killed that woman?"

Heat rose in my cheeks. I closed my eyes, wishing I could escape from the situation.

"I'm so sorry. I understand if you don't want to see me anymore. You probably hate me now, especially after what you shared with me." His hands covered mine.

Opening my eyes, I saw that his face was only about six inches from mine. "I don't hate you. I understand what it means to be afraid and unsure of the right thing to do."

Jon placed his hand on my cheek. "I like you, Adri. I never want to hurt you. The body scared me, and then my mind kept coming up with different scenarios that all cast guilt on my father." He blinked rapidly to clear the moisture in his eyes. "I don't know how to handle the idea that my dad might have killed Charly."

He stood and paced in front of the pool. I rose slowly from my chair. "I don't think you killed her, but I'm scared and second-guessing myself, afraid to trust you."

Jon turned and came toward me. "Will you help me talk to my dad first?"

"Me? Why me?"

"I just—I think it would give me courage."

"Okay, I can do that." I was curious to hear what Neil might say, but I didn't want to walk into a death trap. "But only if we go to the police first." Jon didn't know that a policeman would be arriving soon, so whether he agreed or not, he'd be talking to Officer Kinau.

Jon flinched. "Do you think they'll arrest me for tampering with evidence or something?"

"No, but they might arrest you if they think you're a suspect and are withholding evidence. If you go to them and tell them what you know, it makes you less suspicious."

"I wish I hadn't taken it." He stopped and looked at the bracelet I held. "Is that the same one from the body then?"

"No, I found that one in your board shorts when I was looking for my ring, but I was too scared to say anything." I ducked my head and mumbled. "I didn't want to get myself killed."

Jon stepped toward me. "I'm sorry. If you'd rather not be around me, I understand."

I lifted my head with a question in my eyes. "How do you feel?"

Jon groaned. "Like things are pretty messed up and I need help."

"Well, I want to help you."

"You're not scared of me?"

"Maybe a little." I smiled to soften my words. "I'm not very sure of people anymore, so don't take it too hard."

"Do you trust me?" Jon asked.

"I think so." My words sounded cruel to my ears so I squeezed Jon's arm and looked into his eyes. "What I mean is that I want to trust you. I think you're a trustworthy guy, but I'm still going to be careful."

"You're a smart woman. That's what I like about you." He reached for my hand and interlaced his fingers with mine.

"Well, you might not like me as much when I tell you that Officer Kinau is waiting in the lobby to speak to you and me."

Chapter 18

BEACH WEDDING WELCOME SIGN

Paint the following message with the bride and groom's names and wedding date on a wooden placard with directional arrows

*Malia & Kyle * February 26th Forever*
Sandy Toes
Salty Kisses
Shoes Optional

Courtesy of www.mashedpotatoesandcrafts.com

Jon's eyes widened. "Right now?"

"That's why I was out by the pool. I was waiting to talk to him." I tugged on Jon's hand. "Come on."

"But why were you going to meet with him here?" Jon took a few steps forward and stopped.

"Because I called the police when I found a picture of Charly in the photos Malia gave me for the wedding collage I'm making."

"How did you know it was Charly?"

"I didn't at first. But then I saw a picture of the woman who died, Stacia Fletcher." I held onto Jon's hand and kept moving forward.

"Stacia who?"

I hesitated, wondering how much I should share with him. "It's pretty interesting, but I'd better let the police fill you in." We hurried toward the lobby.

Officer Kinau hadn't arrived yet, so I decided it was time to come clean and hand over the bracelet stashed in my suitcase. "Hey, I need to grab something from my room. Are you okay to wait for a few minutes?" I wanted to trust Jon, but I decided to take extra precautions with the bracelet. He didn't know where I had hidden it, and I didn't want anyone besides the police to handle it.

Jon had his head down, with his arms crossed over his knees. "I guess it's best to get this all over with," he mumbled. "I just wish I knew if my dad did something wrong. I need to talk to him."

"Let's talk to the police first, okay? Don't do anything until I get back. I'll be less than five minutes."

Jon nodded, and I left him sitting there with a pained expression on his face. As I rummaged through my suitcase, I thought of how Jon couldn't bring himself to say the word we were both thinking. What if Neil was a murderer?

I grabbed my laptop in case Officer Kinau wanted to look at any other pictures. My fingers tightened on the smooth black surface—what if the police confiscated my laptop for their investigation? I still had so many questions that I needed answered, and so far the Internet had helped me unravel a portion of the mystery. Hopefully, I'd be able to keep searching for answers. When I returned to the lobby with the bracelet in the pocket of my laptop bag, Jon grabbed my hand and gave me an intense look laced with anxiety.

"I don't want to tell the police, but I have to confront my dad before the police bring him in. I'm sure they'll tell us not to talk to him, not to scare him off."

"They may be right," I said.

Jon shook his head. "No. Dad won't ruin Kyle's wedding. I want to talk to him first to give him a chance to turn himself in if he did this. Don't you think it would be better for him to go to the police on his own?"

"That's a good point." I looked at my hand in his and wondered about the emotions rocketing through my body. With Jon, things were different, but I still had the tentativeness that had defined me for some time. And now I was in the middle of a murder investigation and my own sleuthing had just cracked it wide open. A feeling of dread washed over me, coupled with the questions hovering over the green-eyed Stacia/Charly I had discovered at Tunnels Beach. I didn't want to think that Neil might have killed her, but that was where the police would look first.

"I guess we'll see what they say." Jon blew out a breath.

Officer Kinau was talking to the security officer when we returned to the lobby. He shook my hand, his grip firm. "Thanks for meeting me, Ms. Pyper."

"Thank you for coming. Jon was here when I came down earlier, and he'd like to talk to you as well."

Kinau nodded at Jon. "Well, that's good because I have some questions for you too."

The police substation in Kalaheo was probably where Kinau would have liked to talk with Jon, but because he was at the hotel, we decided to use the security office to discuss the information I wanted to share.

We met in a small office, and as soon as the door closed, I pulled the bracelet out of my bag. "Here's the bracelet that Charly was wearing when she died." I handed it to Officer Kinau.

He lifted his eyebrows. "Thank you. This might prove to be an interesting piece of evidence."

We sat in folding chairs, and I purposely kept my eyes averted from Jon. The office smelled like stale french fries. It made my nose itch, but I kept my hands in my lap, worried that any movement would make me look guilty by association with the Connellys.

"I'm interested to hear how you're involved with this woman." Kinau's brow furrowed slightly as he studied Jon.

"I'm afraid that I made a mistake in not contacting the police about my suspicions," Jon said. Kinau listened intently as Jon struggled to tell him the details that could implicate his own father in murder. My palms grew moist with sweat, and I tried to hide the nervous twisting of my hands under the table. I reminded myself that Kinau was a good guy and that he would help us. My friend Tony was a police officer back home and he'd always told me he'd do his best to help me with anything I needed. Thinking of that made me relax, and I rested my hands quietly in my lap.

Jon stumbled through his explanation of the day we discovered Charly's body. Kinau listened, nodding his head and taking a few notes. I interjected with my own discovery that Charly Wilks was most likely a fake name for Stacia Fletcher.

"That information looks accurate," Kinau responded. "We had a tough time locating any family members and so we looked at her work. When we called Fontana Inc., they said she'd been fired and didn't have any information on next of kin."

"That's odd." I wanted to say that it also didn't make sense with my theory that Stacia's company had sent her to spy on Tri-C, but Jon beat me to it.

"That's a load of crap." Jon leaned forward, his fingers splayed out on the table. "Her company sent her to spy on my father's company. We have proof that she was stealing files and may have been successful in getting some of our research information into the hands of other GMO engineers. We didn't know who she was working for, but this all adds up."

"We'll definitely be looking closer into that possibility. It will help if your father will cooperate and turn over the evidence he collected against his secretary."

Jon hesitated. "I haven't really talked to my dad, but I had wondered if he recognized her as well."

Officer Kinau skewered him with an icy gaze. "So you say you recognized the woman but didn't report that?"

Jon hung his head. "It sounds terrible now, but at the time I was confused, and I didn't want to start pointing fingers. When her identity wasn't released, I started to doubt myself."

"And your father didn't say anything about the possible identity of the woman?"

Jon shook his head.

Kinau tapped the bracelet, glanced at me, and then spoke to Jon. "You tampered with evidence when you took this, and because it's been six days, this appears highly suspicious."

Jon's forehead creased with worry, and he shot me a pleading glance before Kinau continued.

"However, I understand your intent. I'll need your full cooperation as we continue this investigation, or we may be pressing charges against you."

"Yes, sir," Jon replied. "I want to help."

I swallowed my sigh of relief at the change in direction. Kinau wouldn't press charges for Jon's involvement, and he seemed to believe what we were telling him. Kinau began to ask Jon several questions about his whereabouts last week on Monday and Tuesday. Jon gave him detailed information, along with names and numbers of people that Kinau could contact to confirm his alibi.

My throat tightened as I watched Kinau take notes. Jon glanced at me with tension in the lines around his eyes. Then

Kinau looked up and nodded. "We'll need to bring your father in for questioning. Do you think he'll come quietly?"

"I know it looks like my dad had something to do with this, but I just can't believe it," Jon said. "I mean his whole life has been devoted to making the world a better place, improving agriculture so that people won't go hungry. He's a philanthropist at heart. I know he was angry about Charly's betrayal, but I can't imagine him killing her. There has to be some other explanation."

"That may be true, but do you think your father will come in for questioning?" Kinau repeated.

"Yes," Jon answered. "I know he won't like it, but he'll cooperate."

Kinau nodded. "Well then, can you tell me where I might be able to find him today?"

"He'll be at the office. He's busy getting everything ready before my brother's wedding." Jon inclined his head toward me. "That's why Adri's here. She's the wedding planner."

"I remembered hearing that." Kinau smiled at me and tapped his pen on the table. "I'm going to let you two go, but ask you to please contact me if you have any other information that you feel might be relevant. Anything at all." He slid a card to Jon.

"I brought my laptop in case you needed to look at any more pictures." I squeezed the sides of my laptop.

"Could you send me the photos via email?" Kinau asked.

"Sure, I'll send over the zipped file right now." I popped the screen up and waited a moment for it to flicker to life.

Kinau didn't seem too worried about the pictures, and he wasn't asking for my laptop. Perhaps they had discovered more about Stacia than they were letting on. "Okay, I just sent the pictures."

"Thanks again for your help, Miss Pyper."

My palms were clammy in Jon's grip as we exited the security office with Kinau following us. Jon's alibi must have been solid for Kinau to let him go. I allowed my shoulders to relax. I'd noticed the subtle shift in his posture when Jon told Kinau that Neil was at the office. I had a pretty good idea that he wasn't at the office and that Jon and I were about to find out exactly where he was.

Jon waited until we were in the car before he sucked in a breath and spoke rapidly. "I texted my dad before we met with Officer Kinau and asked him to meet me at the Opaeka'a Falls lookout. I told him it was an emergency. He'll be waiting for us."

"Jon, are you sure we should talk to him before the police? What if it's interfering with the investigation?"

"I have to look him in the eye and ask him if he killed her." Jon gripped the steering wheel tighter. "I can't turn him over to the police without knowing the truth."

"And what if he lies? Do you really think you'll be able to tell if he's hiding something?" The tension in the air around us crackled.

"He's my father," Jon spoke softly. "All I can do is try, but I owe him that."

My phone buzzed with an incoming text from Heather but before I could open it, she called. "It's your mom."

His brows drew together. "Don't give anything away. She's probably calling about the wedding, right?"

I nodded, but guilt pricked at my conscience as I picked up the call.

"Adri, did you get my text? I'm so happy with how it turned out," Heather said.

"Uh, I was just about to open it when you called. One second." I toggled through a couple screens until I was looking at the photo Heather had sent with a message about Malia and Kyle's welcome sign for the wedding. "You're right. This is perfect." I studied the image of a wooden sign painted with white lettering that read: Malia & Kyle, February 26th Forever.

"My friend helped me with it, and I'm so glad it turned out," Heather gushed. "Don't you love how the sign is pointing in two different directions?"

"That is a fun touch and works well because the luau will be in the opposite direction of the wedding." The sign had one arrow with the words "Sandy toes" and another arrow with the words, "Salty Kisses". Underneath the arrows, it read "Shoes Optional". "Thanks for your help with this, Heather. I couldn't have done it better myself."

"I'm glad I could help," she replied. "Are you at the hotel?"

I licked my lips and looked at Jon. "I'm just out checking on a few things, but I'll be back later."

"Okay. Have you seen Jon? I can't seem to locate him or his father today."

"I talked to Jon earlier. He said something about things being really busy at the office." It wasn't a complete lie, but I wished I could be forthright with Heather.

"I'll check over there again. Talk to you soon."

After Heather ended the call, I let out the breath I'd been holding. Jon reached over and took my hand. "Thanks for covering for me. She has tried to call me a few times, but I didn't trust myself to talk to her. I don't even want to think about what this would do to her."

"I'm sorry about all of this. I'm sure we'll get it cleared up." My voice didn't sound nearly as confident as I hoped it would.

Jon seemed nervous as we pulled into the parking lot, but I watched him shake it off as he helped me from the car and escorted me along the sidewalk that flanked a view of the Opaeka'a Falls. My breath hitched when I saw Neil. He stood casually, relaxing against the railing as if everything was normal and he had nothing to do with the drowning of an innocent young woman. Immediately after that thought, I wondered how innocent Charly was in the situation. She didn't deserve to be murdered, no matter what she'd done, but what if there was much more to the story than we thought we'd figured out? As we walked toward Neil, I marveled at how he could appear so calm if he had killed her.

"Thanks for meeting with me, Dad." Jon gave his father a one-armed side hug. "Hope you don't mind if I brought Adri along."

"There's always room for a pretty face." Neil winked at me, and I scolded myself for blushing. "So what's the emergency?"

"Let's walk over here." Jon indicated the other end of the sidewalk. His voice was slightly strained, but overall he was doing a good job of appearing calm and cool.

"Sure." Neil walked a few paces and leaned against the low rock wall.

"I asked you to meet us because I need some answers." Jon looked his dad in the eye and leaned forward, his voice just above a whisper. "We know that Charly Wilks is dead. More importantly, she's the woman Adri discovered at Tunnels Beach."

Neil's eyes widened and he glanced from me to Jon. "What are you saying?"

"Dad, I need to know why you didn't tell the police you recognized her."

Neil dropped his gaze. I noticed his hands were clenched. My chest constricted. I was holding my breath in anticipation of what Neil would say.

"I should have told them, but I was worried about how it would look." Neil lifted his head and there was concern in his eyes. "I mean, what are the chances that her employer would be the one to find the body? That's too much of a coincidence."

"Dad." Jon's voice was firm. "I need you to tell me everything you know about Charly."

Neil's face hardened. "She was stealing secrets from our company. I haven't been able to figure out which company she worked for, but they have to be behind it. She was spying on us, gathering intel for the nutrient seed."

"So you killed her when you found out she was stealing?" Jon said.

"What?" Neil shook his head. "Jon, how could you think that I—" His mouth hung open, and he looked between me and Jon.

I decided it was my turn to speak up. "Mr. Connelly, do you remember the bracelets you brought to me yesterday at dinner?"

He furrowed his brow. "What does that have to do with any of this?"

"Jon saw one on Charly's wrist when we discovered her." I decided to leave out the part where Jon removed it to protect his father.

"She was wearing the sample?" Neil rubbed a hand over his face, and when he did, I saw that he was also wearing the Tri-C bracelet. He noticed the thin gold band with the company logo on his wrist and twisted it around, studying it for a moment. "How could she be wearing the prototype? There were only three made. I thought—" He dropped his hand and looked at Jon with a question in his eyes. He opened his mouth, closed it, then seemed to regroup. "But why didn't you say something about the bracelet that day?"

"I should have," Jon answered. "But then I started doubting what I'd seen, and when the police didn't identify her body, I thought maybe it was someone else. But Dad, I need to know the truth. Did you have something to do with Charly's death?"

"No. I was just as shocked as you were to find her body at Tunnels. And I still don't understand why they haven't identified her."

I squeezed Jon's hand as if to tell him not to share what we knew about Charly's true identity.

"You need to go to the police and tell them everything you know," Jon said. "If you don't, they'll arrest you for murder. They know who she is now."

Neil straightened and his face turned pale. "How do you know that? Have you already talked to the police?"

Jon frowned. "Yes, and they'll probably be at your office when you get back. Please do the right thing, and go with them to answer their questions."

Neil twisted the bracelet on his wrist and looked at Jon with an expression full of hurt. "Did you set me up?"

"No, Dad. I came to warn you. The police would be angry if they knew I was here talking to you, but I needed to know if you killed Charly."

"And did you get your answer?"

Jon looked out at the vista before us and blew out a breath. "I want to believe you, but all I see is a good motive for murder."

"But I fired her last week. We cleaned up the files she was trying to steal, encrypted them, and sent her out the door. The last time I saw her was Tuesday."

"I wonder when she died." Jon looked to me, and I shook my head.

That information hadn't been shared with us yet, but if Neil was telling the truth, he hadn't seen her since three days before her body was discovered. I looked Neil Connelly in the face. "How do we know you're telling the truth?"

Neil planted his feet on the sidewalk and his eyes hardened. "I've been working my tail off at the office, and the rest of the time I've spent with my family, preparing for Kyle's wedding. There wasn't much opportunity to commit murder."

"She's not saying you did it. We're just asking because the police are going to ask you the same questions." Jon reached out and squeezed Neil's arm. "Would the lawyer at Tri-C be able to help you?"

"Yes. I'll have him come with me to the police station." Neil straightened and took a step away from us. "I'd better get going. I don't want the police causing a bunch of problems at the office when they don't find me there."

"Good point." Jon stepped in the path of his father and hugged him. "I'm sorry this happened."

Neil hugged his son, but his shoulders slumped as he stepped back. How much had Jon just damaged his relationship with his father by asking him about Charly's murder? I watched Neil walk briskly to his white Lexus and drive off. Jon turned back to the wall, pushing his hands against the rocks and staring out at the falls.

The Opaeka'a Falls were a brilliant white in the distance and the green vegetation surrounding the area was on par for Kauai's beauty. I hadn't taken a moment to appreciate the scene before because my insides were churning. I sidled up next to Jon and allowed myself to take a deep breath. He put his arm around me and gave my shoulder a gentle squeeze.

"That really hurt my dad."

"I know. I'm sorry." I wrapped my left arm around his waist, and he pulled me into his chest.

"Did I do the right thing? Maybe I shouldn't have talked to him."

I leaned my head back. "What do you think?" It was a loaded question, asking much more than the words indicated.

Jon swallowed. "I don't think he did it, but it doesn't look good for him if he doesn't have a solid alibi for whatever the time of death was."

"What is it that makes you think he didn't kill her?"

"He's my dad. I just—it feels like a betrayal to even consider it."

I nodded and rested my head against his chest. Jon held me, and I tried to sort through the conversation we'd had with Neil. It was terrible to think that he might have killed her just before family started arriving for his son's wedding celebration. It was horrid to think of him killing her at any time, but it didn't make sense to me that he would risk something happening to his family during such an important event. Unless he was confident he'd get away with it. Is that what killers thought? Did they always feel so confident that no one would discover their heinous crimes?

"What are you thinking?" Jon moved his head, and the stubble on his chin brushed against my cheek.

"Um, I was thinking about Charly, and I just thought of something." I stepped back to look at Jon. His eyes appeared greener today, and I focused on the goodness I saw in him as I thought about his father. "It doesn't seem like a powerful enough motive for your dad to kill her over stealing files. If he caught her, then wasn't the problem solved? And if he did kill her, he would never have suggested that we go snorkeling at Tunnels."

The way Jon looked at me, with hope in his eyes, made me wish I hadn't vocalized my thoughts. It would be so painful if the police arrested Neil and charged him with murder. Or would it hurt worse if Neil confessed to the crime?

Chapter 19

MARRIAGE ADVICE

Never go to bed angry. Always kiss me goodnight.

Courtesy of www.mashedpotatoesandcrafts.com

"You're right. I forgot that." Jon squeezed my hand. "It was Dad's idea to go to Tunnels. Mom and Kyle thought we should take you and Malia to Ke'e beach instead. Mom and Dad were arguing about it the day before."

"It still doesn't look good that your dad recognized Charly and didn't tell the police, but that part at least is understandable."

Jon moved his hands up my arms. "She couldn't have been dead long. I don't think my dad has had a minute to himself for the past two weeks. I'm sure he'll have an alibi."

"So you're certain that he didn't have anything to do with Charly's death?"

Jon hesitated, rubbing at the neatly trimmed sideburn on the right side of his face. "All I can trust is my feelings. I know it looks bad, but it just doesn't feel right. My dad couldn't kill someone."

"I don't know what to say, other than I'm sorry." I gave Jon a weak smile.

He wrapped his arms around me and held me close. "Thanks for understanding," he whispered.

I hugged him back, resting my cheek on his chest. The air was thick with feelings and my mind struggled to know what to do with them all. Part of me wanted to melt into Jon's arms, to feel his closeness and to comfort him. The other part of me resisted, telling me to run and close my heart to any dangerous emotions. My forehead tingled as Jon brushed his lips near my temple.

"I never want you to feel scared again. I wish your heart would give me a chance."

Jon rested his chin on my forehead, unaware of how his words stirred something inside me. I wanted my heart to open its iron gate and let someone in, too. I hated to admit it, but I'd been lonely over the past couple years. The loneliness wasn't easily recognizable because of all the companion emotions at war for my attention. Fear, anger, betrayal, grief—they were all best friends with loneliness.

I leaned back and looked at Jon, my gaze flicking to his lips. The hint of a smile curled the corner of his mouth upward on the left and he bent closer to me, his eyes asking permission for something that I wanted but wasn't sure I could handle. Some part of me must have answered yes because Jon put his hand gently on the back of my neck as our lips met.

He kissed me softly, and I wavered for half a second before kissing him back. He paused with a breath of space between our lips, his hand moving to my waist. I leaned forward and covered his mouth with mine, and he pulled me closer. A spark of fire flashed against the gates of my heart, and I allowed myself to revel in the past few days of Jon's company. He was funny and charming. He'd saved me twice from precarious life-threatening situations, but he hadn't imposed on my wishes. Jon was so different from—but no, I wouldn't think of his name, his face, or the way he'd kissed me.

Before my mind brought up images of my ex-boyfriend— the last person I had let get close to me, I opened my eyes and stepped out of Jon's embrace.

But he pulled me back into his arms. "You're safe. I'm not going to hurt you. I'll never hurt you." He stroked my jaw with two of his fingers. "I'm not him. I promise. I'm a good guy."

I leaned my head on Jon's chest and blinked against the moisture in my eyes. How had he known what I was feeling? He only knew a brief account of my history, yet his every action seemed considerate of how I might be feeling. This was different. There would be time to figure things out, but I held onto the one assurance I had. Jon was different. I hadn't felt this way about any of the guys I'd dated in the past, and I wanted to get to know him better.

I surprised Jon by kissing him again. He moved his body closer as he returned the kiss, his hands tangled in my hair. His lips caressed mine. My heart thumped against those iron gates. Jon kissed the sides of my mouth and trailed three kisses down my neck, and then he sighed and held me close again.

His voice was husky. "I vote we stay here and try out this kissing thing some more."

"That sounds nice, but—"

The jangle of Jon's phone interrupted me, so I waited for him to answer the call.

"It's Kyle. I better get this." Jon stepped away and leaned against the wall as he spoke. I was going to say that sometimes people hold secrets we'd never think were possible, but just because I had issues with trust didn't mean that Jon was wrong about believing his father.

Jon ended the call with a curse. "Something's happened at the test farm," his voice held an edge of panic.

"What? Is someone hurt?"

"I'm not sure, but the entire test plot for our new seed has been destroyed." He pushed his hands through his hair. "Come on. I have to get over there now. Someone's vandalized a bunch of property, too."

I gasped. "But who?"

We jogged to the car, and Jon helped me inside before peeling out of the parking lot. "Kyle's there with the police now."

"How could someone even get through the gate?" I trailed off as my research answered my own question. "PFI. Those people did this."

"Who?"

"Pure Foodists International. They set up a rally here, and I'm pretty sure a group is staying at the Hyatt. Their aim is to raise awareness and destroy GMOs."

Jon swore. "There's dozens of those groups. They've had rallies here before but never caused any problems." He shifted into a higher gear. "What makes you think it's this particular group?"

"I've had several run-ins with Mrs. Amelia Harper. She's with PFI and has threatened me several times over double-bookings with Malia and Kyle's wedding. I did some homework and maybe a bit of sleuthing and found out what they're up to. But I didn't think they'd do anything illegal." I didn't tell him that I'd even tried to join up with their group to get information, but they denied access to me and anyone else smart enough to try to figure out their plans.

Jon pulled off the paved road and drove up to a gate that hung open. A white SUV was parked just inside the gate with a Tri-C emblem on the driver's door. "That's Kyle." Jon pointed toward the open field. He cut the engine and jumped out of the car. I followed him, half-jogging to keep up.

ATV tracks crisscrossed over the path, and I saw where they swerved into the field tearing up the once-neat rows of corn seedlings. Garbage and debris dotted the dark black earth and angry gashes from some kind of equipment had torn up half the field.

Jon knelt in the dirt and picked up a trampled seedling. His face hardened with anger and he swore again. "How would they know to target this plot?"

"What do you mean?"

"Remember the special nutrient seed I told you about?"

I nodded. Kyle was across the field, stomping in our direction.

"This was the first test plot." Jon threw a mud clod. "Literally years of research went into the planting of this little parcel of land." He stared at the dark soil and muttered, "And several hundred thousand dollars."

"I'm so sorry. You said Kyle contacted the police?"

"Yes, they've already come and started an investigation." Jon kicked at the dirt. "We can replant, but it will be several weeks from now. We'll have to prepare another batch of the nutrient-rich seeds."

The destruction before me was mind-numbing. Even though it was only tiny corn plants and muddy earth, I recognized the danger behind the threats that Mrs. Harper had sent my way. This seemed to be a direct hit, and it made me nervous. What if PFI planned to do more?

I followed Jon around the field and did my best to commiserate with him and Kyle, but after a while I returned to the convertible, carefully removed my muddy shoes, and leaned the seat back. Everything was spinning out of control and there were too many emotions to process at that moment. I closed my eyes and thought of Luke. I brushed my fingers across my lips and wondered why I wanted to know how it would feel to kiss him. The sun was warm on my skin. I dozed until the car started moving. With a yawn, I opened my eyes and stretched.

"I'm sorry about all that," Jon said. "Did you have a good nap?"

"Yes, I dozed off for a minute. Sorry I couldn't be of more help." I rotated my neck to release the kinks from sleeping against the headrest. "I think all the stress is zapping my energy."

"No problem. There's not much anyone can do now, but we'll do our best to start over."

Jon dropped me off at the hotel, and I went inside and cleaned up. The ringing of my phone interrupted my shower. I wrapped a towel around myself and dried my hands before sliding my finger across the screen flashing with the name of Jonathan Connelly.

"Is everything okay?"

"My mom just called," Jon's voice broke, and I could barely hear his next words. "They've arrested my dad for murder."

"No! But how? There couldn't be enough evidence."

Jon sounded as if he had been crying. "They think Dad killed Charly."

The shock hit me like a punch to the gut. I found myself struggling to find enough air for the next breath. "No. He didn't do it. Can't his lawyer help him?"

"I guess they're talking now. They said he'll get a reduced sentence if he confesses. I think he's considering it."

"But why would he confess? He didn't kill her."

"I don't know what's going on," Jon mumbled. "I'm heading home. I'll let you know if I hear any more."

"I'm so sorry. I wish there was something I could do to help."

"We have to figure this out. My dad didn't kill her. There has to be something else going on."

"Don't worry. The truth will come out."

Jon ended the call. I slumped on the bed swallowing my tears. Truth. I thought of what I'd just said to Jon. The words were to comfort him, but I had meant every one of them—despite the fact that some cases did remain unsolved. I asked myself the same question that was probably haunting Jon. Had Neil actually killed Charly? No. The immediate answer was no because none of this made sense. He'd left us with determination to prove his innocence. Something had happened between the time he'd left Jon and me and when he'd met with the police. I dialed Officer Kinau's number. He answered after several rings.

"This is Adri Pyper. Officer, you have to help me. Neil Connelly didn't kill Charly Wilks."

"I'm sorry. I can't really discuss that."

"But he didn't do it. You can't let him confess to a crime he didn't commit. Someone is going to get away with murder."

"I know it's hard to believe, but he'd be doing the right thing by confessing. That girl deserves justice." His voice sounded clipped.

Anything I said would be futile, but I tried anyway. "Look at the evidence. There's something wrong with that bracelet she was wearing."

"What do you mean?"

"I'm not sure. I have to do some checking first, but that bracelet was a prototype. I don't think Charly was even supposed to have it. There's something about it."

Officer Kinau ended the call with forced politeness, and I clenched my jaw, swallowing the anger and frustration welling up inside. My favorite purple pen sat on top of the lined notebook I'd been toting around Kauai. I flipped to a blank page and jotted down notes as fast as I could. I wrote down everything I could remember, starting with the discovery of Charly's body last Friday. Turning back a few pages, I searched through my previous notes and questions to see if anything connected the dots of the mystery involving Stacia/Charly.

I called Jon ten minutes later. He sounded worse when he answered the phone. I didn't know what else to say, so I launched into my questions.

"Do you remember your dad saying something about the bracelet sample—that there were only three made?"

"Well, yeah."

"I need you to get me permission to go and talk to the person at Tri-C who would know what happened to those samples."

"My dad was wearing one today. I know his was the original prototype. He showed us right after it was made," Jon replied. "You'd need to talk to Osamu—he was in charge of those, I think."

"Can you call ahead and get permission for me to go inside and speak with him?"

"I think so, but Adri, are you sure you want to follow this lead? I don't think there's anything we can do at this point."

"There's plenty to do. All we have to do is find the real killer."

"I'm meeting with another lawyer in ten minutes or I'd come with you." Jon's voice sounded tired.

"Don't worry about me." I ended the call and hurried to the fourth floor and banged on the door to Luke's room.

He opened the door, his expression wary.

"I need to borrow your rental car."

Luke raised his eyebrows. "Okay?"

"Neil Connelly was just arrested for murdering Charly Wilks—the woman whose body I found at Tunnels Beach."

Luke shook his head. "I know. Malia called me. She is completely freaking out. I told her there was no way they'd get this straightened out by Saturday."

I rubbed my left ear as I thought about the calls I hadn't answered from Malia. They had started coming right after I talked to Jon, but there was nothing I could do to help her until

I proved Neil's innocence. "I think we can help Neil and help Malia in the process."

"How? The police wouldn't have arrested him unless they had some solid evidence. I don't think there's much we can do about that."

"Neil didn't kill Charly." I spoke the next words almost without thinking, "Do you want to come with me? I can explain everything."

Luke raised his eyebrows. "Well, it is *my* rental car."

"C'mon then. We need to get over to Tri-C Enterprises."

"Where's that?"

"It's not far. I have the address loaded into my phone's navigator."

"Okay." Luke slipped his flip-flops on and followed me out the door. "But how are you going to help prove Neil's innocence if he really did kill that woman?"

"He didn't kill her."

"You said that, but how do you know?"

"Because he had no motive." We walked briskly to the car, and Luke opened the door for me. His skin looked golden from the Hawaiian sun, a nice complement to his dark hair.

Luke put on his seatbelt, and I showed him the address and started the GPS navigator. "There's something that doesn't add up with some of the evidence in this case."

"And you're going to figure it out?"

"Don't sound so shocked. I'm pretty smart and observant." I gave him a smug grin. "There's kind of been a lot going on that I haven't told you."

Luke shook his head. "You haven't been being careful, have you?"

I bit the inside of my cheek. "Let me explain."

And for the next ten minutes, I debriefed Luke on everything that had happened, every suspicious move including Mrs. Harper and PFI, but I didn't feel brave enough to tell him how I had found the bracelet in Jon's swim trunks. Luke had already given me the evil eye a few times, but I didn't let him interrupt. When I finished filling him in, I leaned back against the seat.

Luke shook his head. "What a mess. But I agree, things aren't adding up right. This reminds me of a *Castle* episode—do you really think you can figure this out, Beckett?"

I laughed. Luke loved the same weekly detective show as much as I did, even if he did like to tease me about it. "We're going to talk to Osamu. Turn right here." I pointed at the GPS and then at the stop sign we were approaching. "He works at Tri-C, and he designed the bracelets and special-ordered the samples. There were only three of them. It sounds like Charly was never supposed to have one. Neil is wearing one. We need to find out what happened to the other two."

"Thanks for letting me come along. Please don't do any more sleuthing on your own." Luke pulled into a parking slot and fixed me with a look that was part pleading/part bossiness.

I nodded. "You can be my partner as long as you behave."

"Does that mean you think I'm as good looking and smart as Castle?"

"I'm not answering that one."

Chaos was a good word to describe the setting of Tri-C when we arrived. The receptionist looked frazzled and several groups of employees were clustered, talking and gesticulating, while some sniffed and wiped their eyes. It must have been quite a blow to find out about Charly's murder and Neil's arrest seconds apart. We only had to wait about five minutes before Osamu came out.

He wore a white shirt and red tie and his black hair had a sprinkling of white around his ears. He looked to be in his fifties. He greeted us without a smile and led us to his office. I explained that we were there to help Neil and needed to know about the samples of the gold bracelets.

"We gave the prototype to one of our stateside clients and kept the other two," Osamu said. "As you noted, Mr. Connelly took them."

"Wait, he took them both? Do you know who he gave the other one too?"

Osamu shook his head. "I'm sorry. I don't know, but I do know he was going to get them engraved."

I sat up straight. "Really? Do you know how he was going to do that?"

"I think Charly was going to do it for him."

"Oh. That makes things more difficult." I tapped my fingers on my notepad. "Did he mention what he was going to engrave on the bracelets?"

"I thought it was initials."

"Thanks for talking with me." I shook his hand. "Do you mind if I call you if I have another question?"

"Not at all. Here's my card." Osamu handed me a business card, which I pocketed. My unanswered questions created a tornado of what ifs concerning Neil's innocence and who was really behind Charly's murder. It was so close, close enough to reach out and grab it, but at the same time the elusive truth taunted me. I gritted my teeth and didn't make eye contact with the receptionist as I exited the building with Luke.

Chapter 20

GUAVA CAKE

1 yellow cake mix
1 1/3 cups guava nectar
3 eggs
1/3 cup vegetable oil
1 (8 ounce) package cream cheese, softened
1/3 cup sugar or 1/8 cup Stevia
1 teaspoon vanilla
1 cup of whipped cream
2 cups guava juice
1/2 cup sugar or ¼ cup Stevia
1/4 cup cornstarch

Grease and flour round cake pans. Bake cake according to package directions, substituting guava juice for the water. In a medium mixing bowl, beat cream cheese with hand mixer until fluffy. Add sugar and vanilla and beat. Slowly fold in the whipped cream and refrigerate until ready to use. In a medium sauce pan, bring the 2 cups guava juice and sugar to a boil.

Make a paste out of the cornstarch and a small amount of water. Remove guava juice from heat and stir in the cornstarch mixture. Return to heat and bring back to a boil for one minute. Cool in refrigerator.

Ice the cake with a thick layer of the cream cheese mixture. Glaze the top of the cake with guava gel. Refrigerate until ready to serve.

Courtesy of www.mashedpotatoesandcrafts.com

I waited until we got in the car to unleash my ideas on Luke. "We have to find the initials on that bracelet. I think it will lead us to the killer."

"I don't know. What if it had Charly's initials on it?"

"I don't remember seeing any initials on the bracelet from Charly's body, but I guess I wasn't really looking for them. If they were small, I could have missed them."

"Could Neil have engraved them somewhere that only the wearer would recognize?"

"That's a good point." I jotted down Luke's idea on my notebook. "Do you think we could stop by the police station and talk to Officer Kinau about this?"

"Sure. All he can do is say no, right?"

I nodded as I entered the address to the Kapa'a police station into my navigator and set it.

"Listen, Adri. About the other day." Luke glanced at me, and I forced myself to appear unaffected.

"It's okay. Don't worry about it." I doodled in my notebook, keeping my gaze averted from his face. It didn't work because I still saw him in my mind—his blue eyes that always held more than what he let on, pulling me closer to him with a magnetism I couldn't ignore. The dimple in his chin reminded me of his laugh and the way his chiseled jawline relaxed when he let his guard down. When I thought of the Harley he drove back home and how good he looked in jeans, I nearly groaned out loud.

"But I am worrying about it." I could feel him looking at me. "I know you're getting fed up with my issues, but I wanted you to know that I appreciate you. It's hard to be patient with myself. I must drive you crazy."

I laughed. "You just described me."

He tilted his head. "Oh?"

"Everyone has issues. I'm afraid of things, but I don't want my fears to keep me from living my life so I keep pushing forward, even when I'm uncomfortable."

"Is that what you're doing with Jon?"

Heat rushed to my face. "He's a really nice guy, and you're wrong about him. He's not a player."

The muscle in Luke's jaw twitched. When he didn't speak I continued, "Why are you jealous of Jon? Every time I spend time with you, you end up pushing me away."

Luke stiffened as if I'd slapped him. "I'm not jealous. I just hope you're not pushing past your comfort zone so hard that you're missing the big picture."

"And what's the big picture, O mighty lens of the universe?"

He shook his head. "Sorry I brought it up."

His apology only made me angrier. "When was the last time you ever pushed yourself past your fears?"

"Stop it, Adri. I'm not fighting with you."

He gripped the steering wheel, and I looked down to see that my own fingers were curled tightly into my palms. I leaned my head against the seat and blew out a breath. "Why won't you talk to me? Every time we just skirt the issues, I'm left feeling confused and angry that I tried to reach out to you again. What do you want?"

Luke pulled into the police station and parked the car. He turned and grabbed my hand as I reached for the door. "Wanting something and being able to have it are two very different things."

I frowned, trying to decipher what he was saying.

"I'm not trying to push you away." He covered my hand with both of his. "You're the only one who really sees me. I can't hide from you, and that scares me."

I opened my mouth to retort, but he shushed me. "I'm not trying to be a jerk. I'm sorry if I keep coming across that way."

It was hard to stay mad at him when I heard the sincerity of his words. "I know you're not a jerk on purpose, but it sure wouldn't hurt if you figured that part out a little quicker."

Luke covered his heart. "Ouch." He leaned forward and tucked a strand of hair behind my ear. "Don't give up on me, okay?"

My cheek tingled where his fingers had brushed it, and the temperature inside of the car was rising. I held out my hand. "Truce?"

With a laugh, he shook my hand. "Truce."

"Let's go get some answers."

Luke mumbled something about that's what he was trying to do, but I chose to ignore it as we entered the police station.

We waited for nearly ten minutes before Officer Kinau met with us. I told him about the bracelets and how they had been engraved. "I know the bracelet is now evidence, but I wondered if you could check? Or if maybe we could take a look?"

Officer Kinau frowned. "I don't know. We're busy here. There's a lot going on right now." His patience with me was wearing thin, and I wasn't sure what I could do to convince him to consider Neil's innocence.

"You don't have the murderer in custody. I think that bracelet may contain a big clue as to who that is."

"Okay, let me see what we can do. The evidence is no longer here, it's at the lab, but I'll make a call and see if they can check it out. If we find anything, I'll get back to you." He stood to leave.

"Wait. Can you check Neil's bracelet? He would have been wearing it when he came in today."

Kinau studied me and gave me a curt nod. He probably wondered how I knew that Neil was wearing a bracelet, but I wasn't about to give that away. "Thanks so much for taking time to talk with us."

Luke and I left the police station and headed back to the hotel. We rode in silence for a few minutes while I jotted more notes, crossed out possibilities, and finally doodled in my notebook. "I wish I would have taken pictures of that bracelet when I had it, but I probably still wouldn't have noticed any initials."

Luke raised an eyebrow—a reminder that he didn't know everything yet. Great, now he would think even less of Jon. "I guess I forgot to tell you about how Jon took the bracelet off Charly's body when we found her in the ocean."

"What?" The car jerked as Luke just about swerved off the road.

"Maybe I should wait to tell you the rest until you park the car."

"That might be a good idea." The car picked up speed as Luke hurried toward the hotel. When we parked, he helped me out and kept a firm grip on my hand. "Let's walk down to the beach and talk about this."

We skirted the main part of the lobby, in case Mrs. Harper and her thugs still had ideas about threatening me, and headed out past the swimming pools, cabanas, and happy vacationers that stretched to the golden sand on the beach. We stopped about ten paces from the ocean and Luke turned to face me. "Did Jon have something to do with Charly's death?"

"No." I held up my hands. "It sounds way worse than it is."

"I'm listening."

"Jon saw the bracelet on her arm and thought he recognized her. He knew how it would look for his dad, so he took it off."

"That doesn't make sense. You don't just hide evidence in a murder investigation because you're worried your dad did it."

"He turned it into the police."

"On his own?"

"I found it in his board shorts and confronted him."

"Okay, I won't ask what you were doing with his board shorts."

"Luke!" I tried to slug him, but he moved out of the way.

"But still, think about it. Was Jon really covering for his dad, or someone else?"

I rocked back on my heels. Luke had a point. Jon hadn't hesitated to confront his father about the murder, yet he had hidden the bracelet for two days and never said anything.

My phone rang as I considered the new angle Luke had just brought to my attention. It was the police station. "Hello?"

"Adri, this is Officer Kinau. I wanted to let you know that we checked Neil Connelly's bracelet. It had tiny initials carved on the inside of the band. We think they were N.C. for Neil's initials. We talked to Neil, and I'm only sharing this information with you because you're the one that brought it to our attention. Can I trust you to keep this confidential?"

"Yes, sir. You can trust me."

"We questioned Neil about them, but he said it didn't mean anything. Just a mark on the sample. I don't believe him." Officer Kinau paused, and I heard other voices in the background. "Neil denied having the bracelets engraved, but I think he's lying. Whatever is on that bracelet could lead us to evidence that will either exonerate him or put him away for good."

"I just talked to a man at Tri-C named Osamu. He claims that Neil was taking two bracelets to be engraved. Why would he lie about it if it could prove his innocence?"

"That's a good point. We'll check into it. We're retrieving the evidence now so we can find out what is on the other bracelet. If I can, I'll let you know."

"Thank you. I appreciate this." I wanted to say more but didn't know the best way to express my thanks when Neil was still believed to be the top suspect in the murder investigation.

"Please be careful, Miss Pyper."

"I will." I ended the call and chewed on my bottom lip for a moment.

The ocean filled my ears with roars and I slumped down into the sand.

"Adri?" Luke crouched next to me. and I held the phone in front of me, watching the screen wink against the sunlight. "Do you need to lie down?"I shook my head as beads of sweat broke out across the back of my neck. Neil knew something, but why wasn't he cooperating with the police? I had been so sure of his innocence, but what if I was wrong?

"Who was that on the phone?"

The sand blurred before my eyes. "It was Officer Kinau."

Luke cleared his throat. "Um, are you going to tell me what that's all about?"

"I want to, but Officer Kinau asked me to keep it confidential. Do you think I should tell you?"

Luke rubbed his hands over his face. "Agh. Of course you should tell me, but I understand if you can't."

I vacillated for a moment. "You're a lawyer. Can I get into trouble for telling you?"

"No, and if you end up helping the police because you told your expert lawyer friend and he ended up thinking of a great idea to find the real murderer, it would definitely be okay."

"You definitely have issues."

Luke tickled the sides of my waist and I jumped away from him with a shriek. "Okay, you have a point. I'll tell you." I lowered my voice and relayed my phone conversation with Officer Kinau.

"The initials will identify the killer. That's what I think," Luke said.

"Unless the initials are C. W. for Charly Wilks, or maybe even S. F. for Stacia Fletcher." I shook my head. "But no, that would mean Neil knew her true identity, which he didn't."

"Are you sure about that?"

I knew what Luke was thinking. If the initials did indicate Stacia's identity was known then it would look even worse for Neil. I thought back to just a few hours before when Jon and I had confronted Neil. He had proclaimed his innocence, and we both believed him. There were still doubts, but inside, I couldn't make sense of the fact that Neil had been arrested for the murder. "Why would someone hide evidence to a murder they didn't commit?"

Luke blew out a breath. "The only reason I can think of is to protect someone they love."

"Do you think that Neil is covering for someone else in his family?" I pictured his sons, Jon, and Kyle, and his wife Heather. Each of the Connellys were kind and genuine. "No, it couldn't be family, but who?"

"I was going to guess family," Luke ventured. "But that doesn't look good for his sons."

"I know. It's so confusing."

Luke held out his hand. "Come on. I'll help you inside."

He pulled me to my feet, but I was off balance and ended up stumbling into his chest. "Whoa. Are you okay?" Luke put his arm around me, steadying me, and then he stepped back keeping a hand under my elbow.

"Just dizzy. I think I'll lie down for a while." But what I really wanted was for him to hold me, smooth my hair, and whisper that everything would be okay, and I didn't need to be afraid anymore. For a moment, when our eyes locked, I thought I saw something in Luke's gaze. A part of me wondered if he was seeing the same thing, but I took a step forward and the magnetic pull was broken. He put his hand on the small of my back as we walked toward the hotel, and he kept it there until he dropped me off at my room.

I kicked off my sandals and curled up on the bed, my skin burning where Luke had touched me. If I closed my eyes, I could pretend for a minute that everything was simple, but I'd eventually have to open my eyes again. If I did and Jon had something to do with Charly's murder, I didn't know if I'd ever be able to trust anyone again.

Chapter 21

BEST BEACHES TO VISIT IN KAUAI

For snorkeling: Ke'e Beach, Tunnels, and Lydgate Beach Park
For sunbathing: Poipu Beach, Secret Beach, Donkey Beach
For watching wildlife: Beach House Beach, any beach around Poipu for whale sightings

Courtesy of www.mashedpotatoesandcrafts.com

The beeping of my phone alerted me to two new voice messages. The first was from Malia.

"Hey, Adri. I know you've been at the police station, trying to help Neil. Kyle and I appreciate your help. This is a nightmare. Please cancel everything for our wedding. I'm so sorry about all of this. Don't worry about me and Kyle. It'll all work out."

I archived the message and swallowed the lump of tears in my throat. Poor Malia. This was supposed to be a dream destination wedding. We'd planned for over six months to get everything just right. I thought about her veil waiting at the concierge desk—just one more detail in this dream wedding gone impossibly wrong. I dialed her number, but it went straight to voice mail. Maybe the stress was too much and she'd simply turned her phone off, but it didn't seem like her. The only option was to leave a message in return, telling her that I would take care of everything.

After I left the message, I stared at my phone for a moment, struggling to deal with the torrent of emotions circling around the failed wedding plans. Resisting the urge to call Malia again, I looked at the next message in the queue and pushed play.

"Hi, this is Heather Connelly. I'm really worried about Jon. We're all upset and you've helped him a lot so I wondered if you might be able to come over to the house. I hope you don't feel like I'm interfering." Her voice cracked. "I just don't know what to do. Give us a call if you need a ride."

I knew Jon was hurting. I'd definitely head over to the house. I thought about calling Heather back for a ride, but it didn't feel right. I'd already used Luke on one adventure today, and I didn't think he'd appreciate giving me a ride to see Jon. Taxis were too expensive, plus I didn't want to hassle with ordering one, and walking the six miles to Jon's house was out of the question. No options presented themselves for easy travel, so I decided that first I would make sure everything was cancelled at the Hyatt.

Even if Chelsea was manning the concierge desk, it'd be worth it to find out if Malia had picked up her veil. I gathered my things and tried to straighten my slumping shoulders as I headed to the lobby.

My chest tightened and released when I saw Chelsea. There would be no more confrontations because Mrs. Harper would win, not because I'd consented, but because the groom's father was under arrest for murder.

Chelsea's eyes were red and her cheeks were splotchy. I didn't ask why she'd been crying. She fixed me with a vicious glare as I sat down. "I need to cancel all of the Connelly/Wright wedding plans. I'm sure Mrs. Harper will be thrilled to know that she will get her way."

If possible, Chelsea's eyes narrowed more. "Yes, I've already flagged all of the events. I heard about Mr. Connelly."

"How?" I asked before I could stop myself.

"I'm trained to do my job. Thanks for the notification. We'll refund the agreed upon amounts, but the retainer is non-refundable at this point, you've passed the forty-eight hour window."

I nodded. "Yes, I know. Can you tell me if Malia Wright was able to pick up her veil?"

"She did. I gave it to her yesterday. Little good it will do her now."

I was about to say something else when someone came up behind me.

"Chelsea Forrester. You're under the arrest for destruction of property."

I whirled around to see a set of officers brandishing cuffs in her direction. Her face paled as they rattled off a list of offenses and pulled her hands behind her back.

"You're making a mistake. I'm not involved with any of that."

"You PFI people must have handed out a script at your rally because they've all said that exact thing. Good thing for us you didn't notice the cameras set up. Everyone is coming in for questioning, and I doubt you'll be returning here."

Chelsea began sobbing. "I did it for Stacia. She wasn't supposed to get hurt. Those Connellys killed her. You should be arresting that whole family." Her cries echoed against the marble in the lobby and bounced off the high ceilings.

I leaned in closer to try to discern what Chelsea was babbling about. She knew Stacia? My mind whirred with the sudden connections unfolding. If Chelsea was being arrested in conjunction with PFI's illegal activities and she knew Stacia, did that mean Stacia was somehow involved with PFI?

Although she was still crying, and protesting loudly, Chelsea went with the officers. Several patrons stopped to watch the scene unfold. Minutes later, I witnessed the henchmen of Mrs. Harper being hauled off. Though I stood around for a good fifteen minutes, I never saw Mrs. Harper.

In all the commotion, Chelsea had left her computer on and logged into the events. I should have felt guilty, but the name of Stacia kept reverberating in my mind. With a few clicks, I was scrolling through Chelsea's messages. There were several cryptic notes about events scheduled through Mrs. Amelia Harper. I minimized the window and searched to see if Chelsea was logged into anything else that would provide information. When I pulled up her email account, I hesitated for a second, but again, my fingers flew to the search bar of their own accord, typing in the name of Stacia. I bit down on the inside of my cheek when the search produced several emails from Stacia Fletcher. I scanned through two emails, each mentioning the upcoming rally and how they were going to change the world.

My heart hammered inside my chest as I selected a third email.

"Excuse me, Miss. Can I help you?"

I yelped and jumped from the chair startling the young man who had approached me. He wore a neatly pressed concierge uniform and stood with his back straight. "Uh, sorry. Chelsea was helping me but then she got arrested. I didn't know what to do."

"Yes, that was—er, uh, maybe I can help," he stammered.

He started to come around the side of the desk, and I leaned down and minimized her email screen as I angled my body away from the computer. "Can you double-check that all events for the Wright/Connelly wedding have been canceled?"

"Oh, I'm sorry. That's tough when someone waits until the last minute to bow out."

I nodded. He thought I was just talking about cold feet. I guess I was, if those cold feet were at the bottom of Kauai's ocean. Disaster didn't seem to be a strong enough word to describe the past twenty-four hours.

"It's been taken care of." The young man typed on the keyboard and peered up at me. "Anything else?"

"No, thank you. I appreciate your help."

I headed for Luke's room and banged on his door.

"What? Is something wrong?" Luke swung the door open, and I stepped backward at the sight of his bare chest. His muscles were well defined and man, those delts. I was gaping, and I commanded myself to get a grip. Luke's lips twitched. He motioned to his room. "Why don't you come in?"

"Uh, okay, but just for a minute." I followed him in as the door clicked behind me. Luke's room was neat, and a similar setup to mine. He stepped over to a pair of chairs next to a TV and motioned for me to sit. I launched into my latest find. "Stacia/Charly wasn't working for the GMOs. She was working for PFI, and she was planning to go to the rally. I need to call Officer Kinau, but I have to tell Jon, too, because I think this could be the line we need to get the police to look at someone else for her murder."

"PFI. That's the fanatic group against GMOs, right?" Luke stood and crossed to the balcony, pulling the curtains open wider.

"Yes, and that's not all. The concierge here that's been giving me a hard time—Chelsea—she was involved with them too. The police just arrested her."

"Man, I keep missing all the excitement. I was just heading out for a swim." Luke's swim shorts hung low on his hips, and he tightened the drawstrings. "This vacation isn't quite as relaxing as I thought it would be."

"Uh—yeah, that's part of the reason I stopped by. I need to go over to the Connelly's house to talk to them. Heather called and left a message. She sounded pretty upset, and I want to help if I can."

"Oh." One corner of his mouth fell, but I appreciated the effort he was making not to scowl at me.

An awkward pause ensued in which I tried to convince myself that it wasn't a big deal to ask him to use his rental car again.

"Are you here because you need another ride?"

My pride won over. "No. I'm going to get a rental. With the way everything has turned out, I'm going to need one for the rest of my stay here. Malia canceled all of the wedding events."

"I know. She called me."

"She did?"

"Yeah, she wanted to apologize for dragging me out here for nothing."

"But, wait—they'll still get married, won't they?" My eyes burned with tears, and I swiped my hand across my face, blinking rapidly. Everything was falling to pieces. "Malia deserves happiness. I wish I could fix this mess."

"Hey, none of this is your fault." Luke knelt in front of me and placed a hand on my knee.

My breath stilled, and I saw the compassion in Luke's face. My bottom lip trembled as I let out a shuddering sigh accompanied by a few tears streaking down my cheeks.

"Malia will be fine." Luke spoke in a soft voice. "Kyle is still going to marry her, and I know they'll be happy. It just won't be the fancy affair they'd originally planned."

I watched Luke's chest move up and down with each breath as he knelt in front of me and clasped my hands. My emotions were out of control, and the room felt crowded. I stood abruptly and Luke stumbled back, but recovered and stepped next to me. "I hoped we could salvage it somehow, but I guess it's too late." When I made eye contact with Luke, I knew that he understood me. It made me feel vulnerable.

In a move that surprised me, Luke pulled me into an embrace—against his bare chest. I tensed, but my second thought was that this was where I wanted to be right now. My arms went around his torso, and I relaxed against him.

When he spoke, his chest rumbled against my ear. "It's going to be okay. It sucks right now, but I think Malia will still get her happily ever after."

My cheeks lifted with a smile as I remembered the wedding reception where I'd met Malia last summer. Luke had teased me about his cousin wanting to plan her wedding with

Adrielle Pyper's Dream Weddings: Where happily ever after is your destination.

The silence grew stronger, and Luke kissed the top of my head. If I tipped my head back two inches I'd be right in line with his lips. I couldn't lie to myself—I wanted to kiss Luke— I'd wanted to kiss him last year, but every time we got close to this point he ran. Now it was up to me and as much as I enjoyed being close to him, I couldn't do it. Not with Jon waiting for me and the dozens of unanswered questions I had about the murder and the future of our relationship, which all depended on the answers to those questions.

I stepped back and Luke released me. "Thanks for helping me so much today." I didn't miss the way his gaze flicked to my mouth and then back to my eyes.

"I'm glad to. Why don't you let me give you a ride so you don't have to worry about a rental?"

"That's okay. I may as well take care of it now."

"No, I insist. You're upset. Let me help you."

"I don't want to ruin your night."

"It'll give me something to do. All my plans just got nixed." Luke grabbed the car keys. "I don't know what I'm going to do for the next three days."

"Hmm, me either. That's weird to think of. Okay, I'll text Heather and tell her I'm on my way."

"Just give me a minute to change."

I waited in the hall for Luke while I texted Heather. There weren't any more police officers making arrests when we passed through the lobby. I didn't see Mrs. Harper anywhere.

The information I'd found from Chelsea's computer knocked at the back of my brain insistently. I knew what I needed to do next. I pulled out my cell phone. "I'm going to call Officer Kinau and tell him what I found. I hope he doesn't arrest me for being a nuisance."

Luke laughed. "Now that would be kind of funny."

"You must have teased your little sisters like crazy."

Luke grinned. "They were the peskiest little girls ever, and they did plenty of their own harassing."

I laughed. It was good to release the tension I'd been carrying around all day. I dialed the police station and within a few minutes, I'd relayed all of the information I'd found—without revealing exactly how I'd found it—to Officer Kinau. I made a special note to repeat the connection I'd found between Stacia and PFI. He thanked me and said that they were considering everything carefully in regards to Neil's arrest. I ended the call and decided to push the investigation from my mind for a few minutes.

I glanced at Luke. "Thanks for bringing me. It's nice to have good company."

"I agree." Luke patted my hand and for a half-second, I thought he might hold it, but he moved his back and tapped his leg in time with a song playing on the radio. The steel drums sounded cheerful, and it made me wish that this trip hadn't been so eventful.

"Remember looking out at the Na Pali Coast line?" Luke asked.

"I'll never forget. It's been my favorite moment so far on Kauai."

"How would you like to hike with me up one of those mountains?"

"Really? I'd love to."

I loved the way Luke's grin widened from ear to ear when he was excited about something. "Maybe we could go on Saturday since you don't have a wedding to attend anymore."

Then I remembered something from my handy guidebook. "Wait a minute, that's not the twenty-two mile hike I read about, is it? I don't think I'm up for that. My bruises are still tender from the lava pools." I thought about the investigation I'd landed myself in—I couldn't concentrate on a hike for any length of time until I discovered something to prove Neil's innocence.

"No, not the long hike. There's a short one on the Kalalau Trail. We'd just hike to the Hanakapiai beach. It goes up about a thousand feet from the coast. I think you'd like it, and I know those Idaho lungs will help you hiking at sea level. It'll feel like a cinch."

"How about this? If I can figure out how to help Neil, I'll go on this hike with you."

"Sounds fair enough." Luke refocused on the road, his headlights skimming off the vegetation and trees overhanging everything. "Is this it?"

"Yes, why don't you come in with me?"

Luke turned to look at me, his eyes widening. "What about—"

"I've only been on a few dates with Jon. He's not my boyfriend, and after everything that's happened, I don't know if I'll even see him again. He's a really nice guy. If you'd quit scowling at him long enough, you would see that for yourself."

"Okay, okay. I won't say any more bad things about Jon." He held his hands in the air as if in surrender.

He opened his door, but his phone started ringing. He fished it out of his pocket and looked at me. "It's Malia. Let me take this and I'll come in. It might be a few minutes."

"Okay. I'll see you in a bit."

Luke answered the phone. "Hi, Malia. How are the lovebirds?" He waggled his eyebrows in my direction and I frowned, my curiosity pricking. I hadn't been able to talk to Malia yet, but maybe I'd get the chance soon. Luke hadn't seemed quite as worried about her and Kyle, and I wondered if it was because he knew something I didn't.

"Actually, I'm just dropping Adri off to the house. She came to talk to Jon about something." Luke shooed me out of the car. I swatted at him before jumping out. He was close to Malia, and he'd mentioned that things would turn out all right for her. I wanted to know how that was going to happen amidst all the heartache in the Connelly family right now.

A motion light clicked on, blinding me for an instant as I approached the front door. My phone rang next, the ring tone startling me in the stillness. I nearly dropped the phone when I saw that it was Officer Kinau calling me back.

"Miss Pyper. I wanted to let you know that we were able to take a look at the second bracelet and it also had initials engraved on the band." He hesitated and I leaned forward, straining to hear above the buzzing of insects flitting around the light. "They were J.C. The initials of his son, Jonathan."

"Yes, but that doesn't make any sense."

"Actually, it might. In the meantime, it might be best to steer clear of the Connellys until we figure this out," Officer Kinau warned.

I looked up at their front door. "Well, that will be hard to do as I'm here with the family to offer support. But I will be cautious."

"Call me if you think those initials have any significance beyond Jon Connelly."

"Okay." The phone beeped as we disconnected.

I stepped back and sat on the front porch, the impact of two letters might mean that I couldn't trust my heart after all. Was I doomed to always choose the wrong man? I thought about what Officer Kinau had said. J.C.—why would the woman be wearing a bracelet with Jon's initials? It didn't make sense. Did she have another alias that we hadn't discovered? Had she stolen the bracelet?

My heart stuttered. Neil hadn't offered more information about the bracelet for a reason. If he had it engraved for his son, Jon, the one who was supposed to take over Tri-C, he would know that the bracelet would implicate his son. I shook my head. It still didn't make sense. Jon had told his father about removing the bracelet. But did Neil know that the police had possession of the second bracelet? All of the questions made my head spin. With that many possibilities, an answer must be floating nearby. I just couldn't see what it was.

"Adri? What are you doing sitting out here?" Heather stepped onto the porch.

"Oh, my phone rang as I was about to knock on the door. I was just finishing up the call." I showed her my cell phone and stowed it in my purse.

"Well, come on in. Jon will be so glad you've come. It's sweet of you to help him right now." Heather put her arm around me and led me into the house. "You're probably hungry. I hope you can stay and eat with us."

"Thanks." I followed her into the kitchen. "I'm so sorry about everything that's happened. I want you to know that I'm certain Neil didn't do this."

Heather's eyes filled with moisture. "Thank you. That means a lot."

I looked around the room, noting the silence in the house. "Is Jon home?"

"No, he ran out to get a couple things for dinner. He should be back soon."

"Oh, I didn't realize he'd be gone." I thought about going to check on Luke, maybe interrogating him about whatever he was talking to Malia about. Maybe it wasn't a good idea to bring him, considering Heather's emotional state. I decided to wait a few minutes before mentioning that another guest would soon be joining us.

"Let me get you a drink." Heather poured a glass of lemonade and handed it to me.

"Could I have a drink of water first? I'm pretty thirsty."

"Oh, that's fresh squeezed with only a tiny bit of Stevia, it's practically water." She put the glass in my hand. "Try it. It's Jon's favorite."

I nodded and took a sip. "Mmm," I said, even though I wanted to say yuck. There was a strange metallic hint of something in the lemonade. Maybe it was the Stevia. I wasn't experienced with the natural sweetener Jon apparently loved.

Heather watched me, her smile seemed forced. "I feel bad. You're waiting on me after everything that's happened. Is there anything I can do for you?"

"Actually, yes. I wanted to walk out on the beach and listen for the black-crowned night heron. If you listen close, you can often hear them fly overhead in the evening. The sound always comforts me, but I was anxious tonight about going out alone."

"Would you like me to come with you?"

"That would be lovely." Heather rubbed her temples and then straightened, motioning toward the back of the house.

I followed her out the patio doors, onto the open deck and the stairs that led down to the beach. Luke must still be on the phone with Malia, so maybe we'd be back in the house by the time he was finished.

Chapter 22

SHARP KNIVES & SCISSORS

Dull knives and scissors are a hazard in the kitchen and craft room. Sharpen at least once a year to avoid injury. To sharpen scissors at home, cut sandpaper. Use a relatively fine 150 or 200 grit sandpaper, cut with the rough side down, with about 2-3 scissor strokes.

Courtesy of www.mashedpotatoesandcrafts.com

The moon was half-full, whispering its light between the breaths of clouds whisking over its surface. The shoreline was about fifty yards from the back of the house.

"Let's go down by the ocean first. It's beautiful tonight," Heather said.

I followed her, slipping off my flip-flops as we approached the edge of the water rushing up to meet the sand.

"I love the way the light plays on the water at night." Heather sighed. "There's nothing like it."

"It's spectacular." I listened to the rush of waves and thought how the ocean must be especially calming to someone like Heather who lived right next to it.

"Oh, there's a sea turtle." The water shimmered and I looked out where Heather indicated and squinted through the darkness. A flash of movement to the side caught my attention, and I jumped to the left as something heavy came down across my back.

I cried out as I stumbled into the water, covering my head and scrambling away from whatever had hit me. Heather swore. I dove into the water, my knees skidding along the sand as I swam against the waves crashing to the shore. I heard the wave coming, felt the shift and pull of the water, and dove deeper as it washed over my body. When I resurfaced, I sucked in a breath and screamed. "Help! Help me!"

The clouds covered the moon and all was blackness around me, with only the distant lights of the Connelly home on the beach ahead, and their neighbor's farther down the sandy strip. Another wave pushed me closer to the shore. I swam against it, unsure of what had happened to Heather. She was trying to kill me. It was her! She'd killed Charly. I dove back under the water, my arm knocking into a rock, a frantic feeling of doom closing over me. The ocean was dangerous with its land mines of lava rocks and coral dotted close to the shallow waters of the beach. I raised my arms to protect my head in case the waves slammed me into the rock.

A hand grasped my leg. I kicked and screamed, my voice gurgling as I was pulled underwater. My hands came in contact with the gritty sand of the ocean floor, and my fingers grazed a rock. I reached out again and grabbed onto the rock—it would make a good weapon. But my body was yanked backward before I could get a hold of anything.

I sputtered and sat up when I touched the ground underneath me. I had just taken a breath when I heard a whoosh and something hit my head. Hard. Bursts of light broke through my vision and I fell backward, turning as the water ran over my face. I needed to breathe. My lungs screamed for oxygen; every part of my body convulsed against my effort to hold my breath in the liquid death that threatened me from every angle. I lifted my head, and the pain was so intense, I teetered on the edge of consciousness. I couldn't be sure that I'd actually moved my head, but when the cool breath of night air touched my cheek, I turned my head, and inhaled.

I pushed myself above the water with my hands, but I couldn't move my legs to support myself. Someone was pulling on my legs. I turned and the moon broke through the clouds to illuminate Heather. She had a hold of me, and I saw the netting she was entangling my legs with. Black spheres that must have been weights hung from the edges.

"What are you doing?" I cried out. "Neil didn't kill Charly. You did. Help!"

"No one can hear you. The tide's moving out. Save your breath. You're going to need it," she chuckled.

I blanched. Who was this crazy woman? "Why?" I cried.

"All he cared about was his precious company."

I was confused for a moment at her answer. "Wait. Neil doesn't know that you killed Charly."

"Oh, he would have figured it out the minute he saw my bracelet on her arm if you hadn't taken it."

A horrified gasp escaped my throat. She thought I'd taken the bracelet from the body. "You put your bracelet on her body? But Neil thinks that Jon killed her—the initials—they were J.C."

Heather straightened. "Not Jon, those are my initials. My full name is Jillayne Heather Connelly, but I've always gone by Heather. Neil calls me J.C."

Once she mentioned it, I recalled hearing Neil call her a nickname—Jaycee is what I'd heard. I had no idea it had something to do with her initials. "But why put your bracelet on Charly?"

"That tramp had been trying to take it from me ever since she first came to work for Neil."

"But I thought the bracelets were just made." I squinted in the darkness, trying to find what Heather had hit me with. She stood knee deep in the water as the current washed more salty ocean over me. My head was barely above the water. I wanted to close my eyes against the pain, but I forced myself to stay alert, to see what Heather was doing and figure out a way to escape.

"I meant my husband. Neil was sleeping with Charly."

"He was having an affair?" Even as I asked the question, I comprehended the lengths that Charly had gone to in order to get the information to bring down the GMOs. "She seduced him for the files?"

"He was a fool."

"But he fired her. Neil got back the files she was about to steal."

"That's what he thought. It doesn't matter. He chose his company and her over me." She dropped my legs and bent down to pick up a smooth piece of driftwood off the beach. We were closer to the shore than I'd originally thought. I wasn't thinking or seeing straight. Even as I watched Heather grip the piece of wood, I wasn't sure what to do. "It's really too bad that you haven't learned to be more careful on this island. It just seems bound and determined to kill you, doesn't it?"

I remembered the feeling of someone pushing me at the Secret Lava Pools. Heather had pushed me then, but why? She must've thought that I'd figured out Neil's secret affair and Charly's ensuing death even though I had no idea. I heard a wave, a large one, coming behind me. Heather raised her arm and as the piece of driftwood came down, I sucked in a giant breath and rolled away into the wave. The water washed over me, and I continued rolling along the sand. Even with a head injury, I recognized the feeling of going deeper under the water. Several rocks snagged at my arms as I continued to roll. My legs were stiff and heavy with the netting cutting into the flesh of my calves. Pulling and tugging at the ropes was futile.

It took me two seconds to figure out that the only way I would survive was to swim to the surface, despite the weight of the net surrounding me.

My feet found traction against a rock, and I pushed upwards, pulling myself through the water with powerful strokes. My head bobbed above the surface. I forced myself to remain calm as I swallowed a mouthful of air. Heather had a light. She would find me. She wouldn't rest until I was unconscious and sinking to the bottom of the ocean.

The current pulled me farther out towards the moonlight on the water. Once my lungs stopped screaming for oxygen, I concentrated on what else I needed to do to survive. With the water pushing and pulling me, I worked to free myself from the netting tangled around my legs. The ropes burned and slipped against my skin, but I reassured myself that I could get them off. Heather hadn't intended on me being conscious. Why hadn't I seen the trap I was walking into?

With one leg free, I struggled against the dead weight pulling me toward the bottom. Why was Heather trying so hard to kill me? I didn't even know she was the killer until she attacked me. There was still something I hadn't discovered. I was a threat to Heather several days ago and so she'd tried to incapacitate me. What was it?

The net pulled me down under again and I panicked, flailing against rocks to push myself to the surface for another breath. I couldn't scream for help and risk alerting Heather to my conscious state. If I kept my head above water long enough to get my bearings maybe I could swim with the current toward the shore. But first I needed to finish untangling the net that constantly pulled me down. I pulled my leg up and pushed at the tight lashing of the rope around my calf until it bit into my skin. My head throbbed, and I was on the edge of hysteria as I struggled to stay above water.

I remembered Jon's warning about the temperature of the ocean. It was tricky because it felt warm, but it was just cold enough that if you stayed out too long, you risked getting chilled, which led to sluggish muscles and reduced ability to swim through the powerful ocean waves.

"Adri! Are you out there?" a voice called.

It pushed me into motion, and I thrashed through the water, dragging the net behind me as I struggled to put space between me and the voice. A wave rolled over my head and I sputtered, wiping the salt water from my face.

"Adri! I'm not going to hurt you. It's Jon. Tell me where you are."

My ears perked up. It was Jon's voice, both times it had been him calling. He must have been in the water close by. I hesitated. What if it was a trap? There was still a possibility that Jon had helped his mom. Was that why he was sure of his father's innocence? Because he knew that Heather was the real killer?

I swam away from the moonlight, toward what I hoped was the shore, but the weight of the net kept me in place, tugging me below the surface.

"Adri! Please let me help you. Adri!"

He was closer, and I turned to locate him amidst the waves but the moon hid behind the clouds again and everything went black. I treaded water as best I could with a net trailing from my left leg, and listened. A splash to my right alerted me that Jon was close by. I closed my eyes and prayed for help. I didn't want to die.

A memory pinged at my consciousness, and all at once, I knew exactly why Heather had tried to kill me. The dinner at the Beach House Restaurant. I had mentioned seeing something on the body, but I couldn't remember what it was. It was then that Heather must have decided I had taken the bracelet. Even now, she didn't know that Jon had taken the bracelet and turned it over to the police. She thought I was the only person who knew about the initials, J.C.

Jon didn't have anything to do with Charly's murder—I knew that without a doubt now. My remark at the Beach House had been such an inconsequential thing, but it was enough to make Heather worried. She must have known I would eventually figure it out, only with all the wedding plans it'd been swept to the back of my mind, and I'd completely forgotten until I found the bracelet in Jon's pocket.

Jon. I could trust him. He would save me.

"Jon! I'm here. Help me!" I screamed. I had to get out of the water because I knew where Heather was headed. I had to prove Neil's innocence before Heather got away. "Jon!"

"Adri! I'm right here." He was right behind me, swimming furiously, his strong arms stroking through the water. He grabbed hold of me and started to pull.

"No. Heather wrapped a net around my legs. It's weighted, dragging me down. I can't get loose."

"Hold on. I'll get you loose." He had a snorkeling mask on, and he dove under the water. Something jerked on my leg. I tried to hold still and clenched my eyes tight as I was pulled underwater again. He tugged on the net and it scraped against my skin, but I moved my ankle more as Jon untangled it.

"I've got you." Jon pulled me above the surface. "You're almost free. The net got caught around a big rock down there. Can you hold on for one more minute?"

"Y-yes." My teeth chattered. I swept my arms back and forth, filling my imaginary basket with apples as I treaded water like I'd been taught when I was ten years old. It was much different in the ocean as wave after wave rocked me back and forth. Water rolled over my head, and then I was free, my body cascading toward the beach.

Jon resurfaced and spit out his mouthpiece. "Hold on, Adri. We're almost there."

He grabbed my arm, and I held onto his wrist with both my hands and kicked with him toward the surface. When my toes skidded along the sand, I cried out in relief. Jon hauled me onto the beach, and we both lay there breathing heavily as the water lapped at our feet.

A light blinded my eyes, and I closed them and groaned.

"Sorry, I'm just checking your legs for injuries."

He moved my legs. They felt like two pieces of driftwood, numb from the cold water and lack of circulation, but my right toes tingled. I figured that was a good sign. "My head."

"We need to get you to the hospital. I think you need stitches."

"No, I don't want to move anymore. Please," I mumbled.

"Don't worry. You're safe now." Jon lifted me into his arms and carried me across the sand. I linked my arms around his neck and kept my head as still as possible against his chest. Every step reverberated like my head was being squeezed in a vice. After a few minutes, I noticed the sensation of warm blood trickling down the side of my face.

"How did you know I was out there?"

"Luke. He couldn't find you in the house, and so he went out back and heard screaming. He was running back to the house for a flashlight when I came in. I told him to call for help, and I grabbed my snorkeling gear." He shifted my weight and took in a breath. "I saw my mom running down the beach. She didn't stop when I called out."

Neither of us spoke for a moment, and when I did my voice sounded raspy, probably from drinking too much seawater and screaming. "She tried to kill me. At first I didn't know why, but then I found out she killed Charly."

"I can't believe it." Jon hesitated and gasped for breath. "I'm so sorry."

I leaned my head back. "We have to tell the police to get to my hotel room. That's where Heather's going. She's probably going there to look for any evidence I found that links her directly to Charly's murder."

"But why did she kill Charly?"

I licked my lips and tried to find the courage to share what I'd discovered. "Your dad was having an affair with her."

"No," Jon cried. "That can't be true! My dad loves my mom."

"I'm sorry," I murmured.

We didn't talk anymore as Jon carried me toward his house. I imagined the anger and betrayal welling up inside him. I thought about how his world had been turned upside down. I heard Luke's voice a few seconds later.

"Is she okay?" he asked.

"I think her head needs stitches, and her legs are pretty torn up," Jon said.

"Put her over here."

I cracked open an eye as Jon set me carefully on a blanket, and Luke wrapped a towel around my shoulders.

"I'm sorry I wasn't there for you." Luke rubbed my arms gently with the towel to dry them off. "I just can't believe it was Heather all this time."

"Did you see her?" Jon asked.

"I was on the phone with the police when I heard a scream. I looked out front and she was driving away in the white SUV. Here, let's get some pressure on that head wound." Luke held up a towel and moved it toward my head.

I cringed as he made contact with the gash on the side of my head. Lifting my arm required more effort than I anticipated, but I held the towel gingerly in place. "Call the police again. Tell them Heather's going to the Hyatt to get into my room." My chattering teeth made it a struggle to form my words. My head was heavy, pulsing with pain. I was aware of a burning sensation coursing through my legs.

"Okay," Luke said. "I think you should lie down."

Jon sat next to me while Luke relayed the information about Heather to the police. Jon cradled me in his arms, lowering my head carefully against his chest. "I'm so sorry. Stay with me, Adri. Don't go to sleep yet."

My eyelids fluttered, and it seemed as if the net was still attached to my body, dragging me under the water. I wanted to sleep, to escape the pain and the fear of drowning as my lungs cried out for oxygen.

"An ambulance is supposed to be coming, but do you think we should head in the direction of the hospital?" Luke asked.

"It'll probably take them about twenty minutes to get here from the time they were dispatched. I think it's best to wait at this point." Jon took my hand from the towel on my head. "Just be still. I'll hold it in place."

Something rubbed my legs and I opened my eyes to see Luke blotting the water with another towel. He looked up at me, worry etched on his face. "You're going to be okay now."

I struggled to keep my eyes open. His face swirled before me. Jon was speaking, but I had an urge to say something else. It was important. With a deep breath, I focused on Luke's face. "I'm sorry I got mad at your heart. I don't think it's broken, Luke. You have a strong heart. Thanks for saving me again."

Luke said something and it sounded like Jon laughed, but the blackness was too deep and I couldn't swim out of it. I let my head sink into the darkness and I floated there, feeling the pain on the edges of my consciousness.

Chapter 23

GET WELL CARD

This card features a miniature box of tissues on the front.

1. *Fold 4 ¼" x 11" piece of cardstock (your choice of color) in half to make 4 ¼" x 5 ½" card base.*
2. *Cut a square, sized for the tissue box, and score it to look like a box.*
3. *Cut a piece of tissue about 2 " x 2 " and pinch one end together. Glue onto the back of tissue box square.*
4. *Glue tissue box onto the cardstock, centering it on the front of the card.*
5. *Stamp a Get Well message either above or below the tissue box.*

Courtesy of www.mashedpotatoesandcrafts.com

Early Friday morning, I was discharged from the hospital after being interviewed at length by Officer Kinau. My head still hurt, and I sported a bald spot with seven stitches where Heather had split my scalp with a piece of driftwood. Most of that day was foggy, with painkillers, police officers, Jon, Luke, Malia, and Kyle all checking on me.

The police had intercepted Heather at the hotel. She had been trying to find a way to sneak into my room, most likely to steal the bracelet as I'd suspected. The word "unstable" had been mentioned several times and so far Heather hadn't confessed, but we were still hoping she would change her mind. I didn't want to testify against her in court. No matter what happened, she would be locked up for a very long time.

Jon told me that Neil Connelly arranged for a private nurse to care for me back at the hotel, which was more than I needed, but I was so happy to be away from the beeps and smells of the hospital that I didn't mind accepting his generosity. Once I was settled back into my room, the manager of the hotel came to visit me and apologized for Chelsea's and Mrs. Harper's behavior.

She'd seen the police escort Mrs. Harper and her henchmen off the premises, and the news had leaked stories about PFI being in trouble. "The news indicated that charges were being brought against them for vandalism, harassment, and attempted manslaughter. I'm not sure of the details, but I know for certain that you won't have to worry about them anymore. PFI will no longer be operating according to the news."

"Thank you." My head still felt muddled, but her words brought a sense of relief to me.

The manager handed me an envelope with a brochure. "This is a voucher for a five night stay in our best suite. It never expires. I know that it can't undo the damage, but I hope it will help in some way. We want you to know that our customers are our first priority."

"Thank you." I took the envelope. "Your hotel is fantastic. It's a perfect venue for a wedding. I'm just sorry it didn't work out how we planned."

"Me, too. Get feeling better, Miss Pyper."

After she left, I set the envelope on the nightstand. The gift was significant. Before I drifted off to sleep again, I wondered if I would ever have a chance to use it, and if I did, who would come with me.

The doctor asked that I limit visitors, so I hadn't seen Luke or Jon since the hospital. It had allowed me time to recover and rest but I was feeling kind of lonely by Saturday morning. My first visitor was Neil on Saturday afternoon. I'd slept most of the day, working my way through the haze of altered consciousness that a battered body and painkillers left me with. My nurse checked on me every couple of hours. She'd helped me bathe, and I was sitting up in one of the upholstered chairs that faced the patio and the ocean beyond.

Neil sat next to me in a matching chair and stared out at the ocean. His eyes were haggard, with dark circles and a haunted look that made me sorry for what he was going through. Neil's mustache moved up and down when he pursed his lips, preparing to speak. "I owe you more thanks than words can express."

My thoughts wandered to his wife, Heather. Officer Kinau had informed me that the police had apprehended her near the hotel, and my quick thinking had made the arrest possible. Heather had been on her way to my room, thinking that she had gotten away with another murder.

I shuddered to think what might have happened if Heather had somehow escaped police custody. I felt safer knowing she was behind bars. I forced myself to smile at Neil, despite the horrible circumstances he was in. Jon had shared that his father was in pretty bad shape after finding out what Heather had done. I didn't want to dwell on Heather anymore but Neil was hurting. "I knew you didn't kill Charly."

With a nod, he pursed his lips. "I was a fool to get into a relationship with her. It was wrong." He scrubbed a hand over his face and sighed. "When I got arrested, I didn't say anything. I thought I was protecting Jon, even though my heart didn't want to accept that he might have killed her. Everything I'd found made him look guilty. Then when he showed up with you and questioned me about the murder, I thought he was asking me to help him. All that time Heather was setting things up to make sure she appeared innocent, no matter the cost." He swallowed and blinked his eyes several times before continuing. "I just can't wrap my head around the part that she could actually kill someone. In a sense, my boys have lost their mother."

The magnitude of this father's love for his son warmed my heart. Neil was a good man who had made some grave mistakes by trusting Charly, and it was terrible what had come of his infidelity to his wife, but he was suffering for his choices.

"Jon and Kyle are lucky to have a father like you."

Neil shook his head. "I have to accept responsibility that I put all of this into motion by what I did wrong. Charly is dead because of me—because I was unfaithful to my wife."

The words hung in the air and I couldn't fully disagree, but I wasn't sure how to respond. I opened my mouth, but Neil held up his hand as if anticipating what I might say.

"Part of me feels like I've ruined Heather, but the other part can't ignore what our marriage has always been like. My lawyer is preparing divorce papers. It'll probably be a difficult process, and one more thing for my sons to deal with."

His guilt was tangible, and I wondered how long he would carry that weight, how it would affect the rest of his life. I leaned forward to see his face better. "Neil, you're right. We all have regrets. I hope you can work through this. Your sons still love you very much. I hope that you've been as forthright with them as you've just been with me."

"Jon didn't want to see me at first, but I finally got to talk to him." Neil rubbed a hand through his hair and his forehead creased with worry. "Kyle pretty much doesn't want anything to do with me, but at least Malia will support him."

"I'm sorry."

"Don't be. I should feel this pain, and I'm not going to forget what I've learned from my mistakes. You've saved my life, Adri. I'm in a mess right now, but at the same time, I feel like I've been given a second chance to turn my life around. Even though I don't deserve it, I'm not going to waste it. My family is suffering, and I'm going to stop being selfish and help them. I know Jon wants to follow Kyle to Idaho and try something different. I'm not going to stand in his way. My sons have my blessing to follow their dreams."

"That's wonderful news. Have you told Jon?"

He nodded. "He's waiting in the lobby to see you." Neil chuckled. "I think there might be a bit of a competition between him and Luke."

My cheeks heated and I ducked my head. My heart thrummed with anxiety in my chest as I thought about facing both men. It was time for me to make a decision between Jon and Luke.

Neil stood and patted my shoulder. "I promised them I wouldn't keep you too long. Please let me know if there's anything you need."

"I will. Thank you so much for getting me out of that hospital."

"It's the least I could do." He wagged a finger at me. "I'm serious about my offer. Anything you need, not just now, but in the future, don't hesitate to call me."

"Okay."

"I'll see myself out. Do you need a few minutes before I send the dueling princes in?"

I laughed, then winced because it hurt my head. "Actually, twenty minutes would be good. Maybe I can try to grow some hair to cover my bald spot."

It was Neil's turn to laugh. "You're one of a kind. I'm rooting for Jon, though." He winked and opened the door. "Good luck."

Even though it was pointless to try to fix my appearance, my vanity hadn't died with a few stitches. I walked carefully to the bathroom and swiped on a bit of mascara. For once, having thick hair was a good thing because I could arrange it to hide the stitches and ugly shaved part of my head. There were still dark circles under my eyes, but I could talk to Jon and Luke without feeling too self-conscious.

My phone pinged with a text from Lorea. I opened it and studied a picture of a get well card with a tiny tissue box on the front. Her message said: **Get better soon, girl! I need to teach you how to have a real vacation.**

Lorea was a great friend. I thought about what she would recommend concerning Luke and Jon—but it didn't make the decisions before me any easier. I wanted to see both of them, but I wasn't sure how I felt about either of the men who'd played a role in saving my life. Drowning would have been the outcome if Jon hadn't come searching for me, endangering his own life by swimming out in the rough waters to find me. I remembered how Luke had carefully dried my arms and legs and how Jon had held me until the ambulance arrived. Most of that night was gone from my memory, but there was something on the edge of my recall from Thursday night that had me worried. I'd been talking to Luke before I passed out, but I wasn't sure what I'd said.

I texted Lorea: **Can you talk right now?**

Within a minute my cell phone buzzed with an incoming call. Lorea's happy face flickered across my screen. She'd called to check on me a couple times, but I'd been kind of incoherent from the painkillers. I was looking forward to a conscious conversation with one of my best friends. Part of me knew what I should do, but the other part needed some reassurance.

"Lorea, I'm off the painkillers. How are you?"

She chuckled. "I'm great. Are you doing okay?"

"I am, just having a little dilemma in the dating department."

Lorea groaned. "Please don't say that you're going to swear off dating again."

"Actually that was one of my ideas. I thought you'd be happy, since you've always been against dating—until recently, I guess."

"Now, now, don't change the subject," Lorea said. "Tell me what's up."

"Well, I'm not feeling so many butterflies about Jon anymore. It's been such a nightmare here with the murder, and his mother trying to kill me. Is it terrible of me to want some distance?"

"Not at all. In fact, if he has any kind of sense, he'll know that you need some space. I'm sure Jon is going to need some time and space as well."

"I'm glad to hear you say that. I started having second thoughts about dating him, and then I felt guilty because I don't want to add more hurt to his life right now."

"Adri, right now you need to take care of yourself. Someone tried to kill you—again. You're far away from home with a head injury. Feeling guilty should be the least of your concerns."

I gazed out the window at the palm trees swaying in the wind. "You're right. I'm going to be brave and take care of myself."

"It's going to be okay," Lorea said. "And I can't wait to see your bald spot."

"No making fun of the victim." I tsked.

"Okay, just a tiny bit. Besides, you'll forgive me when you hear what I have to tell you."

"Hmm, I'm listening." I sank into the loveseat facing the ocean view of my room, grateful for the change in conversation. "I hope it has something to do with this mystery date you've been killing my curiosity with."

"It does," Lorea replied. "I was going to make you wait until you got back but I decided you've had enough suspense."

"You're right there, so go ahead. Spill. I want all the details. Who is this wedding date?"

Lorea laughed and I thought I detected a hint of nervousness in her voice. "Well, you were partly right. It did start out as a pity date. You know me, I didn't want to take a date, but my family insisted. So I asked a good friend if he'd go along with me. He knew it was a pity date, but then we both had such a great time. Adri, we've been out three times in the last week!"

"Well, who is it?"

"You'll die when I tell you," Lorea hedged.

"I'm going to kill you if you don't tell me right now." I leaned forward with anticipation.

"It's a friend of yours, too. A certain detective."

"Tony? Really? That's great!" I wished I could hug Lorea right then.

"Do you really think so?" Lorea asked.

I understood why she was nervous. Tony was a family friend. She was probably worried that I might disapprove or scold her for using him as a pity date. "Lorea, he's perfect for you. Why didn't I ever set you two up before?"

"Because I would have flat-out told you no way."

"Ah, that's right, you would have." I shook my head. "So three dates and what about kissing?"

"Uh-uh," Lorea said. "No more details. Not until you get home. But he's so great. I love his sense of humor, and how he really seems to get me."

"You sound happy. I can't wait to see both of you."

"Thanks, Adri. I was kind of worried to tell you, but I should've known you'd be fine with it."

"I'm more than fine, I'm thrilled."

"Well, hurry home and maybe we can go on a double date."

I glanced at the leis draped over my chair and frowned. "I guess we'll have to see about that."

Lorea chatted for a few more minutes about the upcoming weddings we had planned, and she asked me more questions about Jon and Luke. When I said goodbye, I couldn't stop smiling. Lorea was a no-nonsense woman who often scoffed at the drippy, love-sick brides we worked with, but I had a feeling that all of that was about to change.

Chapter 24

HONEYMOON SNACK BAG

Purchase several snacks, preferably those that can travel through airport security, and put them in a cloth bag or small reusable shopping bag. Include granola bars, nuts, dried fruit, chocolate bars, hard candy, an empty water bottle, travel tissue pack, and any other favorites the bride and groom might like.

Courtesy of www.mashedpotatoesandcrafts.com

Lorea's news lifted my spirits and erased the dread I had over talking to Jon. He arrived a few minutes later and knocked on the door with a staccato rhythm. When I opened it, he stepped right inside and hugged me. "It's so great to see you when you're not half-dead."

"Thanks, I think." I laughed as Jon held me.

He stepped back and pretended to examine me. "I can't see your bald spot. I thought you'd be showing that off. You actually look pretty good."

"Hardly. My legs are a mess." I pointed at the rope burns and bruises. "I guess after everything that's happened, it's not a surprise that I slept most of the last two days."

Jon took my hand, and we walked toward the loveseat flanking the wall next to the bed. "I'm sorry about everything. I know I joke a lot, but I've never been more afraid than I was when I was searching for you in the ocean." We sat down and he put his arm around me. "I've missed you. The nurse wouldn't let me bother you, and my dad said I shouldn't either. I wanted to give you some space."

I took a minute to phrase my next sentence. Jon seemed light-hearted, but I sensed he was covering darker emotions.

"I'm so sorry about your mom."

Jon nodded. "It's weird to think that my parents will be divorced. And my mom's going to prison. It's hard because I've never been that close to her, but I still can't believe she was capable of what she did."

I held back a shudder and took a deep breath. "It has been awful. How are you doing?"

"I'll be okay." Jon's eyes softened. "Did my dad tell you that he's supportive of me going to Idaho with Kyle?"

I nodded, and Jon's breath hitched. He coughed and looked at the floor. "The thing is," he hesitated. "I'm not sure it's the right plan for me anymore."

"Oh?" I couldn't think of anything else to say, but a huge weight had fallen from me. I wouldn't have to add more hurt because it sounded like he had changed his mind.

He lifted his head. "I know what I told you, but with everything that's happened I don't think I can leave Hawaii."

"I think you're right."

Jon sat up straight. "You do?"

"You're a great guy, and I enjoyed getting to know you and spending time with you here, but now you need to give yourself a chance to heal. Don't rush into any big decisions."

He leaned back into the loveseat. "That's great advice, but it doesn't make things easier."

I traced the striped pattern on the cushion with my finger. "It's the same advice that I was given a few years back, and it's proved to be true."

We both were silent for a moment, and then Jon leaned toward me. "Thanks for understanding."

I wrapped my arms around him. "Good luck."

"I'm sorry about everything, Adri." He hugged me and kissed my forehead. "I wish you all the best."

He stood and I smiled up at him. "You too. Take care of yourself."

After Jon left, I was struck with a feeling of lightness that I hadn't experienced in days. The pressure I'd been under had finally been released, and the worries I had over Jon in the future were no longer a concern.

Luke would be coming to see me next, and I remembered what he'd said about not giving up on him. The weak part of me wasn't sure if I should risk trying to break through his armor if it went into place again, but I cared about him and I could no longer ignore my true feelings.

A knock at the door sounded, and I moved slowly to open it. Luke stood there, concern evident on his face. "How are you feeling?"

"Doing better. Come in." I motioned for him to follow me to the set of chairs Neil and I had occupied earlier.

"I wanted to come in first to tell you the good news, but Jon looked pretty anxious." Luke held his cell phone and tapped the screen.

"Good news would be nice about now."

Luke nodded. "I'm happy about this. Hopefully you'll be okay with it."

I scrunched my eyebrows together, curious as to what he meant. He handed me his phone and I focused on the picture. It was of Malia and Kyle, and it looked like they were at Waimea Canyon. My eyes flicked to the words trailing along the bottom of the picture, "We're married!"

"They eloped?"

"Yes, and I hope you're not mad that I helped."

"Of course not." I looked at the picture again with a bittersweet pang for Malia. "I'm so glad they could still be married today."

Luke nodded. "Me, too. I didn't get to walk her down the aisle, but I think she still found her happy ending. Here's another picture she sent for you." He slid his finger across the screen.

It was a close up of the couple. Malia looked radiant, and Kyle appeared smitten. The caption read: "Tell Lorea thanks for the help with my veil. I love it!"

Malia had yellow and pink plumeria clipped into her hair next to the veil and the effect was stunning.

"You'll have to send that to me."

"I'll do it right now," Luke said. "Malia wanted me to surprise you, that's why she didn't send any pictures to your phone yet."

"Do you think they'll be okay," I asked.

"Kyle's taking everything pretty hard, but they decided to move forward so they could have a fresh start." He looked up from his phone and shrugged. "I'm not really sure how they'll deal with everything once they get back."

I pulled my toes through the carpet. "I talked to Neil. He's suffering. I hope he'll be able to reconcile with his family."

"It'll take time, but he seems humbled. I think that will help." Luke rubbed his jaw and then leaned forward, his mouth quirked in a funny smile. "Speaking of reconciling—that reminds me of something."

"What?"

"You don't remember, do you?"

I lifted my hands. "I can't be held responsible for anything I said while under the influence of narcotics."

Luke laughed. "Well, if it's all the same to you I'd like to keep those words. They meant a lot to me." He stood. "Do you mind if we stand on the balcony for a minute? Or are you too tired?"

"That would be nice. I need to get out of this room, but I keep falling asleep." I let him take my hand and lead me out on the balcony. The ocean breeze ruffled my hair and my scalp tingled near the stitches. When I glanced at Luke he was watching me with a serious expression. I cleared my throat. "Are you going to tell me what I said?"

He squeezed my hand. "You said you were sorry for getting mad at my heart."

My face burned and I pulled at my fingers, wanting to cross my arms over my chest, but Luke didn't let go, instead he pulled me closer to him, resting his arm on my shoulder. "I'm not making fun of you."

"Yes, you are." I kept myself apart from him by a half-inch.

"No, I'm not. You also told me that I have a strong heart. But what I thought was interesting is that you thanked me for saving you."

"Well, if you hadn't been there, Jon would never have known I was there. I would have drowned."

"True. But he's the one who saved you with some pretty fantastic swimming."

"I'm grateful that both of you were there," I said.

"You also told me you didn't think my heart was broken," Luke murmured. "I've been thinking about that for the past two days."

I wasn't sure what to say. Luke had told me enough times that the death of his wife had basically ruined things for his future love life, he just didn't feel capable of loving someone like that again. He was almost like a Dr. Jekyll and Mr. Hyde because one moment, he could be sweet and sincere and show his vulnerable side and the next he had clammed up and let the anger at his loss boil over again, mad at the world and those who were happily married.

"I think you're right." Luke pivoted so he could look me in the face. "My heart isn't broken anymore. And you were right when you said that Dana wouldn't want me to live my life this way. I was angry because those words pierced my soul. The reason I came to talk to you today is because I wanted to tell you I'm going to do better from here on out. I'm leaving the old Luke behind, and I'm going to take a chance on happiness."

His blue eyes were intense, the familiar spark between us sizzling. I thought of the time we'd spent together, and how much I'd wished that Luke would open up and quit hiding behind the facade of the angry divorce attorney. I wasn't sure, but it seemed like he was asking something and that made my throat tighten.

Luke pulled his bottom lip between his teeth. "You're thinking about Jon, aren't you?"

I shook my head.

"I didn't know you two were that serious."

"No, we're not. Actually, I was going to tell him I needed space, but before I could, he said that he'd changed his mind about moving to Idaho. And I wasn't thinking about him just now. I was thinking about you."

Luke's face brightened. "That is the best thing I've heard today." He studied me. "But what's wrong?"

My heart pounded as I thought about what I wanted to say to him. "It's just, you scare me Luke."

His eyes widened. "Really?"

"Well, not like that. More in the sense that I'm afraid of what you'll do. Every time you get close to feeling something, you run and usually get mad at me in the process."

"I'm sorry, Adri. I never meant to hurt you." He let his head fall into his hand. "I have a real problem with timing, I guess."

I decided to be just as blunt as Lorea would in this situation. "Luke, what are you really saying? Are you asking me something?"

He lifted his head and placed his hands on my shoulders. "I want to know if you'll go on another date with me—if you'd consider dating me?"

I couldn't say no to the hope in his face. "I would love to go on a date with you again, on one condition." I held up my finger. Luke nodded before I even spoke. "If I say something you don't like, you can't get angry at me. You have to think about it and *talk* to me about it."

"That sounds like a tough condition, but I'll do it." He pulled me in to his chest and hugged me. "I want you to be happy, so I'm willing to give you space to figure out what you want, but I'm also ready to date you if you're ready."

I encircled his waist and hugged him back. We stood there for a few more seconds and Luke let his arms drop to his sides. "My flight is scheduled to leave in the morning, but I'm worried about leaving you. I'm also bummed that you tried to be shark bait to get out of hiking with me."

I laughed and slapped his arm. "I would much rather have been hiking with you, but don't worry about me. I won't be far behind you. I'm leaving Monday."

"Will you be up for the flight?"

"Neil transferred me to first class, so that will help."

Luke touched my cheek. "I want to take care of you. I'm going to change my flight so I can travel home with you. Would that be okay?"

"That would be nice. I don't want to mess up your plans though."

"Adri, the only plans I have right now involve you."

Warmth spread throughout my body as his words sunk in. Our pasts had plenty of hurt but I was confident we'd both come out stronger because of our trials. I just didn't know what the future held.

Luke had been confusing me since the first day I'd met him, and he told me he was against marriage. I rolled my eyes when I thought about how he'd made fun of my wedding planning business, and I'd let him know how ticked I was about that. But he had changed and I believed it was an honest change.

There was a spark there, and we were both finally ready to see if it might ignite. Part of me worried that his heart might never heal enough to love. There would be time to figure it out, and maybe if he wasn't wearing his cynic's armor, things would be different on our next date.

"I'm willing to take a chance on you," I said.

Luke dipped his head and kissed my cheek. "See you soon."

My face warmed with his kiss. I smiled as I opened the door. "Mahalo."

Book Club
Discussion Questions

1. How would you feel if you discovered a body or stumbled onto clues in a murder case?

2. Have you visited any of the islands of Hawaii? Kauai? If so, how would you describe the difference between the islands?

3. Compare and contrast your own home town with a tropical paradise like Kauai. What would you miss about your hometown?

4. Adri is hesitant about dating because of her past. What advice would you give to her in regards to starting a new relationship?

5. Discuss the clues that you noticed as the mystery unraveled. Which characters did you suspect?

6. A red herring is a tool used to misdirect a reader's attention and suspicions. Discuss the red herrings you noticed in this book.

7. How do you think Luke's childhood and subsequent experiences in adulthood have shaped him into the person he is? Think about your own life experiences, what traits would you attribute to certain experiences in your past?

8. Adri enjoyed creating crafts and wedding tips with a Hawaiian theme in this book. Check out the chapter headings and discuss any that you've tried.

Learn more about Adri and her crafts at
www.mashedpotatoesandcrafts.com

Sneak Peek of Proposals and Poison

Enjoy this sneak peek of the third book in the Wedding Planner Mysteries available now.

Chapter 1

Date Idea Jar

Set a jar with popsicle sticks next to a sign that says:

DATE JAR

Share your BEST date idea for the new Mr. & Mrs.

Instruct guests to share their ideas and put each popsicle stick in a decorative jar to give to the bride and groom.

Courtesy of www.mashedpotatoesandcrafts.com

The afternoon sun had the asphalt steaming when I closed the door of my wedding shop on my way to run errands.

Summer was notoriously busy for weddings, and July promised no respite from the work ahead. I couldn't complain about my workload, though, because it made me happy to finally be in a place where my life was falling into a somewhat predictable routine. It also kept me from obsessing over my relationship status with Luke Stetson.

At the moment, Luke was in court, working a messy divorce case that was ballooning into so much drama he'd had to cancel on me three times in the past two weeks. The case involved the sister of Lily Rowan, one of my new clients. Lily was the happy part of the story, because she just got engaged to Tim Esplin—the vet I would take my cat to this afternoon. Lily wanted a November wedding, and since it was already July ninth, I was pushing to get the most important decisions made so we could progress with the rest of her plans.

My phone beeped, and I looked at the reminder on my calendar. In one hour I would be meeting with Lily to talk about the theme she and Tim wanted for their celebrations.

Sliding my finger across the screen, I dismissed the reminder, only to once again see the text from Luke. He'd canceled our lunch date by text this morning and still hadn't called. I wondered when the case would be over, and if he'd have more free time or get bogged down in another case.

Well, my work almost kept me from obsessing about Luke for, like, two minutes, I thought, frowning. As I slid into my car, I considered the question that had entered my mind right after Luke canceled our lunch date. Would Luke Stetson, divorce attorney, ever be able to love again? And should I,

Adri Pyper, wedding planner, be spending time (a.k.a. pursuing a relationship) with him?

The elusive answer shimmered like the heat from the pavement, just out of reach. I shook off thoughts of Luke and cranked the air conditioner up on my way to the consignment store located just a mile from my shop. Everybody's Closet had a summer fling sale going on with new merchandise, and Necia kept me in the loop since I was always on the lookout for vintage and unique decor to use in my weddings and parties. It was the height of yard-sale season, and Necia usually got in all the leftovers from people's garage sales. I loved going to yard sales and finding great bargains, but too many weekend weddings had me missing the early morning sales. Everybody's Closet was the next best thing.

The parking lot only had one other vehicle, a single-cab white pickup that didn't belong to Necia. She usually walked to work in the summer months. I pulled in next to the pickup, right in front of the store, and put my car in park. When I looked up, my eyes locked with those of a man standing in front of the doors, holding a rifle.

The silver metal of the stock gleamed in the hot afternoon sun, and I blinked, waiting for my brain to catch up to the strange sight before me. The man was short and stocky with dark brown hair, and as I studied him, he smiled and moved his rifle, pointing it toward the sky. I sucked in a breath when the man stepped forward. My windows were down, and the sound of robins trilling cheerfully carried across the parking lot. He said something in a different language. It wasn't

Spanish—I spoke a little, and his words had a Slavic sound to them. Regardless of the language, I was pretty sure he was swearing.

I fumbled for the window and door lock controls. My throat went dry as the man looked at me again and fired a shot into the air. I covered my ears and screamed, reaching for the gearshift to back out of the parking lot. My hand slipped and my car went into neutral. When I moved to put it in gear, the car died.

By then I was in a full-on panic. I turned the key, and thankfully my car started back up. I pumped the gas and put the car in reverse, but the gunman was faster than my frightened wits: by the time I backed out of my parking space, he was already peeling out of the parking lot, heading for the main road.

What had just happened? I wasn't sure whether I should call the police department or dial my friend Tony Ford, the local detective. Then, with a start, I thought of Necia. What if something had happened to her? I jumped out of my car and ran through the front doors of Everybody's Closet, the bronze bell clanking as I charged in. "Necia!" I called out.

"I'm right here, and I'm okay." She came around the corner, wearing a red-white-and-blue-striped apron. "Did you see that man with the gun?"

"Yes, and my brain froze. I didn't know what to do. It all happened so fast. Was he in here?" I pummeled her with questions, breathing hard.

"No, I just came from the back and saw him standing there holding a gun," she said, her breaths coming in short gasps. "Then he walked off and I heard a gunshot. I already called the police and they're sending someone over." Her light-brown hair was pulled back into a messy bun, and a few strands framed her heart-shaped face. She was in her late thirties and practically lived at her store.

"That was so weird. What do you think he was shooting at?" I turned to look at the parking lot. My hands shook, and my heart thumped hard in my chest. I took a deep breath, proud of myself for not freaking out after witnessing the man discharge his gun.

Necia raised her eyebrows. "I have no idea, but I don't suppose it would hurt to go outside and look around."

We stepped outside and I shielded my eyes against the sun, tucking one of my blonde curls behind my ear. The parking lot was empty, and a few trees lined the edge of the property. The birds were quiet, and besides the occasional passing car, there was hardly any noise. Necia and I looked at each other, and my fear was mirrored in her eyes.

"I can't imagine what he was doing with a rifle in town like this," I said. The Sawtooth Mountain Range that loomed around Sun Valley attracted its fair share of hunters, but that guy was completely out of season. I didn't know of many hunts held in the sweltering heat of July.

"Let's go back inside while we wait for the police." Necia held the door open for me and followed me inside.

"I came here to look at your new items, but now I don't feel like I can concentrate." I glanced at my watch—already past two—and grumbled. "I'm going to have to reschedule an appointment, because I'm sure Tony or whoever comes from the police will make us fill out a statement."

"That's true." Necia took out a ballpoint pen and clicked it a few times. "Wasn't it last year around this time that a policeman came to my store to see you?"

"Uh, yeah, and now Tony is dating Lorea, so I've been seeing even more of him lately."

Necia chuckled. "That's good to hear. She's a great match for him."

"I think so too." Lorea Zubiondo was my assistant and partner in crime when it came to planning weddings and creating stunning wedding gowns. Over the past year and a half, we'd helped plan over twenty weddings, solved a few mysteries, and created fantastic crafts and recipes for my website, Mashed Potatoes and Crafts. Her first date with Detective Tony Ford had been sort of a pity date to her sister's wedding, but they'd hit it off, and I'd never seen Lorea quite so twitterpated before.

The clanging of the bell interrupted my thoughts, and I looked up to see Tony standing in the doorway. He was well over six feet tall, with a full head of light-brown hair. In his dark suit and tie, he was an imposing figure, but his boyish smile was what made Detective Ford so good at what he did. He disarmed people with that smile and the smattering of freckles across his nose, but I knew better than to underestimate him. Tony was smart, and an excellent detective. "Good afternoon," he said. "I'd say it's a pleasant surprise to see you here, Adri, but it's not a surprise at all. You are always in some kind of trouble."

"I am not." I held up my hands. "I didn't do anything. Didn't even get out of my car and some crazy guy started shooting."

"Hmm. Why don't we start with a few questions?" Tony gave us his signature smile. "Necia, were you inside the store when the incident occurred?"

"Yes." Necia told him what she had seen.

"What about a description?" He looked at both of us. "The most important detail I need right now is his vehicle. Did either of you see what he was driving?"

"Yes, I pulled right up next to his pickup." I pointed out to the parking lot. "It was white."

"I thought it was gray," Necia said.

"No, I'm sure it was white." I looked at Tony and then at Necia. She furrowed her brow and looked at the ground, as if trying to conjure up an image of the vehicle.

"Extended cab?" Tony asked.

"No," both of us answered in unison. I smiled at Necia as I added, "I'm pretty sure it was just a two-door, regular bed." I paused, trying to recall any other detail about the pickup. By that time, my blood pressure had skyrocketed and my memory was saturated with fear, not leaving much room for other details.

"Ford, Chevy?" Tony prompted.

I shook my head. "I don't know. Maybe a Ford?"

Necia rubbed her forehead. "I didn't get that good of a look, and I'm not really great with truck models, anyway."

"Anything else in particular you remember about the vehicle?" Tony pushed the button on the radio attached to his shoulder and gave a quick description of the pickup, citing that it was possibly white or gray. That sort of bugged me since I knew it was white, but maybe he had to report what both witnesses thought they had seen.

Thinking about the pickup cleared away some of the fuzziness in my head. I willed the memory to come into sharper focus. "I think there was something in the back of his pickup. Maybe something red?"

"Something?" Tony repeated, and he gave me a half smile.

I resisted the urge to smack him in the arm like I did so often to my older brother Wesley, who happened to be Tony's best friend. "I know it's odd, but I don't know what it was. Just that something was in the back of his pickup, hanging over the edge."

Tony nodded. "That could actually be an easy thing to spot if it was there. Necia, did you notice anything?"

"I can't be sure." She clasped her hands together and rocked back on her heels. "My view from inside the store was limited."

"Hang on." Tony spoke into his radio again, reporting the possibility that I'd just brought up. How many policemen were roaming the semi-quiet streets of Hailey right now, looking for this mystery vehicle?

"Now, how about a description of this guy?" Tony asked.

I closed my eyes and focused on the memory of the man standing in front of the store. "He was short. I think shorter than me." I held out my hand to indicate about how tall I thought the man was.

"So probably about five-six or five-seven?" Tony looked at Necia, and she nodded.

"And he had bushy, dark brown hair," Necia said.

"Receding hairline?" Tony asked.

"No, a full head of hair, but no facial hair," I answered. "And he had on a white T-shirt with some kind of green picture or logo on the front. I didn't recognize it. Oh, and he spoke a foreign language. Not Spanish. Maybe German?"

"Do you speak German?"

"No, but I've heard it plenty of times and it reminded me of those sounds."

He was about to ask another question, but stopped when a second police car pulled into the parking lot. "That'll be Hamilton. He'll have you fill out a statement."

I held in my groan when I saw the police officer get out of his cruiser with a clipboard. I'd gone my whole life without so much as a speeding ticket, but in the last few years I'd had so many dealings with law enforcement, I knew just what to expect. Officer Hamilton would repeat most of the same questions and get us talking in the hopes that we'd remember something significant, some clue that maybe we didn't already mention. And then we'd have to fill out the witness statement and possibly answer a few more questions.

"Let me make a phone call and reschedule an appointment," I said. "Then I'll get that filled out."

I dialed Lily's number and rescheduled our meeting for Thursday—another two days to wait. "I'm really sorry about this, Lily, but I have an appointment for my cat next. I've already had to reschedule the appointment twice. Do you mind?" I would be taking my cat, Tux, to the vet, who happened to be Lily's fiancé. I'd probably be fifteen minutes late after running home to get Tux, but I was banking on typical waiting room delays to make up for the detour in my plans.

"No problem. I understand," she replied. "It'll give me some time to talk to my stepdad about our plans."

"Thank you," I said. "Maybe I can ask Tim what he thinks about the wedding colors." I laughed at my own little joke.

"Tim is actually pretty good with details," Lily replied. Her voice wasn't as chipper as usual, and she didn't even chuckle when I mentioned Tim and the wedding colors.

"I could possibly go over some things with you in the morning before work since you're right next door," I offered. Lily Rowan had been my neighbor since I'd moved back to Idaho from San Francisco, and we often chatted in between our comings and goings from work and life.

"Okay. That might work," Lily said.

"I'm looking forward to showing you some of the designs we have in this season. And Lorea has three new gowns that just came in." I infused extra brightness into my voice, hoping it would lift her spirits and have her more eager to meet with me.

"Thanks, Adri. That'll be fun. I'll talk to you later." She still didn't sound super excited, but at least we had an appointment.

With a frown, I ended the call and submitted myself to another round of questions. While Necia and I related most of the same information, the Blaine County sheriff pulled up in a black Ford pickup. He talked to Tony and then headed our way. He asked us a few questions about the description of the rifle, and we did our best to answer.

I took the clipboard from Officer Hamilton and hurriedly wrote down every detail that I could remember. I included all of my contact information, even though I wanted to write *You know where to find me!* on the dotted line.

I filled up the page and handed it back to Hamilton before Necia finished writing details in her neat and tiny script. Hamilton took the form over to the sheriff and Tony walked back toward us.

Hopefully I could leave now. I glanced at my watch. It was nearly three thirty; if I didn't hurry, I'd be late to the vet. I was disappointed that Lily hadn't been able to reschedule for later today, because she hadn't seemed herself over the phone. I wanted to talk to her to see if I could reassure her about planning her upcoming wedding. Maybe Lorea could help me think of a way to cheer Lily up.

"Is that frown work-related?" Tony asked.

I rubbed my hand over my frown. "Yes, your paperwork made me miss an appointment and I had to reschedule."

"Sorry about that. I know summer is a busy time for you wedding gals."

I laughed. "Yes, and you seem to be taking up quite a bit of time lately for one talented seamstress I know."

Tony grinned, and it was the kind that had the edges of my mouth pulling up in a smile to join the happiness in his face. Man, he had it bad for Lorea, and that was a good thing. "We've been dating for five months now. I surprised Lorea when I remembered that."

"She told me. I can't believe how fast the time has gone. It doesn't seem that long ago that I was in Kauai." Beautiful beaches graced by rugged mountains and the smell of plumeria had my toes itching for the Hawaiian sand, where I had planned a destination wedding earlier in the year. Those thoughts led to Luke, and my heart did that silly little stutter again.

"Hello?" Tony waved his hand in front of my face, jolting me back to the present. "I can see those wheels turning in your mind. Don't be planning my wedding already."

This time I did smack him. "Not thinking about you."

"Oh? Who's on your mind?"

"Never mind. Are we done here?" I interrupted him before he could follow that line of questioning.

"We're taking this seriously." Tony took the clipboard that Necia handed him. "I don't know what that guy thought he was doing, but discharging a gun within city limits is a misdemeanor at best. Since he fled the scene, he's looking at a few more charges. We'll be in touch, but let us know if you think of anything else." He handed Necia his card. "There'll be some officers coming and going today, keeping an eye on your store."

"I appreciate that," Necia said. "Maybe you can come by tomorrow, Adri?"

"I'd like to. I'll have to see what my schedule looks like. See you two later."

I gripped my keys and waved with two fingers. My car had been baking in the sun for over an hour, and heat emanated from the interior when I opened the door. I started it and cranked the air conditioner to full blast. My phone chimed with an incoming text just before I put the car in drive, so I slid my finger across the screen and saw Luke Stetson's smiling face.

Luke: Want to meet me for dinner?

Me: What? The mighty attorney has time for dinner?

Luke: :) Yes, and I want to see you.

Me: Would love to.

Luke: Rocky Mountain Pizza?

Me: Sounds delicious!

Luke: Pick you up at 6:30?

Me: I'll be hungry.

Luke: :)

I suppressed the girlish squeal I wanted to let out. Okay, maybe I did squeal a little and immediately forgave Luke for being so busy the past few weeks. When he'd canceled our lunch date earlier, I'd been annoyed and sort of depressed, but now even the sun seemed to shine brighter. I reminded myself not to get my hopes up—after all, it was still a date with a divorce attorney. Hunger and a rapidly increasing pulse did funny things to my brain.

With the upcoming date on my mind, I forgot all about the gunman in front of Everybody's Closet and drove to my house to pick up Tux.

Chapter 2

Paper & Lace Heart Bunting for Guest Book Table

Cut out 15-20 hearts in varying sizes from papers matching your wedding décor. Glue or mod podge lace on every other heart. Hang the hearts from twine, ribbon, or cording. Attach to the guest book table. You could easily create the bunting with other shapes to highlight your wedding colors.

Courtesy of www.mashedpotatoesandcrafts.com

The veterinary clinic in Hailey smelled like dog food and antiseptic spray, but it couldn't overpower the smile that kept coming back whenever I thought of a date with Luke. A rumbling purr and a nudge from Tux brought me back to the present. I was sitting in the vet office, holding my cat and dreaming about Luke, instead of working on the new weddings I had booked for the fall. Maybe I shouldn't let myself get too excited. Luke's capacity for a relationship was still questionable.

Tux meowed and stretched his little white paws forward, a contrast to the sleek black fur covering his entire body, except for the V-shaped patch of white on his chest that looked like a tuxedo cravat. He pushed his black head against my hand. Cats were simple and so easy to love. Maybe I should get Luke a cat—it'd be a good place to start for someone who made a living helping people tear apart their love stories.

The bell above the door jangled, and Tux hissed at the chocolate Labrador that had just entered. The dog's tongue lolled to the side in the summer heat. He looked like he hadn't even noticed my cat.

"Hush, Tux, or I'll have to put you back in the carrier." I held firmly to the scruff of Tux's neck until he settled back onto my lap. The dog snuffled at the floor, straining against his leash.

The vet assistant swung a door open and checked her clipboard. "Tux?" she asked, looking toward me.

"That's us." I stood carefully, cradling Tux and keeping his face away from the dog.

"You're late. Follow me," she said in a curt tone.

I hurried after the short-haired blond assistant—her name tag said "Vickie"—into a small room scrubbed clean, with lingering scents of the various animals who filed through every day. "I'd recommend putting your cat in the carrier on your way out," she said. "You were lucky he didn't get mauled by that dog."

"I'll do that," I responded. "I'm very sorry about being late." I'd waited for about ten minutes despite being twenty minutes late, so I wasn't sure why it bothered her.

Vickie seemed especially grumpy, so I pasted on a smile to combat her negative wavelengths. She didn't smile as she entered in the information I'd given her on Tux. Looking her over, I noticed that her nails were neatly trimmed and painted bright purple.

"I like your nails." Maybe a compliment would soften her. I really did like her nails, because purple was one of my favorite colors.

"Thanks." She looked up and glanced at me, and then at my cat. "It makes me smile on those days when I don't want to." She finally smiled, but it looked kind of grim. I wondered how many animals she'd worked with today, and what she seemed to have against me or my cat.

I held Tux and spoke to him in soft tones while Vickie took his vitals. I think we both took a deep breath when she left the room.

"I wonder what was eating her," I whispered to Tux. He didn't have a chance to answer with his usual plaintive meow before the vet, Dr. Tim Esplin, entered the room. He was just barely taller than my own five feet ten inches, and he had a full head of wavy brown hair with neatly trimmed sideburns.

Tim didn't wear scrubs; instead, he wore a classic snap-closure cowboy shirt, Wranglers, and boots. He fit the part of a down-home country vet, and his upper-class fiancée, Lily, didn't want him to change one bit.

"Good afternoon, Tux," Tim said as he approached my cat. "Adri, it's nice to see you. I wasn't sure how much you got away from all those gowns and doilies."

I laughed. "I manage to sneak away once in a while. Just running errands today." I placed Tux on the table. "He sure has grown since I found him last year."

Tim nodded. "You've done well with him. Most strays aren't this lucky. I just had to put one down yesterday that someone brought in."

I grimaced. "That's true. I'm lucky to have Tux too," I said. "We watch out for each other."

"Pets are the best for that." Tim examined Tux carefully, and my cat purred.

I thought of how he'd mentioned putting down a stray, and frowned. "Do you have to do many euthanizations?"

"Usually only a couple per month," Tim replied. "It never gets easier."

"Does it hurt the animal?"

"No. It's just like a shot, and they go to sleep. We make them as comfortable as possible." Tim carefully administered a shot to Tux, who mewed in protest but then quieted.

"That's a hard decision to make." I rubbed under Tux's chin as he purred.

"We do all we can before we go to that point, but if we can't find a home for them, we're required to euthanize. In the case of a sick animal that's suffering, it's what we do to provide peace."

"My uncle used to say that'd be the way to go," I said.

Tim arched an eyebrow. "Unfortunately, some people agree with him, and it's become a problem in recent years."

He refocused on Tux, but I felt like I'd put my foot in my mouth somehow. So I decided to change the subject to something less grim. "I'm meeting with your sweetheart to talk shop and get some things on the calendar this week."

Tim smiled, but something around his eyes hinted at an underlying concern.

"Is something wrong?" I asked.

Tim shook his head. "Not with us, but ... well, sort of. Lily is so upset about this whole divorce mess with Rose. Has she said anything to you?"

"No."

"I don't know what to do. She's talking about postponing the wedding because she doesn't want to get married on the heels of Rose's divorce. I don't want her to feel pressured, but I do love her." Tim hesitated, and then let out a breath. "I want Lily to be my wife. I can't lose her." He handed Tux to me, and I moved my cat into his carrier and shut the door. "I'm heading out early today to spend some time with Lily to get her mind off Rose."

"I didn't realize she was that close to her sister."

"Actually, she's not." He threw away some paper towels from the exam table and washed his hands. "Lily is the one who told me Rose was an unfit parent for Jasmine."

"Oh?" I wasn't sure how much I should pry, but since they were my clients I decided to venture. "How old is Jasmine?"

"She's six, and Rose *is* a terrible mother. She has never put her daughter first in anything. That poor little girl has had to ride the parade of Rose's boyfriends while she and Javier have been separated, and then Rose is busy slinging mud at him and turning Jasmine against her father."

"Oh dear. I'm sorry. I can see why Lily is concerned. Divorces are always difficult."

Tim put a hand on the back of his neck. "That Luke Stetson is a cutthroat attorney. Javier definitely picked a good one. He's fighting for full custody of Jasmine, and he just might get it."

I cringed, and then coughed to hide my surprise at hearing Luke's name with the term *cutthroat*. He was good at his job, but I hadn't heard him described that way before. "What makes you say that about Luke?"

"He works overtime to find the nitty-gritty details. Just yesterday, I heard—"

Vickie knocked on the door and opened it. "We have a dog that just came in—needs stitches, heavy bleeding."

Tim straightened and headed after Vickie. "Sorry to run, Adri."

"No problem. We're done here anyway. Good luck." But I wished we hadn't been interrupted. I would have liked to know what he was about to say concerning Luke.

Pick up your copy today to read the rest of *Proposals and Poison*!

Thrills for the Heart

FOR A LIMITED TIME

Sign up for Rachelle's
VIP Mailing List
to get your *FREE* book.

Get started here:
www.rachellechristensen.com

About the Author

Rachelle is a mother of five who writes mystery/suspense, nonfiction, and women's fiction. She solves the case of the missing shoe on a daily basis. She enjoys raising chickens and laughing with her husband. She graduated cum laude from Utah State University with a degree in psychology and a minor in music.

Rachelle is the award-winning author of twenty books, including *The Soldier's Bride (a Kindle Scout Selection), Diamond Rings Are Deadly Things, Hawaiian Masquerade,* and *Christmas Kisses: An Echo Ridge Anthology.* Her novella, "Silver Cascade Secrets," was included in the Rone Award–winning *Timeless Romance Anthology, Fall Collection.*

Join Rachelle's VIP mailing list to learn more about upcoming books & get your free book at http://www.rachellechristensen.com